COME WITH ME

ERIN FLANAGAN

THOMAS & MERCER

Text copyright © 2023 by Erin Flanagan

Published by Thomas & Mercer, Seattle

www.apub.com

Amazon, the Amazon logo, and Thomas & Mercer are trademarks of Amazon.com, Inc., or its affiliates.

ISBN-13: 9781662510328 (paperback)
ISBN-13: 9781662510335 (digital)

Cover design by Ploy Siripant
Cover image: © Kriengsuk Prasroetsung / Shutterstock; © Karina Vegas / ArcAngel

Printed in the United States of America

For Christina Consolino, Meredith Doench, Katrina Kittle, and Sharon Short

It is difficult to say who do you the most mischief, enemies with the worst intentions, or friends with the best.

—*Edward Bulwer-Lytton*

Chapter One

GWEN

January 2012

Gwen entered the conference room in a new navy suit, her pantyhose shushing with each step. A slender blonde woman in her early twenties sat at the head of the long table, her legs tucked under its glass top. Gwen could see her immaculate plum-colored suede stilettos. It had snowed earlier that morning, and the sidewalks were slushy and slick where they hadn't been shoveled. Had Gwen attempted wearing those shoes, they'd be salt stained and gritty.

"Are you Ms. Knowles?" Gwen asked. Ms. Knowles was the head of HR at Dack & Anders, the media company where Gwen would be interning and writing copy for the next four months.

The woman locked eyes with her, and for a second Gwen wondered if she would open her mouth and something as sophisticated as a British accent might come out. She looked the type: cosmopolitan, possibly foreign. A woman destined for love affairs and no carbs.

She shook her head. "No, I'm Nicola," she said. "Another intern." She did not have a foreign accent, but her voice also didn't sound local to Ohio—the vowels too crisp, like the snap of a $100 bill. Nicola leaned her long body forward to shake Gwen's hand, and Gwen was so surprised by the warmth of Nicola's skin she let her own hand rest limply as Nicola pumped it three times with a firm grasp.

Already, Gwen felt she was behind in knowing how to make a good first impression. How had this woman kept her shoes so clean? Gwen's suit was from JCPenney, an early Christmas present from her mother, and frumpy now next to Nicola's floral blouse and pin-striped pants. As Gwen turned the engagement ring on her left hand and took a seat, she reminded herself this was an internship, not the start of her life: that would come in June when she married Todd. Sometimes when she was away from him, she felt herself sinking, waiting for his air and light to buoy her back to the surface.

A mousy girl sat across the table, near the window. "I'm Missy," she said, waving from a few feet away. Her hair was pulled up in a banana clip and she wore a tartan plaid sweater. Gwen hadn't even noticed her until she'd spoken, but was somewhat relieved to see Missy was wearing snow boots, a puddle forming at her feet. Gwen at least had worn sensible pumps.

"Gwen," she offered, and smiled at her. "Are you an intern as well?" she asked. Gwen knew Dacks had hired three interns for the spring semester.

Missy nodded. "I'm so excited," she said, and did a little chair dance. "Are you both from Glenn State too?" Nicola and Gwen both confirmed. "What are your majors?"

"English," Gwen said, and Nicola shook her head. Was she saying Gwen wasn't an English major?

"It doesn't matter," Nicola said.

Missy furrowed her brows. "What doesn't matter?"

"Your major," Nicola clarified. Her voice was tinged with both boredom and conviction, as if what she was saying was so obvious it barely needed saying, yet it also flew in the face of everything Gwen had heard from professors and advisers the last four years: "Your major will determine the rest of your life. Every paper is as serious as a CT scan."

"What do you mean your major doesn't matter?" Gwen asked.

"Neither do your grades," Nicola added.

Gwen felt herself lean forward, drawn to the sophisticated woman. Maybe it was just that she was saying all that Gwen wanted to hear. Her grades had continued to slump, semester by semester, the more time she spent with Todd, and she knew her father would have been disappointed she hadn't reached her full potential. *But why do I even need good grades?* she'd say to herself. Todd was on track to take the tech world by storm; she didn't need an English degree to read picture books to the babies they'd have soon.

"Well then," Gwen said, "what *does* matter?"

Nicola smoothed a hand down the blonde braid slung over her shoulder. *Who can pull off French braids at work?* Gwen wondered, although the answer sat in front of her.

"What matters is what happens from here on out," Nicola said. She pointed at the floor, the gray-and-green carpet where her four-inch heel, that wonderful plum shoe, rested. "All that bullshit we learned in college in our finance majors or our English majors, none of that matters because it happened in a vacuum. One class, then another class, then another." Nicola rolled her hand over and over to mimic repetition, the speed of her words dizzying. "You'd get a grade, but then those professors would move on to a new set of students and another stack of papers and forget about you. They probably can't even put a face to a name anymore—you're just one in a cattle call." She spoke quickly but cleanly, each syllable enunciated. "Here is where we really start to make an impression. Get face time with the people who can help us get ahead. They don't care if you got As or Bs or Cs. What they care about is what you do from here on out, what initiative you take. We're in the real world now with real stakes. And ladies?" She leaned forward, as did Gwen and Missy. "What's the one thing we know for sure?"

3

Gwen had never wanted so desperately to get an answer right in her life. She held her breath, hoping to god it was a rhetorical question.

"That it's a man's world, and we need to claw our way into it. We," Nicola said, drawing a circle between the three of them, "need to stick together. We need to help each other as much as we can. It's going to get ruthless out there, so we need to say right now that we have each other's backs, okay?"

Missy was nodding, but Gwen felt herself pull away slightly. Ruthless? Stick together? It was an internship, not the start of battle. They were going to be in a cubicle together, not a foxhole. She was biding her time until June 7 at 5:30 p.m., when she would stand at the front of the First Lutheran Church, followed by circulating appetizers and an open bar.

"There are five rules that are going to help us get ahead," Nicola said, and held up her hand, her fingers splayed. Missy dove into the large leather purse at her slushy feet and pulled out a yellow notebook and a black pen.

"Number one," Nicola said, and pushed a finger in the air to accentuate the point.

Missy leaned over her notebook, ready to write. There was a plastic flower taped to the end of her pen.

Gwen turned toward the small window behind the desk, a swirl of snow in the air. After the appetizers, they were serving salmon fillets and new potatoes, a vegetarian option available. Todd had lobbied for chicken, but Gwen had held firm: it was always so dry, so underwhelming; salmon held a wow factor.

The snow came down pretty as a picture, like she was trapped inside some kind of boring, industrial snow globe. Maybe they should have gotten married last month during the holidays. Maybe she should have just called it quits on the degree and started her real life, but her father had been so proud of her for going to college, the first in the family. It was one of the last things he'd said to her before he died her sophomore

4

year: "Finish your degree. It'll be a nice backup." Tears unexpectedly welled in her eyes. Grief was like that—so sudden and inconvenient and often at the most unexpected times.

"Gwen?" Missy said, and her voice pierced through Gwen's ruminations. "Are you okay?"

"I'm fine," Gwen said, and shook her head to dry her eyes. "Allergies."

"Rule number three," Nicola continued, and as fascinating as the woman was, Gwen looked back out the window, distracted. Nicola was now speaking only to Missy, who was writing down each word in a script so neat it resembled calligraphy.

Gwen already knew the only rule that mattered: as long as someone loves you, all will be fine.

Chapter Two

NIKKI

August 1994

Nikki held hands with Celeste in the back seat of their mother's Buick. She and her sister liked to see how quickly they could tap matching fingers against the other's knuckles. It was a way to pass the time while their mom played the picture game.

In the fields on either side of the car, cornstalks rattled like a flock of birds taking flight. Their mom, Onita, leaned against the hood of the car, which was pulled over to the side of the gravel road. A pickup going the opposite direction pulled in front of them through the wet Ohio heat.

The driver stepped out, wearing blue jeans and a thin cotton short-sleeved shirt with pearl buttons, his chest thick and hard underneath. Celeste looked away, her mouth in a thin line. She did not like the picture game.

The man closed the heavy door of his Dodge behind him with a crack. A metal ram's head hood ornament was bolted to the front of the truck, the curve of its horns covered in dust. Nikki's daddy had had the same one and kept it shiny clean even in August when the dust was up, but he was gone now.

"What seems to be the problem?" the man asked. He adjusted his feed cap, pulling it off his sweaty head and back down again. Nikki tap-tap-tapped her fingers against each knuckle of Celeste's hand.

"Car trouble, I guess?" Onita stayed put, leaning against the engine and waiting for him to walk closer. Nikki didn't know how she could stand it: the hot metal against her bottom. Their mom wore a short denim skirt and a hot-pink tank top with thin black bra straps visible on her shoulders. Her underpants were lying on the front seat—pale yellow with daisies. She wore dusty, turquoise flip-flops on her feet.

"I hate to see a damsel in distress," the man said, and Onita's head cocked to the side.

"That so? You Prince Charming?"

He threw his head back and laughed, and Celeste's fingers stumbled on the rhythm. Mom asked his name and he told her Harold.

"Anyone call you Harry?" she asked, and he said his friends did. "Is that what you want me to call you?" He paused before agreeing.

His gold wedding band glinted, choking his finger. Onita didn't wear her ring anymore. Nikki and Celeste had gone snooping for it when their mom was in town, but it had vanished along with the rings their dads had worn. Nikki had watched her mother slide her father's ring off his finger at the funeral parlor where his empty hands laid one on top of the other on his chest, his hair parted and glistening, the comb lines as even as rows of corn. He wasn't Celeste's real dad. The girls were only half sisters, but as Celeste liked to say, two halves made a whole.

Onita told the man she'd hit something a mile or so back and there was a noise coming from under the car. "You want me to take a look?" he asked, motioning to the hood.

"It's not the engine," she insisted. "It's something underneath."

"You certain?" he asked, and she said she was.

He managed to wedge himself under, sliding his Levi-ed fanny beneath the car with a few grunts and a push off the heel of his boot.

"I don't see anything," he said. He spoke up so Onita could hear him, but his voice was dim, echoey, in the back seat.

"Well why don't you come out and tell me if you can see anything then," Onita said. She broke the rules and looked at the girls, throwing a wink. It made Nikki feel like they were in on this with their mom. It wasn't her and the man, but her and them.

Onita planted her two worn flip-flops wide on either side of his ankles, straddling where he'd shuffle out from under the car. Nikki sat up and leaned toward the unrolled window. This was her favorite part of the game. The man was always so surprised! It was like a magic trick.

First to appear were his knees, then his waist, then his pearl-buttoned belly, and then his shoulders. Finally his wattle-like neck, his rough chin, nose, and eyes.

Onita looked down, her hands on the side of the car, her torso leaned forward so she could see him, the blanket of her hair creating shadows. "I'm sorry," she said. "I didn't mean to take your picture."

The man stared up between her spread legs, his mouth open like he'd seen god. They always did.

There was a stretch of time when Mom and the man were quiet, assessing, until eventually he scooted the rest of the way out and put his left hand in his front jean pocket.

"I'd like to show you my truck," he said, his voice now deep and watery.

"I'd like that," Onita said. Sometimes they wanted to show her something in the truck, not the truck itself. Each time, she would take the first step and the man would follow behind. She'd open the truck or car door and lean in, sometimes putting her knee on the seat, that skirt getting even shorter. Nikki couldn't wait to be that tall.

She felt a pressure on her knuckle. "Don't watch, okay?" Celeste said.

"Okay." There wasn't anything to see anyway. Sometimes she heard things, like a coyote in the distance. She didn't understand why her sister didn't like the picture game. It meant later tonight they'd get McDonald's or Big Boy and could order a soda to share with free refills. Sometimes the man would come to their house for visits from then on, but sometimes not.

Celeste pressed harder on her sister's knuckles, her hand slowing down the rhythm. "I'm serious, Nikki. Don't listen."

"I'm not," she complained. Celeste always thought she was doing what she shouldn't be doing, and sometimes she was, but not now.

Celeste pulled her hand away from Nikki's and ran it over her face. Dust had settled on her skin from riding gravel roads with the windows open. It didn't seem fair it could be so humid and so dusty at the same time. Celeste leaned back and closed her eyes. Her eyelids, thin and veined, quivering with whatever was behind them.

"I have to pee," Nikki told her sister, the pressure just starting to build. The number one rule of the picture game was *Don't leave the car.*

"Tough," Celeste said. Nikki reached for her sister's hand, but Celeste pulled it away. "It's too hot."

All Nikki knew was her hand felt empty. She put her palms together and folded down her fingers, thumbs entwined, trying to capture the weight of a hand in hers.

It wasn't the same. Not even a little.

RULE #1: DON'T LET ANYONE MAKE YOU FEEL SMALL

Chapter Three

GWEN

June 2022

Gwen trailed her fingers over Todd's forearm. The hair was thicker than hers, coarser, and when he had the cuffs of a button-down oxford turned two times and pushed up to his elbows, his skin was deliciously irresistible.

It was early summer. The weather was warm, and their favorite farm-to-table restaurant, the Crowded Plate, was not yet overly chilled by air-conditioning. She sat next to him as he told a story she'd heard a hundred times. The kind of story spouses know by heart, words she could repeat in his exact intonation. She inhaled deeply the smell of citrus slices from their cocktails, the vinegar of their wine, as she watched Todd in the mirror across from them. Her hand stroked his wrist in the reflection as the other couple, a husband and wife, laughed at all the right beats and Gwen smiled along.

She'd always loved showing Todd off in social situations—her gregarious, charming husband who always had the right story or joke at hand. It allowed her the role of wallflower, which she had always preferred, although she wondered sometimes if others questioned why he was with her.

She moved her attention to Lori, who was wearing a cream blouse with a lace collar. They both had one child at home; Gwen's daughter, Whitney, was eight, and Lori's son was six. Gwen wondered if Lori felt like she, too, was playing dress-up. How long had it been since Gwen had straight-ironed her hair, applied eyelashes, and squeezed her mom-wide feet into a pair of red mules? What she wanted was to be curled against her daughter's side, their breaths in tandem, reading the latest Percy Jackson. But instead, she smoothed down the front of her black wrap dress—the only cute thing in her closet that seemed to fit—and then rested her hand again on Todd's wrist, the hair above his watch tickling her fingertips.

He caught her eye in the mirror and smiled, and she knew there was no way the couple across from them could tell they'd been fighting up until the moment they slid out of the car. Or maybe not fighting, but there was tension like a crackle of electricity in the air. Todd was stressed about work; he was always, it seemed, stressed about work, and Gwen's job was to ease that tension as best she could. She was an invisible elf in the background, making meals, folding clothes, and scheduling the lawn care.

This kind of compartmentalization—*now we are fighting; now we are charming*—was common in their marriage. Common in most marriages, Gwen assumed. *Now we are doting parents; now we are disciplinarians. Now I have throw-up on my T-shirt; now I am your sexy wife.*

She leaned toward Todd to kiss his cheek, surprised at the heat roiling from his skin. She pulled back and looked at him. Sweat beaded on his forehead, wobbly in the tea lights, even though it was cool in the restaurant. She could see sweat stains seeping from his armpits; no wonder he'd rolled up his sleeves. "You okay?" she whispered.

He turned to her and she blinked, surprised by his glassy eyes. How had she not noticed this earlier? How much had he had to drink? She

14

looked at the Stranahan's on the rocks still in front of him, the liquid now a watery amber, the ice nearly melted. It was only his second drink.

"Todd?" she said, and he turned away roughly, rubbing his jaw and pressing his palm across his forehead, wet now with perspiration. "Todd? You okay?"

He smiled tightly. "I'm fine. It's just hot in here." His eyes flicked to the couple across from them—potential clients he wouldn't want to alarm. In the car on the way here, Todd had been worried about the restaurant choice, what they'd talk about, how to actually make the ask for their financial support. Todd wasn't the nervous type—that was Gwen's role—but she'd noticed a hiccup in his confidence recently. This was the first time they'd gotten dinner with this couple, and it had been going so well—the wives talking about their children, careful not to judge or compete.

Todd scratched at his neck, already irritated from his second shave of the day. His fingers caught in the collar of his shirt, and with a peak of adrenaline, he jerked the shirt open, a button catching on the hole and popping off. It skittered across the wooden table, a tail of thread still attached, and fell off the edge.

Evan, the husband in the other couple, stood up quickly. Todd fell into the table, and a full water glass toppled to the wood floor and shattered. "Jesus. I think he's having a heart attack," Evan exclaimed.

"A what?" Gwen asked. The words made no sense. Todd ran fifteen miles a week and had a resting heart rate of fifty-two. Just ask him; he'd tell anyone who would listen. He did yoga, for Christ's sake! He couldn't be having a heart attack.

"Is there a doctor?" Evan yelled. "Is anyone a doctor?"

The sound of his loud, authoritative voice brought Gwen back to the moment, thankful he'd taken charge. Someone else knew what to do. A doctor, that's what they needed. It would become another story they'd tell a different couple—the one where Todd collapsed at a restaurant and was brought back from the brink.

A woman came over, still wiping her mouth with a napkin. She set the napkin calmly on the table. "I'm a nurse," she said, and put a strong hand under Todd's elbow, guiding him gently from his chair and rolling him onto the floor on his back in one swift motion.

My husband is on the restaurant floor, Gwen thought. She could see his rib cage stuttering under his shirt, the concave of his stomach moving in and out as he struggled for air.

"What's happening?" Gwen asked. Watching his labored breath, she tried to breathe deeper, but her own breath caught, her lungs unable to fill. A panic rose, starting in her chest. Whitney would be in bed by now with no idea her entire world was tilting on its axis.

"A heart attack," the nurse confirmed. The kitchen door swung open silently and three of the staff hovered in the entryway, watching. "Do you have a defibrillator?" she said, and one of the cooks, a young woman with tattoo sleeves peeking out of her chef's coat, shook her head.

"Are you his wife?" the nurse asked, and Gwen nodded. "Did you call 911?"

Gwen's face flushed. "No—" Jesus, she was useless. How had she not thought to call 911?

Lori waved her phone. "I did."

"Did they give you a time estimate?" the nurse asked, but the sirens were within earshot now, the *wheep-whoop-wheep* sound reverberating. Gwen imagined she could see the lights through the large front window, but that was her own panic, red and pulsing behind her eyes.

"Is he going to be okay?" Gwen asked. Todd had stopped moving—when had that happened?—and underneath the red skin puffed on his cheeks, she thought she detected a bluish pallor. Good Jesus, was he going to *die*? She caught a hysterical laugh as it burst out of her throat.

She turned to Lori, shock slapped across the other wife's face. "I'm sorry," Gwen said, although she wasn't sure what she was apologizing for. Their ruined dinner? Her husband collapsing? It was a phrase she said as reflexively as breathing. What would she tell her daughter? What possible words might make sense?

"I'm sure he'll be fine," Evan said, and Gwen turned toward the deep comfort of his voice. She grabbed on to those words like a life raft, scrabbling the weight of herself onto it.

"He'll be fine," she echoed, and slipped her hand into Todd's, squeezing his palm and fingers, unresponsive and heavy in hers. *Deadweight,* Gwen thought as the nurse broke the front flaps of Todd's oxford farther apart, sliced the V-neck collar of his T-shirt with a steak knife, and ripped it the rest of the way open. His chest was silent and still.

Two EMTs burst through the front door, a stretcher suspended between them. A third followed with an orange-and-black metal box: the defibrillator. He sank to his knees in front of Todd's bare chest as the first two EMTs efficiently slid him onto the stretcher.

The man removed the backs of two large sticky pads and pressed them onto Todd's chest.

Gwen squeezed her eyes shut and listened as her husband's body bucked in the air and crashed back to the floor. Lights flashed behind her eyelids as she counted to three in her head. She could hear his body seize again, and an unconscious grunt left his mouth—or was that the EMT?—followed by the weight of him falling back onto the stretcher.

Gwen opened her eyes, helpless, and felt hands on her shoulders, her body turning into a person's chest, engulfed in a hug as her eyes were turned away from her husband.

"He's going to be okay," Lori said, and Gwen opened her eyes enough to see she'd stained the woman's cream blouse with tears. In the eerie quiet of her favorite restaurant, Todd bucked a third time, and Gwen knew nothing would be okay ever again.

Chapter Four

GWEN

July 2022

Gwen walked through the doors of TeckPocket with Whitney gripping her hand. Since Todd's death, she'd stopped taking her daughter to summer camp, had stopped letting the girl out of her sight. Whitney had been prone to monthly night terrors since she was three or four, but now they came every few nights, her screams seeming to shake the very foundation of the house.

"I'm going to leave you out here with Gibson," Gwen said, pointing to the rose gold and muted orange pattern furniture by the reception desk, the chairs on the verge of being out of style. TeckPocket was the business Todd had started out of college, along with his cofounder, Jack. He'd been the idea guy and Jack the practical one who knew numbers like a native language.

"Hey, Whitney," Gibson said. "What are you reading these days?" Gibson had known Whitney for years and was one of Whitney's favorite people, but she looked beseechingly at her mother.

"Can't I come with you?"

It pained Gwen to say no, but instincts told her this wasn't a conversation to have in front of her daughter.

Jack breezed out of the back offices a beat later in Nike shoes and moisture-wicking clothes. He also was a runner, and Gwen wondered if all tech bros worried their hearts would explode like Todd's had at thirty-three. He'd texted earlier in the week to ask her to come in for a quick chat, and something about the casualness of it all—a quick chat—had put Gwen's teeth on edge.

She assumed Jack wanted to know where she stood on the partnership and that maybe he'd want to buy her out, but she didn't know if she was ready to get rid of something so intrinsic to Todd. Just that morning she'd held his dumb disposable toothbrush for at least three minutes, her hand hovering over the garbage pail, before putting it back in their shared ceramic cup.

Jack said hello to Whitney and enveloped Gwen in a hug. It felt like she'd been hugged more in the last four weeks than the rest of her life put together. So much of it had been her body squished against an unfamiliar one, an acquaintance or one of Todd's colleagues, the awkwardness of intimacy she didn't want. The only chest she wanted to be against was her husband's, with the familiar scent of their laundry detergent on his shirt, and that mix of cedarwood, fresh air, and pencil shavings.

Jack was the first person Gwen had called from the hospital after the babysitter, unsure of what needed to be done. *Do I leave the body here? Do I take Todd's wallet and shoes?* She'd been in shock, and sometimes wondered if she still was. Jack had sent his wife to pick up Whitney, and then had come to the hospital to drive Gwen home. It wasn't until nearly a week later Gwen remembered they'd left Todd's car at the restaurant, and when Jack drove her to pick it up, she panicked to see it gone. Another thing taken from her. Jack was the one who realized it had been impounded, of course, and he'd called around for the right impound lot and paid to get it released. At every step, it seemed like she was supposed to know what to do, but she felt lost.

Jack peeled a five-dollar bill off a stack from his pocket and handed it to Whitney. "You remember where the vending machines are?" he asked, and she nodded, perking up a little.

In Jack's office, Gwen sat on the other side of his desk, her knees together and tipped to the side, her toes pointed.

"How've you been?" Jack asked, and she answered with the usual prattle about how she was getting on, taking it day by day. She hated this conversation, just hated it. It felt like her grief was a drive-by accident on the side of the road.

"What's this chat really about?" she asked, after a few volleys back and forth, and Jack cleared his throat.

"Finances," he said.

"I assumed." Gwen glanced at the thick file on his desk. She'd always left the finances to Todd. She supposed she should be embarrassed traditional gender roles were so enforced in their house—he handled the money, she handled the childcare—but they both seemed happy enough to let it stand.

"It's not good," Jack said solemnly, and Gwen felt a convulsion of unease. She was used to the sour weight of her grief, the awful gut punch of Todd's death catching her off guard, but this felt different. Creeping.

"Not good how?" she asked, and Jack pivoted.

"How much had Todd told you about how the company was doing?"

She'd known they were in a dip, or at least that's what Todd had called it. A dip or a blip? She couldn't fully remember anymore, her brain feeling like a sore tooth encased in cotton. A few months ago she'd found water damage upstairs in the master bath and started to gather estimates for a new roof. Todd had told her to hold off, even as the stain was seeping toward the closet. "I know you've had a not-great quarter," she said, and Jack snorted. Gwen leaned farther forward, the panicked feeling spreading from her chest to her limbs.

"It was more than a quarter."

"How much more?" she asked, and he pushed the file toward her with one finger.

She turned the manila folder right side up and peeked inside, trying to make sense of the numbers. Many were red. There were graphs, all crashing toward the bottom right edges. "I don't understand?"

"We've been hemorrhaging money for some time," Jack elaborated. "And it's fine—tech is a game of ups and downs—but the downs have been going for a bit now, and, well, it's a game where it matters when you get out." She looked at him, her eyebrows furrowed. A game? Get out? Todd hadn't gotten out; he'd *died.* "A year from now, two or three, we probably would have been fine, but right now . . ." He let the words trail off. "I'm sorry, Gwen."

"Sorry for what?" she asked. "What does this mean?" She had a feeling she knew: this was bad. But there was bad and there was *bad.* She could put off the new roof for a while; a pot next to the toilet to catch the drips was not the end of the world. As far as tech companies went, TeckPocket was a dinosaur. They'd been running a decade, and it seemed every brilliant idea from Uber to DoorDash was launched moments after Todd began formulating the idea, the taste of it already in his mouth. He had assured her for years that, while they weren't billionaires or even millionaires, it was like drafting behind a semi and saving on gas mileage, although Gwen knew if you did this too aggressively it could be dangerous.

"Todd really believed in this company," Jack went on. "We both did. *Do.* He funneled everything back in to get us over the hump."

So she owned stocks? She shook her head. "I still don't understand."

He flipped a few pages deeper into the file. "Your retirement," he said, and pointed at a number so laughably low she'd be able to repair one shingle on the roof, maybe two. "Todd made withdrawals. It's all gone back into the company."

She looked at him, confused. His mouth was like that of a Muppet talking nonsense. There was no way he could be saying this while he sat there in a $300 moisture-wicking shirt. Todd had been so good about handling the money, always talking up their retirement. He'd started a Roth IRA when he was nineteen and loved to tell everyone that tidbit along with his resting heart rate.

With a dawning realization, a new future flicked before her like a fluorescent light trying to catch. She was only thirty-two; she could rebuild her retirement. She'd grown up lower-middle class and had known lean times before. Sure, Whitney hadn't, but she was a child and would learn. Retirement, she had time to pad, but if their savings was gone, what about *now*?

She reached for the file and pulled it into her lap, riffling through the pages for the life insurance policy. Blood thumped in her ears, fast and hot. Finally she recognized the faded blue logo from their insurance. How long had it been since she'd seen an envelope with that logo at home? Had Todd changed the address to work? Had he been deliberately hiding it?

She grabbed for the paper to pull it to the top, and it sliced into the tender flesh of her finger in a quick, sharp pain. Her eyes watered, the words blurring on the page. Even so she could read the important ones: *lapsed, expired.*

"This can't be," she said, and Jack kept his eyes averted. He was the numbers guy. Todd was the one well versed in dealing with clients and delivering bad news.

"I know it's a blow," he said in the understatement of the year, and Gwen rubbed her watering eyes. Her hand came back smeared with black, the first makeup she'd worn since the funeral. That morning she'd held her mascara wand in a shaky hand, ready to face her life. Now she probably looked like a Rorschach test, and whatever Jack saw there made him wince. "But we're getting on track. I have potential investors coming in this afternoon. And while I won't be able to offer you anything officially, if Susie and I can be of any help, a place to live for a while maybe, we're—"

"A place to *live*?" she interrupted. "What about our *house*?"

"Well," Jack fumbled, "you'll most likely need to sell to cover—"

Gwen stood abruptly and turned toward the hall.

"Gwen?"

She found Whitney in the lobby, a half-eaten Snickers in her hand. Had she kept the change from Jack's five-dollar bill? Gwen hoped so. She wrapped her hand around Whitney's wrist, a smear of chocolate now on her hand.

"Come on, sweetie," she said. "We're going home."

Chapter Five

The next afternoon, Whitney was marooned on Gwen's huge bed, lulled by whatever was on the iPad. "I need to take care of some stuff downstairs, okay?" Gwen said, and leaned over to kiss her daughter on the forehead. She knew she'd been depending too much on screens since Todd's passing, but it was the only thing Whitney seemed to enjoy, the only thing that gave Gwen enough time to hide in the closet and muffle her crying with her husband's favorite sweater. Her daughter had dark circles under her eyes, a shattering look on an eight-year-old face.

"Can I have a Popsicle?" Whitney asked, and Gwen promised she'd bring one when she returned, a cherry one, her daughter's favorite.

Downstairs, Gwen pulled out the file Jack had given her and read through it in detail. Everything was there—their mortgage and credit card statements, the electric bill. Jack had pulled the most recent month for each, explaining that Todd kept all his passwords on a piece of scratch paper in his desk. That was the kind of man she'd trusted with her future. A charismatic people person, but perhaps not the businessman she'd assumed. She vacillated between anger that her husband had left them in this position and left them at all, and the bone-deep want to hear him explain his decisions in his low, reassuring voice. If she could just hear his plan, all would still be okay.

She flipped through the pages, relieved at least to see their very large mortgage up to date and their electric paid in full, but it was the other statements she couldn't quite fathom. Another Visa. A Mastercard. A Diners Club Card for the love of god—who even had one of those? The balances were staggering. Each of the cards was at the limit. Her heart sank as the word pulsed in red at the top: *overdue*. When she looked at the charges, her mind skipped to the worst possible scenario: hotel rooms and jewelry she knew nothing about. So she was baffled instead to find charges to the electric company and their favorite restaurants, the everyday bills of their lives. How long had they been racking up debt, paying 18 percent interest on appetizers and drinks?

Gwen barely had a clue where to begin, but she knew first things first: she had to find a job. Although she didn't even know what she'd want to do, much less what she'd be qualified for. Picking up dry cleaning, whisking a perfect risotto, and online shopping didn't exactly seem like positions in demand.

It had been a decade since her last employment—an unpaid internship her senior year of college. Before that it had been odd jobs like dog walking or babysitting or the Writing Center at Glenn State. Nothing certainly that screamed *career*. Did she just go to LinkedIn, create an account, and say "hire me"?

She decided to start where she'd last stopped and pulled up the website to Dack & Anders, the media agency in Dayton, Ohio, where she'd interned. She'd spent most of her time answering phones for one of the executives, booking his travel plans and organizing his calendar, creating PowerPoints with preset background designs. It was 2012, and she hadn't been particularly good at her job (unpaid, so not *really* a job, she'd told herself).

She read the "About" section on the website, refamiliarizing herself with the company. It was a long shot that anyone there would remember her from ten years ago (and given her lackluster performance on the job, maybe it was best they didn't), but it was the last line on her résumé. It was obvious Dacks had changed a bit in the last decade, no surprise there. They'd expanded to video and social media campaigns, and had a national and international presence, using their hometown location of Dayton to their advantage. "If we can reach an audience from here, we can reach from anywhere," one of the log lines on the website said.

She toggled to the company's "Who We Are" page and was surprised to see a name she recognized: Nicola Kimmel, now chief operating officer, COO. Gwen and Nicola had interned together all those years ago along with another woman. What was her name? Mary? Melanie?

No, Missy. Missy had been the boring one, while Nicola was the cool girl (Gwen had been the one with the fiancé). Even now, looking at Nicola's picture, Gwen could tell that was still true. While most of the executives had photos taken against a bland gray background like a grade-school picture, Nicola's picture had been shot outside, the sunshine perfect on her face, the bone structure Gwen had been so intimidated by cutting like a sharp blade. She still had the long blonde hair she had in college, tucked behind her ear and sleek behind one shoulder. She had the same white teeth, the same big nose. But rather than try to hide her nose under shading as Gwen would have (badly), she'd pierced it with a thin ring back in college, drawing attention and daring someone to look away.

She wasn't surprised to see Nicola had risen through the ranks, but Missy had been more Gwen's speed. One weekend, she'd taken a gift-wrapping class at Hobby Lobby and asked Gwen to join. Any socks Missy wore that weren't black she called "fun socks." Gwen would have guessed all those years ago that she and Missy would be the ones to become close or at least work buddies, but that hadn't happened; Nicola had claimed Missy all for herself. They'd been a cozy twosome, Gwen always on the outside, although part of that had been on her. When they did invite her out for drinks after work, she wanted to go home to her fiancé, Todd, who had now died and left her this mess. Todd who used to dance chicken legs across his plate at dinner just to make Gwen and Whitney laugh.

A sob worked its way up her throat, and Gwen pushed it down as she punched Nicola's office line into her cell and listened to it ring once, twice, the call answered halfway through the third ring.

"Nicola Kimmel's office," a chipper voice said.

Gwen explained who she was—an old friend who'd worked with Nicola when she started at Dacks—and that she was getting back into the job market. She tried to remember corporate buzzwords that Todd had used. Was "circle back" still a thing?

"Okay?" the woman said. "But I mean, you'd be better off talking to HR."

"Of course," Gwen said, feeling foolish suddenly for having called. Who started with the second-in-command of a major corporation? "I wasn't calling so much for a reference," she lied, "but just to connect and say hi."

"Let me see if she's in—" the woman started, and just like that Gwen was on hold, her cheeks flaming with embarrassment she'd called the COO. She was debating hanging up when the line clicked from music back to a voice.

"Gwen?" the voice said on the other end, and she knew instantly it was Nicola—her somehow posh-yet-tough accent that wasn't placeable in the Midwest.

"Nicola?"

Nicola let out a laugh. "I thought that was you. My assistant said you rang and I almost couldn't believe it. Where are you these days?"

Gwen was a bit taken aback by Nicola's friendliness. She remembered her differently, more focused and closed off, but that's what ten years of worn memory tape would do for you. Plus, they were in their thirties now, completely different people, all of their cells regenerated nearly twice in the space of all those years. "Hello!" Gwen said in return, and for the first time since Todd's death felt something like optimism.

She explained she was in Boulder now. "My husband just passed," she said, waiting for the pause of shock and pity before the person on the other end of the line barreled on with an apology.

"Ugh, you're so lucky," Nicola said, and Gwen was so caught off guard, she laughed. For a month everyone had been doling out the same tepid condolences, and such a black-humored comment surprised her. More than surprised her, it had made her genuinely guffaw.

"Watch what you wish for," Gwen joked back but instantly felt bad. She'd never wished Todd dead. She might have wished him to be more communicative or complimentary or trusting of her abilities, but never had she wished for him gone, and a sting of remorse flashed through her at the joke.

"You're funny," Nicola said. "I didn't remember that."

Despite feeling guilty over her comment, Nicola's compliment was so unexpected, tears filled Gwen's eyes. Since Todd's death she'd been only a widow, and that someone saw her as a woman with a personality felt like walking into sunlight.

"Oh god, you're thinking about moving back to Ohio, aren't you?" Nicola said. "And in July, no less. When it feels like we're living in an armpit. A hairy one."

"You're really selling it," Gwen said, and Nicola laughed again. Maybe Nicola was right; maybe Gwen was funny. Moving back to Ohio from Colorado hadn't really occurred to her—she was calling merely for a reference—but maybe that was an option. In the past week she'd contemplated all kinds of things that she thought were behind her—using fans instead of air-conditioning, store-brand shampoo, green beans in a can versus fresh. Already her mind was chugging through possible advantages, like her mother watching Whitney after school. "But yeah," she added. "I might be."

She'd always loved Boulder—the mountains, the hippie vibe—but since Todd's death, everything was a reminder of what she'd lost. The trails they used to hike together she'd now have to hike alone. The restaurants they loved she couldn't bring herself to visit. Even now, standing in the sunny kitchen and looking out at the deck, it was so easy to imagine Todd flipping burgers or moving the sprinkler or lounging in an Adirondack with an Avery IPA in his hand, still that carefree boy from the library she'd fallen in love with. Gwen felt a pang of missing Todd so strong her stomach cramped. She and Whitney seemed to be circling each other in their grief, unable to break the cycle. Maybe what they needed was a change of location, a fresh start. "A chance to blow the stink off," as her mother liked to say.

"Any work lined up?" Nicola asked, and Gwen was so grateful for the opening she nearly wept.

Play it cool, she thought to herself. "I'm just starting to look at my options."

"I remember you being such a hard worker," Nicola said, and Gwen wondered if she was confusing Gwen with Missy, who *had* been a hard worker, but she wasn't about to contradict the only contact she had in the business world.

"Yeah, I really loved working at Dacks."

"Well, I wouldn't go that far," Nicola deadpanned, and then laughed again. "But listen, I'm sure you'll have loads of offers wherever you end up, but if it happens to be in Dayton, I'd love to set you up for an interview. Maybe in accounts? We've always got something available there. It's been crazy turnover since COVID."

"Really?" Gwen said, hope rising in her chest. "That'd be great." Until this call, moving back to Ohio hadn't really occurred to her, but she felt it now in a rush of wanting. This job, this move: they could save her.

"Sure, and listen, why don't you email me your résumé in the meantime and I'll see what I can do. Nothing wrong with options, even if they're entry level. And if anything, maybe we can make you an offer and you can use it as leverage to get more money somewhere else."

Gwen was speechless. She had received so much kindness over the past few weeks, but it was pity in disguise. Friends had been good about dropping off casseroles in the beginning, but the food had been baked in disposable aluminum pans so they wouldn't need to return to the house of suffocating grief. Gwen's mother, Jeri, had told her once that when Gwen's father died it was like the world had cast her in a cold and invisible shadow. Gwen understood that isolation too well now.

This felt different, like someone trying to help her because they liked her. "Seriously, Nicola, this means the world. Thank you."

"We interns need to stick together," she said, like it was no big deal.

"Speaking of," Gwen said. "Are you still in touch with Missy?"

Nicola paused. "Who?" Her voice had shifted a vibration, like a change in cabin pressure, and for a brief second Gwen wondered if she'd imagined it.

"The other intern?"

"Oh right," Nicola said. "She worked here until a few months ago and left under weird circumstances." Gwen did the math; that would have been around March. "It's not really something I want to go into right now."

"Oh, of course," Gwen said. "I'm sorry."

"No worries," Nicola said. There was another pause, and then the air pressure returned to normal. "Gwen Gries. Really, it's great to hear from you."

"Maner now," Gwen corrected.

"Do you regret that?" Nicola said, and Gwen blinked with surprise. "I mean now that he's gone and you're strapped with the name and have to decide to keep it or go back?"

"I—" Gwen started but didn't know what to say. "It's nice, I guess, having it match my daughter's."

"You have a kid?"

"Yes, Whitney. She's eight." There was an awkward pause where she expected Nicola to ask a follow-up about her daughter or inquire about others. "No kids for you?" she finally said, and then instantly worried she'd crossed a line asking about children. The issue was a hot button rather than the innocuous conversation she'd long thought it was, her own pregnancy smooth and easy, although originally she and Todd thought they'd have more. He kept saying it wasn't the right time; he wanted to close one more business deal, launch one more app, get one more chance to hit it big first.

"Oh no," Nicola said. "Childless by choice. Hashtag. I want to be the fun auntie who spoils them rotten then shoves them back at their mothers pumped up on sugar. How old did you say?"

"Eight."

"My favorite age," Nicola said, and Gwen appreciated how easily she was willing to smooth over Gwen's indelicate question, plus her awkwardness asking about Missy. Maybe Dayton made sense; maybe she needed to be around family right now and away from all these memories. *This job,* she thought. *It could solve all our problems.*

"Thanks again," Gwen said as they got ready to hang up. She glanced at her watch, surprised to see they'd been on the phone for nearly half an hour. She was touched Nicola had been so generous with her time.

"Send me that résumé," Nicola said.

Gwen told her she'd send it by tomorrow, jotting down Nicola's email from the website. "It's thin," Gwen warned her.

"At least something is," Nicola joked, and Gwen laughed again, finally recognizing what this felt like: the beginning of a friendship. One that had sidestepped those awful get-to-know-you coffees where you tried to decide if you're really compatible, or your children get along, or if walking with the other woman in the morning would be better for your mental health than listening to a podcast.

Maybe all those years she feared she was the dud to Todd's outgoing personality weren't really about being a dud at all but about reaching a level of comfort where she could just *be.*

She hung up the phone and opened a fresh Word document. She typed her name and Boulder address at the top and paused. She selected a better font, and then another. What else went on a résumé? What did she have to say? She hadn't worked in ten years other than volunteering at the used book sale at Whitney's school and some other school initiatives, which were mainly women in overpriced running gear talking about why they couldn't eat the pastries even though each had brought a box.

Still, she had nothing to lose, and with that she did the best she could filling in the gaps between her internship all those years ago and what brought her to this day. She composed an email to Nicola that she hoped was a blending of nepotism ("such a fun time during our internship together") and professionalism ("the synergy of my skill set within Dacks") and hit "Send."

The laptop made the *whoosh* noise and Gwen leaned back, wondering what this feeling was. It took her a moment to recognize it: accomplishment.

Chapter Six

NIKKI

August 1996

Nikki held the lunch tray in front of her as a skinny woman in a food-stained white blouse and a hairnet glopped a spoonful of warm milky rice onto her plate. Why hadn't Celeste warned her school would be so hard?

It was the first day of grade school, and already one of the boys had told Nikki her hair looked like a bird's nest, and another—the class clown, who Nikki pegged as a nose picker—had said "a *rat's* nest." He'd said it just loud enough that the kids beside her snickered and word spread. Then he mimicked pulling a tiny, baby rat out by its tail. And that stupid old teacher? She hadn't even looked up from her lesson plans.

Nikki understood she was in first and Celeste was in fifth so they had to be in different classrooms, but now in the cafeteria, she didn't understand why she and her sister couldn't spend lunch together. Why did she have to eat with those idiots from her class who oinked as she walked by? When Nikki had walked into the lunchroom, she'd seen Celeste already seated with the fifth graders. She sat a head taller than the girl next to her, and when Nikki started toward her, the subtle shake of Celeste's head stopped her midstride. There was no breaking ranks within the grades.

Another woman in a similar outfit to the first dumped a spoon of canned green beans on the middle-top section of Nikki's pale-yellow tray. It was about the coolest thing Nikki had ever seen, with four equal-size squares and one larger rectangle. She shuffled two beats to the right, and a third woman wearing a loose plastic glove held out a sloppy joe, meat spilling out the sides. Nikki's eyes widened. She got a sandwich too? This was more than she usually ate from morning to night, except on picture-game days.

At the end of the row, there were upside-down plastic glasses. She watched the boy who had mimed pulling a rat baby off her head as he moved to the three industrial drink dispensers labeled "White," "White," and "Chocolate." *Chocolate!*

She snatched up a glass and followed him as he paused in front of the signs. She already knew from the way he'd confused a *b* and a *d* on the board that he couldn't read. Only three hours into her first day of school, she knew she was at a more advanced level than many of her classmates. She'd spent the last year devouring any books Celeste brought home from school, so she was reading at a fourth-grade level. *Beezus and Ramona* was her favorite. "Those two are white, and that's chocolate," she told him.

"I know, Rathead," he said, and bumped so roughly into Nikki's shoulder as he turned that she had to grip both sides of her tray to keep the food from spilling. Would they have given her another tray if she'd dropped it? Would they believe it hadn't been her fault? In a perfect world she'd get his food, but at six she knew already they were living in a far from perfect world.

At the first-grade table, Nikki slid one leg in and then the other, glad she'd worn jeans and not a skirt. She scooted closer to the tray, her mouth watering. Scattered across the table were small plastic bowls of cinnamon sugar. Nikki felt a flush creep up her neck.

What were those for? Did she put the sugar in her milk? On her sandwich?

She had been the last kid in line for her grade and the second graders were still assembling at the door, so she couldn't observe the other children to see what to do.

She dared a glance at the girl next to her, wearing a Mariah Carey T-shirt.

"It's really good," the girl said, nodding toward the bowl. "I'd never had it before, but my brother told me to try it and I'm glad I did." She smiled at Nikki, and Nikki was mad at Celeste all over again. Why hadn't *she* told *her*? Wasn't her big sister supposed to look out?

"Okay," Nikki said, and took the communal spoon, dipped it in the granules, and brought it over her plate. Her hand hovered—milk? sandwich?—and in a quick decision, she lifted the bun top with her empty hand and sprinkled the sugar on her sloppy joe.

"Oh my gawd," the boy next to her said. It was the same one from the milk dispenser, the one she'd embarrassed for being unable to read.

The girl next to her widened her eyes and put a hand over her mouth. "It goes on the rice," she said, and pointed at the soupy white glop on Nikki's plate. "Like a dessert?"

"Your sandwich," the boy said, and guffawed, snorting as he did, a dribble of chocolate milk escaping his nostril. Nikki felt a tingle of heat shoot down her limbs.

She couldn't think fast enough to lie and say she liked it on the sandwich, and instead panicked, standing too quickly and rattling the table. The cafeteria quieted a decibel, and she caught eyes with her sister.

Rules be damned, Nikki slid one leg out, then the other, her foot catching on the seat. She nearly fell but righted herself on the shoulder of the girl who'd been nice to her, knocking over her milk in the process. "Hey!" the girl said.

"Nicola?" the teacher said, but Nikki shot right past her toward her sister's table.

Celeste held up a finger to stop her then stood up and walked to her teacher, leaning over to speak. The teacher nodded and lifted the lanyard from around her neck, a laminated pass dangling at the end, and handed it to Celeste.

Nikki followed her sister out of the cafeteria, down the hallway. Then her sister took a sharp left and knocked open the restroom door. Inside, she stopped and turned so quickly, Nikki bumped into her. "What happened?" Celeste asked.

"I didn't—" Nikki started, and had to take a deep breath before continuing. "I didn't know what to do with the cinnamon sugar." Her lip quivered and she felt tears burn her eyes. She was such a loser!

Celeste shook her head, impatient. "No, I mean what happened with that boy? I saw him run into you on purpose at the milk station, then he was laughing at your table."

She'd been worried Celeste might hate her for getting the sugar wrong, for ruining a perfectly good sandwich, although Nikki would eat it anyway. "He called me a name. A mean one."

Celeste's eyes narrowed. "How mean?"

She didn't want to repeat it, the shame too real. She put a hand to the back of her head. "It's about my hair."

"I'll take care of him," Celeste whispered, and pulled a comb from her back pocket. "Here," she said, and held it out. "It looks like you fixed your hair with a fork." It was what Onita said to them when they left home looking bedraggled.

Nikki pulled the comb through starting at the roots, grimacing when she hit the offensive knot in the back. No wonder the kids behind her had been snickering all day. Was school ever going to get easier? She didn't know what she'd do without Celeste here to look after her and only wished someday she could help someone else like this. Be the one in charge. Maybe Onita would have another baby.

"Chin up," Celeste said, and pinched Nikki's chin as she handed back the comb. Her skin, clutched between her sister's finger and thumb, began to burn. "You be tough, okay? I'll take care of that little asshole."

Nikki felt a thrill at the swear.

Back at the lunch table, Nikki did her best to ignore the boy across from her, even as he dumped the rest of the bowl of cinnamon sugar on her plate. She ate her sandwich, every sickly sweet and gritty bite. He was about to have bigger problems.

After school, Nikki gathered her shoes slowly, slipping her feet out of her hand-me-down slippers and placing them symmetrically in her cubby. She took her time so she wouldn't be outside alone waiting for her sister. She didn't want to allow any extra minutes for other kids to make fun of her for something she couldn't even see coming. That's what she was learning in her first foray into the world: there were a lot of things she couldn't see coming.

Outside, Celeste pushed off from the side of the school with her foot and smiled at her. "You ready?"

Nikki nodded. There were three yellow school buses lined up outside Harris Elementary for the rural routes. She read their sides, found #2, and started toward it.

"We're going to walk today," Celeste said, even though it was three miles. Still, Nikki knew better than to argue with her. "We've got something to do first."

The class clown—she'd learned the second half of the day his name was Keith—emerged from the school's double doors with a new navy backpack, covered in planets spinning around a sun. Nikki hunched her shoulders, aware of the grime ground into the backpack Onita had bought at Goodwill. She'd wanted pink, or even purple, but this one was black and adult size, knocking into the backs of her thighs.

"Hey, Queef," Celeste yelled. Nikki didn't know what the word meant, only that her sister had made insulting names and bad words an art form.

The boy narrowed his eyes. "What?"

The last of the three buses chugged to life and sputtered forward. Already the schoolyard was nearly empty. He looked left to right as if realizing now it was just the three of them, the teachers inside bent over their desks, their attention on the next day's lessons.

"Come with me," Celeste said, and walked to the edge of the street, the edge of school property. "Unless you're scared of a girl?" she asked.

Nikki looked from her sister to Keith. He tightened his hands on the straps of his spotless backpack, the fingers whitening at the creases. And then he followed.

Chapter Seven

GWEN

February 2009

Gwen didn't understand why the university kept the library so warm. It was a few weeks before spring break of her freshman year, and the heat was cranking through the vents like a sleeping gas. Outside, in the late-evening light, she could see a few students playing Frisbee on the quad despite the cold weather, two girls in parkas heading toward the dorms and drinking twenty-ounce Diet Cokes. She wished she were out there with them rather than locked in the heat trying to stay awake.

She opened her copy of *Cell Biology and Genetics* in the carrel where she'd been working—a single desk with blinders on both sides. It was her favorite place in the library, even if biology was her least favorite subject. She could smell the stacks of older books and keep her back to others, but still hear the pleasant buzz of the people around her. Her concentrated silence was broken every now and again by shoes scuffing against the linoleum floors, the pleasant humming of whispered conversations, hardcover books slapping against desks.

As she moved her finger across the complicated lines of text in front of her, Gwen felt the hairs on the back of her neck stand up. Someone was watching her. She dared a glance over her shoulder, and saw a tall, solid boy sitting at a study table a few feet away.

He grinned, not even trying to hide that he'd been observing her. "You're what I call a Serious," he said. He was better-than-average-looking with a lopsided smile, and that effortless kind of hair that both flopped and curled. Was he flirting with her?

"A serious what?" she asked. She wasn't used to this kind of attention from boys. From anyone, really.

"Just a Serious. Anyone in one of those"—he motioned to the carrel—"is here to get straight As."

Gwen looked at him, perplexed. "Doesn't everyone want straight As?" She actually did get straight As her first semester, thanks to many nights just like this one—a near-empty library on a Friday night—but second semester was harder, all the classes just a bit denser. Why did she have to take biology anyway? When was it actually going to come in handy to use a Punnett square to figure out the eye color or blood types for someone's hypothetical baby? But still, she studied.

She knew it was a stretch for her parents to cover the tuition, and she didn't want to waste the opportunity. She also knew her father was dying of prostate cancer, and she wanted to make him proud in the time he had left, although she refused to face the fact that it could be months and not years. She'd always been Daryl Gries's Little Girl, and without that moniker, Gwen wasn't sure who she was. Maybe a Serious.

The boy at the table laughed, his attention like sunshine, and Gwen circled her knees away from her carrel and toward him. She was wearing a knee-length denim skirt, and while she wasn't the most confident girl in the world, even she knew she had nice legs. "You don't want to? Get straight As?"

His eyes tipped down, then quickly back up. "Some people want to have fun too."

"Never," Gwen deadpanned, and he laughed again.

"Do you ever tutor other students?" he asked.

"You don't even know what my major is," she chided, settling into the flirting. She hadn't had a boyfriend in high school but had hoped that would change in college. Her dad had begun talking about how he wanted to see her happily coupled one day with a man to take care of her. He was on medical leave from his electrician position at DP&L, and nearly every night now, Gwen woke to the hacking of his cough. Sometimes, she'd meet him in the kitchen when he couldn't sleep and they'd both eat a bowl of ice cream.

"Well, what *is* your major?" he asked.

"English."

"Perfect. I'm terrible at that. I can barely claim it as my native language."

"You sound like you're doing okay to me," she said.

He made an unintelligible noise and Gwen laughed. "What's *your* major?" she asked in return.

"Computer science."

"That's a major?"

"I thought it meant I would play video games for college credit, but that's not the case." He leaned forward. "Can I tell you a secret?" She nodded. She knew from the setup it wouldn't be a real secret, but the intimacy of it was enticing. He lowered his voice. "I picked it because the CS/engineering building was closest to my dorm."

She put a hand over her mouth and gasped. "That's terrible. Certainly no way to choose a major."

"See," he said. "This is why I need your wise counsel. I thought it was an excellent way to pick a major. This is what comes from not being fluent in English." He crossed one of his unreasonably long legs. He was wearing basketball shorts even though there was snow on the ground, the hair on his legs a golden brown. He bounced his knee, and she blushed as she realized she'd looked up the gaping fabric, following the line of muscle that bulged on his thigh.

"I am wholly unimpressed with your dedication," she said.

"And I am wholly hoping to corrupt yours," he said. Heat flared on Gwen's cheeks. "Come on," he said, and nodded toward an exit. "It's a Friday night. You should be out having fun. With me."

She tapped her pencil eraser on her book and shook her head. "I don't even know you."

"Todd Maner," he said, and leaned forward, dropping his crossed foot to the ground, his legs so long his knees were higher than his thin hips. She could tell he was still growing out of his boy's body, but that he'd fill out nicely, his chest already broad if still scrawny.

"Gwen Gries."

"Beautiful," he said. "A perfect name." Even when he was saying things that were over the top, it made Gwen blush to have the fullness of his attention spotlighted upon her.

"So how about it, Gwen Gries. Can you leave these books on their own for just a few hours and come eat a burger with me? Help me practice my conversational English?"

"That's not really what the major is about, you know," she teased.

He threw his hands in the air. "See how much you have to teach me?"

She looked down at the stack of books in front of her. She had thought the major would just be reading the nineteenth-century novels she loved, not studying the genome. Her and Jane Austen curled on a fainting couch swooning over Darcy, not critical essays where she had to look up every other word. Maybe instead of being Daryl Gries's Little Girl, she could be Todd Maner's Tutor.

She crossed her arms. "I'm not going to dinner with a complete stranger," she said. "How do I know you're not a serial killer?"

"I have a sister, and it is a well-known fact that not one serial killer in the history of America has had a sister."

She perked up. "Is that true?"

"I have no idea," he said. "But it *sounds* like it should be true." She laughed. "What else? I am an excellent orderer of burgers and have

42

never had a speeding ticket. I'm a Leo. I don't like to read, so I need someone who does to help me sound smart at parties. I think you're cute, and I know you think I'm cute or you would have swiveled those pretty little knees away from me by now." He ticked this off as one of his facts and Gwen smiled, biting the inside of her mouth to try to stop it. "Besides, what does a pretty girl like you need with book learning?"

The question rankled her, but she knew it was more of the flirting, nothing to get upset about. She put her notebook, pencil, and pen in her backpack. "Can we get fries along with our burgers?" she asked.

"Mandatory," he said.

"What about onion rings?"

"Sky's the limit."

She closed the book in front of her, the sound like a clap. To Gwen it sounded like one door closing and another opening. She left the stack of books in the carrel and slung her backpack over her shoulder.

"Ready?" he asked, and held out his hand.

"Ready," she said, and put her hand in his.

She already knew she'd follow him wherever he'd go.

Chapter Eight

GWEN

July 2022

Less than a week later, Gwen's plane touched down in Dayton, the shuddering bump of the wheels hitting the runway a match to her nervous stomach. It had all happened so quickly—reaching out to Nicola, sending on her résumé, and then the call saying the board had loved her, and how soon would she be able to make it to Dayton for an interview?

Gwen gripped the edge of her armrest to keep her balance as they taxied in, trapped in the middle seat after switching so the tall man next to her could take the aisle. It was the first time she'd ever flown alone. That morning, she'd followed signs to park her car in the economy lot at DIA and taken a shuttle to the airport proper by herself, her carry-on between her feet, three dollars clutched in her fist to tip. She ate an Egg McMuffin at her gate, then bought peanut M&M'S for the flight. The adultness of it, the freedom, was delicious.

She'd left Whitney with Jack and his wife and their geriatric Chihuahua, Weed, who was more dog-adjacent than actual dog, but even so, Whitney had been genuinely excited for the first time since Todd died. Gwen's mother, Jeri, had complained Gwen wasn't bringing her only grandchild, and Gwen had reminded her mom this was a work trip, not a social visit, placating her mother by saying she'd stay the night at her house and they'd get breakfast in the morning.

Jeri hadn't come to Boulder for the funeral, to help out, anything, saying her doctor had forbidden her from travel. *Since when?* Gwen wondered, and then felt a new flutter of panic. Would her mother die too?

At the funeral, Gwen and Whitney had sat in the front row next to Todd's parents and sister, the only family present. They'd arrived the night before and done little to help with the arrangements, taking off the same afternoon their son and brother was lowered into the ground. While Jeri hadn't been able to travel, she had called Gwen at 2:00 p.m. on the dot every day since Todd's death to see how she was managing. On one hand, Gwen appreciated the calls for support, but on the other, she resented that her mother obviously had an alarm set to remember to care.

Gwen had yet to tell her mom how bad her financial straits were and how much she needed this job. Jeri had taken pride in the fact she'd never worked, even though they also never broke above lower-middle class. Her mother had said over and over that Gwen's father had left them "comfortable," a word Gwen grew to despise. It meant decade-old towels that never seemed dry, a worn path in all the carpets. Off-brand cola and bandages with cheap adhesive.

At the Dayton airport, Gwen beelined to the first bathroom to change out of her yoga pants and into a navy business suit ten years out of date, the same one she'd worn the first day of the internship. She was proud she could get the skirt zipped, the jacket buttoned, even if they were considerably tighter than they had been before. Twenty minutes later, she was heading down I-75 toward the jagged Dayton skyline. She parked her rented Kia in the three-story garage next to Dacks and smoothed lipstick across her lips, flattened her bangs in the rearview mirror. There was a doorman or security guard—she wasn't quite sure of his job—in the building's lobby who told her to head to floor nineteen and ask for Helene. The elevator had a wall of windows facing the street, and as Gwen rode up, she admitted to herself she felt somewhat cosmopolitan in her business suit, a nice handbag secure on her shoulder, even if she was using a black diaper bag for a briefcase, having hung on to it with the hope the time for another baby might come along.

She stepped out of the elevators onto the light-wood laminate floors, the smooth brass and glass of Dack & Anders. She introduced herself to Helene, a girl who looked impossibly young but was probably the same age Gwen had been when she interned here. She had a slouchy insouciance only the young could get away with, dressed in a satiny blouse and fancy leggings. Irresponsibly high heels dangled on her feet under the desk that was a slab of reclaimed wood. Helene glanced at Gwen up and down, and only then did the shame of Gwen's outfit hit with full force: the out-of-date suit, the blouse (with a bow, for Christ's sake!). It was only by the grace of god she'd gotten a run in her pantyhose from a snaggletoothed toenail and had abandoned them in the airport restroom garbage.

Helene smiled tightly and indicated the open furniture behind Gwen, and told her Nicola would be out soon. Hands shaking, Gwen turned to take a seat in the floral papasan chair in the corner, her reasonable pump catching on the rug as she fell toward the chair, nearly flipping it on its side.

"Are you okay?" Helene asked, still seated at her desk, and it felt like she wasn't asking if Gwen was okay from the fall but okay in general, like a person who maybe couldn't get through the day.

"I'm fine," Gwen croaked back as she settled her purse in her lap, tears threatening to fall. Everything had been so hard since Todd died.

A few minutes later, she heard the clatter of quick, confident steps as Nicola rounded the corner. She looked much as Gwen remembered her, only taller (although that could have been the awkward angle of the chair) and even more glamorous. She'd always had a bit of that heroin-chic look where clothes draped effortlessly, but now she had the benefit of adult money—the fabrics better, the cut curated. She wore a hot-pink blazer with a black camisole, blue denim jeans so dark they appeared almost black. She'd replaced the nose ring with a small emerald that looked impossibly cool, and large leather earrings dangled to her shoulders in front of a waterfall of honeyed hair.

Nicola held out a manicured hand and pulled Gwen out of the chair, laughing. "Aren't these the worst chairs for a lobby? I swear, they're a job interview in themselves. If you can get out gracefully, you deserve the gig." She pulled Gwen into a hug, then released her.

Gwen laughed, too, smoothing down the tight skirt that had hiked up her thighs. Nicola smiled at her, her teeth overly white and straight. They were rich-people teeth. Even though Nicola was outdressing her by a mile, and had even left Helene in the dust, she didn't say a word about Gwen's old, ugly suit as she linked her arm around Gwen's elbow and pulled her toward the hall. Who was Gwen to think she might deserve to work with this woman?

"We'll have a minute to chat before the interview," Nicola said, and turned toward Helene before they rounded out of view. "Is the conference room set up?"

"Conference room?" Gwen echoed as Helene nodded.

"It'll be me and a few other muckety-mucks."

Gwen panicked; when she'd interviewed for the internship, it had been a mere formality with one man from HR who looked college-age himself. "I thought it would just be you?"

Nicola grinned. "I may have talked you up a bit," she said. "It's not quite the job we discussed on the phone."

"What is it?" *Jesus, please don't let it be another unpaid internship,* she thought. She could imagine her framed picture of Whitney next to the taped-up photos of the other interns with their half-shirts and BORGs.

"Don't be mad," Nicola said, and it struck Gwen as a little odd—maybe presumptuous?—that Nicola thought she knew what might make her mad. Husbands dying made her mad. Unknown debt made her mad. "But I shot a little higher than entry level. I couldn't stand the idea of you answering phones and making social media graphics on Canva."

"How much is a bit?" Gwen said, suddenly alarmed.

She followed Nicola into her office. Windows covered one wall, and Nicola settled into the leather chair behind the desk, pointing to an empty seat on the other side. The desk was the same type as out in the lobby—no visible drawers or clutter—Nicola's legs crossed and slanted beneath. "Associate VP of Regional Development," Nicola said.

"I—" Gwen started and lowered her voice, leaning forward. "I don't even know what that means!"

Nicola waved a hand. "No one does. I made it up."

Gwen knew Nicola was one of the top brass, but she didn't assume that meant she could hire anyone she wanted and make up positions on a whim. "Can you do that?"

"I mean, I shouldn't, but . . ." She smiled. "We go way back, Gwen. And let me say, I know your potential. If you hadn't been out of the workforce all these years, you'd be above a job like this. I want to help you get on track."

For a second, it reminded Gwen of her first date with Todd, how quickly things had progressed. They'd had a wonderful time that night after they left the library. Even before they'd ordered a dessert to share, two forks, he was talking about a possible trip together months down the line. She admitted she'd been smitten with him and his charisma, but to be talking about a future that quickly had spooked her. Why did he like her so much? The next day he'd sent her a dozen red roses so ostentatious and expensive, she'd tried to cancel their second date. It was all too much. She'd texted him to say thanks for the flowers and that she'd had a lovely time, but she just didn't think they were headed in the same direction.

And what had he done? He'd called her! Another red flag: never respond to a text with a call. Still, she'd answered, wanting to get it over with. "I fucked up, didn't I?" he said when she picked up—no hello, no greeting—and then barreled on. "My sister told me the flowers were too much, and I want you to know I've never done anything like that before, not to make it more creeper, but . . . I wanted you to know I *like* you."

His nervousness had charmed her, as had the fact he discussed her with his sister, and they went out again that night.

Now, sitting in Nicola's office, she was struck with the same feeling, but hadn't that red flag been for nothing? Todd had ended up being the best thing that ever came into her life other than her daughter—half him, half her. She felt a knot tighten in her throat. She had been right to trust Todd, and she was right to trust Nicola, or at least, what choice did she have? What Nicola was offering was a position with, she assumed, a lot more money. She had no choice.

"What can you tell me about this job that I'm obviously qualified for?" Gwen asked, and Nicola winked at her.

"Attagirl." She peeled two sheets of paper from her desk and passed them to Gwen. Her name was at the top with her address, email, and cell phone number, but under "Job Experience" was text she didn't recognize: *TeckPocket: Vice President of Media Relations.* "I made a few tweaks," Nicola said. "Nothing you can't live up to."

"But I—"

"You what?" Nicola said.

"I never worked for TeckPocket. That was my husband's company."

"Did you ever do any marketing for them? Or PR? What about brainstorming sessions?" It was true that in the beginning, Gwen, Todd, Jack, and Susie had all sat around their one-bedroom apartments eating discount Chinese food they stretched with extra rice as they talked about their vision for the company. Fresh off her internship, Gwen had been the one to make the PowerPoints for investors. "Did you ever take clients out for dinner? Play tennis with their wives?"

Gwen nodded slowly. "Zumba, not tennis."

Nicola waved a hand, dismissing the distinction. "That's networking. That's relations." Gwen told her about the PowerPoints and Nicola nodded. "That's fundraising, see? You helped build that company from the ground up. I should have listed you as a founding partner."

Gwen read the rest of the résumé, trying to concentrate. Like any good lie, it had striations of the truth. At the bottom was her book drive work at Whitney's grade school, under "Volunteering," where it belonged.

Nicola sighed, exasperated. "Did you really think you would get this interview with your résumé as you sent it? Spending three hours putting fifty-cent stickers on the Berenstain Bears books does not a résumé line make." Gwen shook her head. "But I can mentor you. You've got this. You just need to see it yourself."

"How would I—" she started.

Nicola waved a hand in the air to expound on her idea. "Go in with the confidence of a white man. And be sure to let them know how involved you were at Todd's company, even if that wasn't salaried. Think truth, not facts. Don't get too in the weeds with it all, which is a golf term all men love. Keep your answers simple so these guys can nod their heads and get back to playing *Candy Crush* on the toilet."

Gwen stared at her blankly, and underneath that was the simmering question: Why hadn't Todd asked her to be a part of things? She'd had good ideas; she contributed in the beginning when given the chance. Maybe if she'd been there, things wouldn't have ended as they did.

Shortly before 2:00 p.m. Gwen joined Nicola in the conference room with four men in suits. The man at the head of the table introduced himself as Mr. Donovan, the CEO, and pulled out Gwen's chair for her. "Ms. Maner," he said. "A pleasure to meet you." He sat down after her without offering his hand.

Every dinner she'd ever attended with other businessmen and potential investors gave Gwen a read on him instantly. He liked demure but confident, not flirty but somewhat in awe. He wanted to think of women as women and not equals.

She thanked him with her eyes locked to his and smoothed a hand over her lap, ignoring that she was dressed in an out-of-date suit and wishing she'd worn a little black dress with a blazer. Still, she could tell by the way he gave her his attention she had a shot at this as long as she played the part.

Three hours later, Gwen slipped one shoe off and then the other, her swollen feet resting on the rental-car carpet. Even as her big toes throbbed, she smiled. She'd nailed it; she knew she had. And if she hadn't already been confident enough, the way Nicola shook her hand at the elevators, two other C-something-Os watching, and leaned in and said, "Well done," had left little ambiguity she'd get the job.

Nicola had given her a quick sketch of the position before they walked in for the interview—basically sales, meeting with potential clients, selling the business—and she was able to draw on her experiences at TeckPocket as well as her prior experience with Dacks to convince them she was a worthy candidate. In the end, it hardly even felt like lying. What it had felt was amazing to sit in front of a room of strangers—her *peers*—and make the argument why she was worthy. For the last decade of her life, she'd been not so much a person but a person in relation to another person: Todd's wife, Whitney's mom, even her mother's daughter. This had been about *her*.

Her phone dinged in her bag and she picked it up, delighted to see Nicola's name. Up for a drink to celebrate?

Does that mean I got it???

Nicola texted back a winky-face emoji, party-decoration emoji, champagne emoji.

"Yes!" Gwen said, and slapped the car dash, the sting in her palm welcome.

Her thumbs flew across the keyboard. Just tell me when and where!

Chapter Nine

Gwen entered the Century Bar, a downtown Dayton institution, feeling like Melanie Griffith in *Working Girl.* She snaked her way through the long, dark bar, the lights dim enough she was barely thinking about her ugly suit or the god-awful bow (*Shut up,* she told herself. *You got the job!*) as she found a small table at the back, peeled off her damp suit jacket, and slung it over the chair. She took her phone from her purse and texted her mom, telling her she was stopping for a quick drink with the COO—a good sign! she wrote—but would be in touch soon about dinner.

She had another text waiting from Jack's phone that said PLEASEEEEEE let me get a dog!!!!! with a picture of Whitney pulling her best begging face as she held up Weed, Jack's mangy Chihuahua with bulbous eyes. Maybe that Todd had gone into business with a man who named his dog "Weed" had been part of the problem. But Gwen didn't want to think that way and shook her head, concentrating on the wins of the day. Whitney seemed genuinely happy! Gwen had nailed the job interview. Nailed it! And so what if they had sort of false information about her qualifications? She hadn't lied, not really. She'd done what Nicola said and stuck to a version of the truth, if not the facts.

A waiter came around and she ordered a glass of pinot grigio, squinting as the front door opened and Nicola slipped in, the sun glaring behind her. She waved at Gwen in the back, then stopped at the bar, had a quick word with the bartender, and pointed to Gwen's table.

"Guns," Nicola said appreciatively as she sidled up to Gwen and squeezed one of her arms before collapsing in the seat across from her. Gwen constantly chided herself for never getting to the gym, but one of the things she'd done to prep for the interview was to remind herself to take a compliment. "Thanks," she said.

"Mine look like flamingo legs," Nicola said, and stuck an elbow out at a gangly angle.

Gwen laughed and snuck a glance at Nicola's arm when she removed the fuchsia blazer she'd worn in the office, a smooth black cami underneath. The thin straps rested against her collarbones and crisscrossed in the back, a perfect day-to-night outfit with her dark skinny jeans.

There was something . . . unmarried about her look, Gwen thought. None of the women she knew in Boulder were single, and even if they had been she couldn't imagine those faux crunchers wearing anything but stretchy athleisure clothes, much less itchy lace on their décolletage, or earrings that irritatingly brushed their shoulders, hair down and not in a slick pony or even a messy bun.

"What?" Nicola said, catching Gwen's look.

"You're just so *effortless*," she said, and Nicola laughed.

"What is it Dolly says? It takes a lot of money to look this cheap? Same with looking effortless."

The bartender came over with the double Manhattan Nicola had apparently ordered and set it on the table. Nicola held her credit card in the air to him without even glancing at the guy. It made Gwen uncomfortable—it was borderline rude—and yet she was also envious of how commanding it all looked. Nicola was like a feminist Don Draper.

And while she didn't want to be insecure and ruin the good feeling of the interview by being needy, she couldn't help but ask, "So you think it went well?"

"Very," Nicola concurred, biting the maraschino cherry from her drink's plastic sword and chewing.

"I can't tell you what it means that you think I'm up for this job," Gwen said, and Nicola cocked her head. "I maybe shouldn't be saying this to the COO, but I was really nervous. I guess I still am."

"About what specifically?" Nicola asked.

"Well, now that I've got the job, or will soon," she hastened to add, knowing it wasn't official, "I have to actually figure out how to get back in the swing of a forty-hour week. Of leaving Whitney at day care or with my mom." She motioned to her outfit. "What to wear." She glossed over the idea of leaving Whitney at day care; she'd always been there when her daughter finished her elementary-school day to hear about her art projects and classroom dramas. That had been the bargain, she thought again: she would take care of the kid and Todd would earn the money. She'd kept her end of the deal, she thought ruefully as she folded her damp napkin in her hands.

"If it helps," Nicola said, smoothing a palm down to her denim-clad knee, "I think I've managed everyone's expectations."

Gwen crinkled her forehead. "What do you mean?"

Nicola rolled her eyes. "I pointed out how few women we have in the executive track, especially since Missy ghosted, and they had to give you to me. All I had to do was say 'gender equity' and 'lawsuit' in the same sentence, tap my heels three times, and those bro-fools would hire a cantaloupe as long as it female-identified." Gwen felt like she'd been slapped, but just as quickly, a splotchy heat rose up her neck. Anyone could have gotten this job—it had nothing to do with her—which meant just as easily it could be taken away.

Nicola saw her face as she sucked in her cheekbones around the tiny straw in her drink. "I didn't mean that to sound cruel." *God help me if you had,* Gwen thought. "I meant, well," Nicola continued, "even with the edits on your résumé, you didn't think you were getting this on your work experience and interview, did you?"

Gwen felt a ricochet of shame blast through her body. She had nearly convinced herself, all evidence to the contrary, that she had earned the job. *Stupid,* she thought now. *Ridiculous.*

"But Gwen," Nicola continued, resting a cool hand on Gwen's warm one. "I would not have fought for you to get this job if I didn't think you could do it. Trust me, you're going to be great. I have nothing but faith in you."

Gwen fought back the tears pooling in her eyes. "I guess."

"Plus," Nicola said, letting go of Gwen's hand, "I'll be there every step of the way. If you need anything at work, or have any questions, ask me. That's what I'm there for. I'll help you set up your clients, make introductions. I can teach you the software. Whatever you need."

The bartender looked over and Nicola circled her finger in the air: another round. It was all happening so fast—the next set of drinks, the software Gwen clearly wouldn't understand. The bartender nodded and turned toward the top-shelf liquor, and Gwen snuck a glance at her watch. She needed to text her mom and push back dinner again. She wasn't about to tell the woman who'd gotten her a job that she had to go.

"Although," Nicola said, "if you think this is really a forty-hour-a-week job, either you're about to be sorely disappointed or I am." Gwen's stomach looped on itself once again, and she took a large gulp of her wine. "Try sixty, seventy, eighty. You're not going to have much of a life, but you'll certainly have bank."

Gwen thought again about Whitney, reminding herself she was doing this for her. But was that really true if it meant her mother would be supervising Whitney's homework and bedtime? How was Gwen going to get time off to attend the ridiculously adorable dance recitals and soccer games or art shows? A good point, but without the job, would she even be able to afford these experiences for her daughter? She thought of how she'd opened her banking app at the airport to see if she needed to transfer money to cover a breakfast sandwich. A breakfast sandwich! She had to do what she had to do.

As the bartender brought the second round, Gwen excused herself to the bathroom, taking her phone with her to text her mom. Sorry! Drinks going long but work thing and can't say no.

Even texting "work thing" gave her a bit of a tingle. How many times had Todd texted her that very same thing? With a jolt it occurred to her: *Wait, was he just out for drinks like I am now?* She felt a boost of anger at the thought, followed quickly by guilt. That wasn't what Todd was like. He'd loved spending time with her and Whitney, or at least she thought he had. Weekends she would schedule a Sunday Funday for the three of them where they took Whitney to the Fiske Planetarium or Denver Zoo or Meow Wolf with its psychedelic lights that gave Gwen a migraine, but what about time with just her that hadn't included clients or home repair or the complex scheduling of their lives?

Here in an hour? her mom texted back, and Gwen felt another flare of irritation. For the first time she wondered if moving back to Dayton was really the answer. She and her mom had a good relationship when there were twelve hundred miles between them, but what about when Jeri had a front row seat for every decision Gwen made?

Hopefully an hour, she texted, trying to manage her mother's expectations.

Back at the table, her phone buzzed again. I haven't even seen you! her mother had texted back, as if Gwen were here for a social visit. She set the phone upside down with a sigh.

"What's the problem?" Nicola asked, concern etched on her face.

"It's nothing. My mom. She wanted to get dinner tonight, but I'm not sure it's going to work out."

"You don't want to go?" Nicola asked, and Gwen shrugged.

"It's not that I don't want to, it's just—" She smiled at Nicola; she didn't want to burden her with her problems. "My mom's a bit pushy."

"Here," Nicola said, and before Gwen registered what was happening, Nicola had picked up Gwen's phone and held it in front of Gwen's face to unlock. Nicola turned the screen toward herself and studied it for a second, Gwen aghast, and then her thumbs flew across the keyboard. "There," she said, and set the phone back down, screen against the table.

Gwen picked it up and read what Nicola had texted to her mother. I will see you in the morning. No explanation, no apology. Her mother would have a fit.

The three rotating dots appeared and Gwen held her breath, and a few beats later there was a text from her mother.

Fine.

No fight, no pushback. Sure, there might be passive-aggressive hell to pay in the morning, but for now she was off the hook.

Gwen couldn't believe it. Thirty-two years she'd been kowtowing to her mother, and all it had taken was one text for her to back off? She didn't know if she was hurt her mother had given up so easily or relieved. "Thanks," she said, and Nicola shrugged.

"I know something about overbearing mothers." She took the last sip of her drink and held it up, rattling the ice against the glass's side to get the bartender's attention. "You ready for another?" she asked Gwen.

"Oh, I don't know." Her nearly empty wineglass was next to her phone on the table. The lock screen was a picture of Whitney on her bike at Valmont Park, sweaty and happy under her helmet, a gaping hole where her front teeth used to be. Maybe she would get Whitney a dog once they were settled in Dayton. It was rare to capture her daughter with a smile, just like it was rare for Gwen to be out on the town without her. "What the hell," she said, and threw her phone in her purse. "Bottoms up." She clinked glasses with Nicola, who laughed.

"You really are a bit of a dork," Nicola said in that straightforward way she had, and while there was a sting to her words, Gwen laughed too. "But don't you worry." Nicola slung an arm around Gwen's shoulders. "I'm here to help." She clinked their glasses again, a sound so sharp Gwen thought for a second the glasses might break. "Bottoms up."

Chapter Ten

Gwen woke with a sour taste in her dry, gummy mouth. Jesus. When was the last time she'd been hungover?

She eased one eye open and glanced around, her dehydrated heart thumping. She sat up quickly, a stab in her head. Where the hell was she?

She should be in her mother's guest room with its out-of-date maroon-and-forest-green bedspread, but she was in a room she didn't recognize, lying on a yellow velvet couch under a very large abstract blue-green painting that looked like it cost more than Gwen's first car. The ceiling seemed a mile away, the walls twice as high as those in Gwen's house.

Where the hell?

Gwen spotted Whitney's old diaper bag and her purse on the breakfast bar and burst from the couch, relief flooding her that she still had them. She sorted through and grasped both her wallet and her cell. The phone screen was filled with texts from her mom, the last one reading, let me know youre okay!!??

She looked up at the clock: 8:18. *Shit, shit, shit.* She remembered Nicola's terse text to her mother, how she'd known that dam wouldn't hold forever, and this was her mother's revenge. Did she still have time to go over there before her flight? She flipped to her Apple Wallet and looked at her ticket; boarding started in under an hour. She scanned the space, darting for her shoes tucked under the breakfast bar. She was still dressed in her interview suit, the blouse's bow crushed at her collar, the skirt wrinkled and twisted so the zipper rested on her hip.

A door opened down the hallway and a very fit and very sweaty man entered. Gwen's heart rate climbed higher, slamming into her chest like a fist. One of the reasons she wasn't a big drinker was because it had always made her either mean or horny. With a flash of horror, she thought, *Did I meet someone?* How awful it would be to put her mouth on a mouth that wasn't Todd's, but that was followed by the soul-crushing realization that even if she had, she wouldn't have been cheating.

He smiled at her as he removed his earbuds. "Fun night?" he asked, and she wasn't sure if he was asking if she'd had a fun night or they had. Who the hell was he? She held her bag in front of her chest as if she were naked.

"Derek," he said, and held out a hand. She shook it reflexively, his hand warm and slick. He wouldn't introduce himself after sex, would he? "I was in bed when you guys got in last night."

Guys?

But then she remembered Nicola talking about her husband of six years. She'd thought over the music at the second or third bar that Nicola had said Garrett. Nicola had leaned forward, spilling her mixed drink on her knee, saying her husband was an asshole. Gwen could recall Nicola's glassy eyes, the unfocused gaze as she told Gwen she was certain he was cheating on her. At least Gwen hadn't been the only one to blur the lines of professionalism by getting drunk and complaining about her mother.

In the kitchen, Derek grabbed two huge plastic jugs from under the sink where at home Gwen kept the cleaning supplies. One was a vanilla protein powder, the other glutamine. She didn't even know what that was. He unscrewed the vats and added a scoop from each into the industrial-grade Vitamix on the counter along with half a banana, water, and ice cubes. There was a clicking noise above her, and Gwen recognized the sound of heels descending stairs as the Vitamix began grinding and whirling, the engine like an old VW.

Nicola rounded the corner toward the kitchen, waving over the noise. "Well, well," she said cheerily, and Gwen felt a hot burn start its way up her neck. "Someone's finally up." She shot a wry look at her husband as he stopped the blender. "Derek. You're not sexually harassing our guest, are you?"

"Jesus, Nic," he said as he poured the shake into a bottle before pumping his fit legs up the stairs.

"I am so sorry," Gwen started, her heart scattering through her chest. She wasn't even sure what she was apologizing for but knew it was probably the right thing to say. How many drinks had she had?

"You're fine," Nicola said, and Gwen felt a rush of relief course through her like a glass of cold water. Nicola laughed. "You were pretty drunk, though."

"Weren't you?"

"I mean, tipsy certainly, but something tells me I have a little more experience than you."

Gwen cringed to think she came off as such a country mouse. Nicola clapped her hands. "We should get going. I tried to wake you up in time to shower before we left but you were having none of it, and we still need to get your car from the parking garage." She nodded toward a closed door. "There's a washcloth in the bathroom if you want to at least swab your pits."

"Thank you," Gwen said, embarrassed all over again to think Nicola had tried to wake her. Had Gwen been a bitch about it? She was too humiliated to ask.

In the half bath, she wet a washcloth with cold water and winced when she set it on her neck, leaning forward to cup water in her hands and splash it on her face. Her skin felt like it was covered in a thin veneer of dirt, the caked-on makeup and grime so thick. She removed the washcloth and scrubbed her face with hand soap. Riffling through the top drawer, she found a near-empty tube of travel toothpaste and squeezed a half inch on her finger.

Gwen hiked up her skirt and peed a dark yellow stream as she faced the texts from her mother. There were eight in all, the most guilt-inducing being, as a mother you should know how worried I am about you, and the most passive-aggressive being, let me know you're not dead.

Was this what it was going to be like if she moved back to Dayton? Her mom losing it if Gwen didn't check in every hour? As much as she wanted to ignore these texts, she hated the idea of being on the outs with her mom, especially if she was going to need to stay with her while she found a place.

She took a breath and texted her back. I am so sorry mom!!! Job interview went very late and nicola let me sleep at her place. All is fine. Forgot to check phone last night. We'll have lots of time to hang soon when I move back <smiley-face emoji>.

The three dots appeared from her mother, and then nothing. Maybe the most passive-aggressive text was the one not sent. But who could blame her, Gwen thought as she flushed. If Whitney pulled that on her, even at the age of thirty-two, Gwen knew she'd be furious.

Back in the kitchen, Nicola handed her a travel mug of coffee; the smell of it made Gwen's stomach recoil once again, but she held it up in thanks.

"This place is amazing," she said, motioning to the kitchen and living room, desperate for normal conversation.

"Thanks," Nicola said. "We moved in here a few years ago. It's great—quiet neighbors, a gym, reasonable HOA fees."

"Sounds perfect," Gwen said, and took a swig of the coffee, sweetened with sugar and cream. Everything was so orderly, so in its place, it was obviously a house without kids. Nicola threw a granola bar at her and Gwen fumbled it to the floor.

In the passenger seat, being driven to her car by her new boss, Gwen felt like a stupid child, chiding herself for having screwed up so badly after such a great interview. Would they even want to offer her a job now, much less one at the level they'd discussed after she'd gotten so drunk? She shuddered thinking Nicola would rescind the verbal offer and she'd be back to square one. "I am so, so sorry about last night," she said quietly. "That was so unprofessional of me."

"Don't worry about it," Nicola said, quick to reassure her. "It's not like you were doing shots in the middle of Dacks. We're old friends. We went out for a few. It's not that big of a deal."

"Really?" Gwen said, desperate once again for reassurance.

Nicola glanced over at her. "Really," she said. "You get to decide whether this was a big deal or not, so just decide it wasn't and move on. You're an adult; you had some drinks. Don't let anyone make you feel bad about it."

"It's that easy for you?" Gwen asked, genuinely curious.

Nicola shrugged. "Why would I give anyone the power to make me feel small?"

The saying tickled something in Gwen's memory but she couldn't place it. "I really wish we'd been closer during the internship," she said, gratitude rushing in.

"You didn't really seem interested in it," Nicola said, rotating the steering wheel toward downtown as she turned onto Far Hills. That wasn't how Gwen remembered it at all. Missy and Nicola had been so close, she'd always felt like a third wheel when she asked to join them for lunch. Even when she'd been doing something as benign as stuffing envelopes with Missy, Nicola had seemed determined to horn in, glaring at Gwen like she'd taken the last candy bar on earth. Maybe even snatched it out of her mouth. "All you seemed to care about was getting married."

Gwen felt a blush creep up her cheeks. It was true. But she was older now, not so self-absorbed, although had she asked Nicola anything about herself last night? "So have you read any good books lately?" she said, and Nicola made a gagging noise.

"Really? Are we going to have that kind of conversation? I think everyone should be worried about climate change. My good deed is blood drives because I'm a universal donor. My celebrity run-in was Harrison Ford at a Circle K." She shook her head. "I'm not going to do that, Gwen. I'm not going to be your boring friend. Real dirt or nothing." Gwen laughed, and Nicola glanced at her before moving her eyes back to the road. "Remember when you called and asked about Missy?"

"I do," Gwen said. "You said something about her leaving under weird circumstances. Is that real dirt?"

"It was super unprofessional," Nicola said. "She just quit, up and left in the middle of the night. Poof. Ghosted."

"That's an option?" Gwen laughed, but the comment left her sour: there was much she loved about her life, number one being Whitney. And even as she said it, she thought about Missy as she'd known her: the pattern socks, the color-coded pencils, an honest-to-god set of adult underpants for the days of the week. She did not seem like the type to go off the grid.

"Right? But it's not a joking matter," Nicola said, which struck Gwen as odd considering Nicola had joked about her own husband dying. Outside the window, two suburban women with ankle weights walked slowly down the manicured sidewalk, Starbucks cups in their hands. "Things have to be pretty bad in your life to just up and leave like that. She was engaged to this guy, Jonas, and he told me he found this general see-ya in her Notes app saying she didn't want this life anymore. I mean, the Notes app? Super tacky. But I think she thought disappearing was her only way out." She looked knowingly at Gwen. "The guy was sketch."

"You didn't like him?" Gwen didn't want to look like a gossip, but she had to admit she was curious. Maybe it was the same morbid curiosity that drove people to ask about Todd's death.

"I don't want to speak badly about the guy, but I thought Missy could do better. He was an ex-con and had a kid. The daughter was sweet, but it was obvious he just wanted Missy to raise her. Plus, he was super controlling. Derek and I met them for dinner before lockdown, and he was the type of guy to order for her, put his hand over her wineglass if he thought she'd had enough. That kind of thing." Gwen felt her cheeks heat; Todd had done both of those things regularly.

Nicola signaled to the right and then the left, jockeying between cars to get ahead. She looked at Gwen as if sizing her up. "Or maybe she was one of those women that abandons her girlfriends when she gets in a serious relationship." Gwen did her best to look as if she too didn't like those women, knowing damn well she was one herself.

"Men don't understand how much women need other women in their lives."

"For sure," Gwen agreed as Nicola did another quick lane change. An SUV behind her laid on the horn as Nicola nearly clipped its bumper. "But like, how do you mean?"

Nicola hit the gas and flipped the driver off. "Men are stupid if they think they're going to fulfill all of a woman's emotional needs. There's sex, and that's great, but Jesus, do I want to hear about weightlifting and home improvement projects? No, thank you. I'd much rather spend time with a woman. Even if we're just watching a movie or running errands. Or like, what would you rather do on a vacation? Go to the beach or a sports bar to watch football? How is that compatible?"

Gwen bit down harder, a flood of iron in her mouth. "Marriage is about compromise," she said neutrally, but when really had Todd compromised? They'd certainly spent more afternoons at sports bars than the beach.

"Yes, but I think as a society we put too much pressure on that one union. Too much responsibility for one person to do all the emotional lifting." She looked pointedly at Gwen. "And you know that lifting is always done by the woman. I wonder what marriage would be like if we could just agree: listen, we're here for sex and to split a mortgage and to have someone to spend the holidays with. That's it."

Gwen frowned. "That's a sad description of marriage." One of her favorite parts of being married was spending the flotsam of their days together. Cleaning out the garage, deciding Christmas gifts, the common-ground nemesis of the neighbor who fired up the leaf blower early on the weekends.

"Is it?" Nicola seemed genuinely curious. "Or is it maybe freeing to think that's all it has to be? We put all this weight on marriages when what we have in common is sex. I'm saying there are healthier, more meaningful relationships out there." Gwen wondered in a roundabout way if this was a pep talk about losing Todd.

Nicola pulled into the dark parking garage, Gwen's eyes adjusting after the piercing morning sunlight. She pointed out the Kia she'd picked up at the airport. It was the first time she'd rented a car in her own name, another ping of independence she was secretly proud of. She bet Nicola had rented dozens of cars, maybe hundreds, but as Todd used to say, comparison was the thief of joy. Todd, who would often see a guy wearing a cool pair of kicks at a restaurant and grab his phone to order them immediately.

Nicola tucked her sunglasses into her hair and turned off the engine, both women climbing out. "So I guess I'll see you soon," she said.

Gwen had been nervous to ask outright if she still had the job, but there it was. She felt a surge of gratitude. "Great!" she said, pulling the diaper bag high on her shoulder as she reached for her purse with her other hand.

Nicola leaned in for a hug, releasing Gwen with her hands on her shoulders. She locked eyes, and Gwen wondered if these would be her final words of advice, a little something for her to take back to Boulder to fortify her for the adventure ahead.

"And Gwen?" Nicola said. "If you want, I can take you shopping for a new work bag."

Chapter Eleven

NIKKI

August 1996

Keith was eyeing Nikki warily. He seemed lost and smaller now that they were away from the cafeteria and his friends. They followed Celeste to the park across the street, the school buses all gone. The Harris Public Park was nicer than the one where Nikki had spent recess by herself, with its uneven four-square court and weeds in the concrete cracks. This park had a shiny set of monkey bars with a tall metal slide that curled at the bottom.

Celeste kept walking without turning around, and Nikki marveled that her sister was so confident she didn't even check to see if Keith was still following. She stopped finally at a copse that butted against the beginning of farmland, then turned around and jutted out her hip. Celeste and Nikki were both tall for their ages, their arms skinny and long in their short-sleeved T-shirts, bony at the elbows.

Keith stopped a few feet from Celeste, and instinctively, Nikki stilled an equal distance behind him. Last year, she and her sister had found a feral cat in the barn. Celeste had grabbed two of the heavy wooden panels leaning against the wall, and step by step they'd shuffled the panels right and left until the space between them and the cat became smaller and tighter. The cat's tail puffed as he hissed, fangs exposed. Keith had the same look of fear in his eyes right now, although he tried to hide it behind a slouch as he kicked his shiny new shoe in the dirt. Nikki was wearing Celeste's old pair of knockoff Keds from Payless.

"I heard you called my sister a name," Celeste said. One corner of her mouth quirked up as she said it.

Keith drew the toe of his shoe through the dirt again. Nikki felt a flash of anger; he didn't even care about the nice things he had. "I didn't know she was your sister."

Celeste took a step closer. "So if you had, you wouldn't have called her a name?"

"I don't know," Keith mumbled, and Nikki understood two things at once: she felt an evil glee that Keith was getting his comeuppance after being so awful to her, and simultaneously bad that he was in the position she'd been in, cowed at the hands of someone bigger and stronger. It was, she realized, the most grown-up thought she'd ever had.

"What was it you called her, anyway?" Celeste asked. "Nikki didn't want to tell me, so it must have been pretty bad."

He was looking at his feet now, that hypnotic shoe mining a dry rivulet in the ground. "I don't remember," he mumbled.

At that, Celeste's eyebrows shot up. "You don't remember? You said something so mean to my sister she had tears in her eyes, and now you don't *remember*?" Keith kept his eyes on the shoe, that shiny white shoe. Nikki thought she saw his fat bottom lip tremble.

"Hey," Celeste whispered so softly to Keith, Nikki felt her body lean closer. "Look at me."

Keith met Celeste's eyes as she took a step toward him, and Nikki took a step closer behind him. She pictured that tabby from the barn, chest heaving as his back arched in the air.

"What was the name?" Celeste asked again.

"Rathead," he admitted, and Nikki felt an arrow of shame pierce her. It had been her fault; she was the one who left for school without combing her hair.

A thought flicked through her head like an errant tongue: she should step in and defend him. But there was that side-serving of deliciousness, watching him squirm. *He* had called her the name. *He* had started it.

"Why Rathead?" Celeste asked.

"Because of her"—he motioned to the back of his own head—"her hair."

Celeste nodded as if that made sense, but she had another question. "Do you have a sister, Keith?" Nikki didn't know why she'd asked it, but Keith shook his head. "I didn't think so. Any brothers?"

"One."

"Older or younger?"

"Younger. Just a baby."

"Someday you'll understand this then," Celeste said, and took a step closer, Nikki echoing her movement. Keith whipped his head around to look at her and Nikki held his gaze, careful not to smile by default. He'd been so mean to her! Ruining her sandwich and calling her names. She could still feel the grains of sugar between her teeth, like biting down on sweet sand.

"Understand what?" he asked.

They were both a foot away from him now, crowding closer, and Celeste snaked out a hand and clutched his elbow. "Let's go play on the slide," Celeste said, and yanked Keith's arm. He was sniffling now, his child-size planetary backpack slipping off his shoulder.

"I don't want—"

"We can't always get what we want," Celeste said, and Nikki recognized it as a song, one that played on the car radio. Sometimes Onita would drive to town and leave them in the car for hours in the evening, channel 105.7 the only babysitter. Not once had their mother ever come to Nikki's rescue like this. Two half sisters make a whole.

Keith stumbled forward, and as they approached the slide, Nikki realized it wasn't in as good a condition as she'd thought, with flakes of rusty metal at the bottom that looked like they could cut through skin. Probably not denim, but definitely skin. She was suddenly glad that Keith wasn't wearing shorts.

"Why don't you climb to the top," Celeste said, and spun Keith in a half circle, sliding his backpack down his arms.

"I don't—" he started, but he was crying in earnest now.

"I don't care what you want," Celeste said. She passed the bag to Nikki, who clutched it with both arms against her chest. It was heavier than hers. Full of new notebooks and sharpened pencils, she presumed. Maybe even the plastic, see-through calculator she'd coveted at Walmart. She wanted to unzip the zipper tooth by tooth and see, but she knew stealing was wrong.

Celeste turned to Nikki. "Put the bag over there. You can follow him up."

Nikki set the bag by the end of the slide so Keith could retrieve it. She didn't fully understand what was happening but knew better than to disobey her sister, who walked both her and Keith to the rungs at the back of the ladder. Celeste nudged the boy with her hip, which came almost to his shoulder, and he took a faltering step forward.

His right hand gripped the guardrail, and he placed his left foot on the first rung. Nikki watched in amazement as the denim at his crotch darkened, the wet stain spreading down his thigh. He looked at Nikki, his throat convulsing, and Nikki found she had to look away. He was just a little boy, starting first grade like her.

"Go," Celeste said, with more force in her voice. He stepped right foot, left. Right foot, left. "Follow him up," she said to Nikki, and Nikki didn't know what to do but obey. She ascended the steps, the smell of dark urine wafting down from Keith's pants.

When they were halfway up, he whispered to her, "Please don't push me."

Was that what Celeste wanted her to do? She couldn't imagine doing it, but wouldn't admit that to Keith. "Go," she said, echoing her sister.

At the top was a small metal ledge where Keith crouched down. "Don't push me, please," he pleaded again. He sat on the ledge and placed one foot out and then the other. His legs stank, as did his shirt now, too, stuck to his back with an acrid, adultlike sweat.

Nikki looked around him to Celeste, waiting at the bottom of the curved slide. "Come on!" she yelled up at the boy. He was scared, looking from one sister to the other quickly, his eyes bobbing back and forth as his hands gripped the sides of the slide.

Nikki reached out one finger and tapped his shoulder, light as a feather, and Keith screamed. He shot down the slide, pushing with his hands to keep moving in the wet denim.

At the bottom, he stopped just shy of the rusted area, Celeste to his right. She snatched out her hand and grabbed a fistful of Keith's red hair. She bunched it in her fist, lifted his head, and slammed it down on the metal.

Nikki felt it before she heard it, the smash reverberating through her fingers, gripped to the side of the slide. This was followed by the clanging noise of it, buzzing through the oaks, a cawing sound of a surprised bird ringing right behind.

Celeste leaned down and said something to Keith that Nikki couldn't hear and he scrabbled off the slide, bawling, one hand holding the side of his bloody face, the other reaching for his backpack. He ran a few feet, then slithered to the side as if he'd just turned circles too quickly and lost his balance. He fell and dirt ground in his knees, but he righted himself and shot toward the street.

Celeste looked up and smiled at her sister, motioning her down. Nikki gripped the sides of the slide, careful not to gain speed, stopping before the blood-matted metal, one drop trickling its way farther down.

"He won't bother you again," Celeste said. "I promise."

Nikki reached for her sister's hand so Celeste could help her down from the slide. "Thank you," she said. The clang still rang in the air, or she thought it did. Was thank you the right thing to say?

Celeste squeezed her sister's hand. "You're welcome."

Chapter Twelve

GWEN

July 2022

By the time Gwen landed in Denver, she had the offer waiting in her email. The money was better than she would have hoped, but they wanted her to start in a little over a *week*. She needed to get Whitney registered for school, find a place to live, pack up her house, figure out day care. How was she supposed to accomplish that in nine days? She thought about Nicola and added *new work bag* to that mental list.

After Gwen put Whitney to bed, she called her mom to ask if they could stay with her until she found a place. "Hopefully only a few weeks. A month at the most."

"A *month*? Why don't you rent a place? One of those furnished apartments or suites by the airport?" Gwen rolled her eyes. Was this payback for missing breakfast? It wasn't like her mother to not want to host. She was far from a social person, but had always enjoyed having them home, walking Gwen through the house to show her any new blankets she'd crocheted or knickknacks she'd acquired after a feisty eBay exchange.

"Because we're *family*," Gwen said, hoping to guilt her mother into it. "And Whitney would be disappointed to stay anywhere else."

It was a stretching of the truth. Last time she, Todd, and their daughter had stayed at Jeri's, they'd been on top of each other the whole trip. Whitney had slept in the double bed with her and Todd. *That had been last Christmas, right?* But no, Whitney would have been too big to join them in the small bed. They'd lost the Christmas before that to COVID, and the one before that, Todd's family had visited Boulder. The one before *that* had been a trip to Costa Rica through TeckPocket. Had it really been that long since she'd been home? Guilt seeped in as she thought about flying all the way to Dayton the day before, yet not finding time to see her mom.

"I'm sorry I didn't see you when I was there," Gwen said, her voice softened. "It was just such a quick trip."

"I know," her mom agreed. "And I'm not mad."

Gwen felt a whoosh of relief. She could not stand when someone was mad at her, warranted or otherwise, but still. Why was her mother being cagey? It was true Gwen had always been a daddy's girl, but she and her mother had also found their common ground after his death, although she'd been passed by that point like a baton from her father to Todd. "Then what is it? Why wouldn't you want us to stay there?"

"Of course you're welcome here, Gwennie," her mother said. "It's just I don't want to hear word one about how my house isn't up to snuff."

"What are you even talking about?" Her mom had kept an immaculate house her entire life.

"Not everyone can afford a fancy-pants housekeeper. I'm just saying." "I'm just saying" was her mother's favorite period at the end of every discussion.

"Mom, I'm sure your place looks great," but even as Gwen said it, she wondered if it was true. Did this have to do with the health problems that had kept Jeri from traveling to Colorado for the funeral? Just what was waiting for Gwen in Ohio?

◆   ◆   ◆

Jack's wife, Susie, showed up the next morning with a clipboard in one arm and Weed in the other, the dog dressed in a red-and-gray ringer tee. Susie set Weed down and gave Gwen a hug, ending in an efficient clap on the back. Gwen had always been the warm wife, the one who showed up with rolls or a cheese dip, while Susie had an Excel sheet with action points. The women had been friends for over a decade, but quantifiably so; their husbands' partnership was the end of their commonality.

Whitney ran from her room at Weed's first hacking bark, collapsing on the carpet next to him as he took a few wobbly steps and bent to pee. He had patchy white fur that glowed from the pink skin underneath and a black growth of some kind on his wiener. He barely even passed for a dog, but still Whitney was taken with him, acting like Lassie had found another kid in the well.

Over the next two days, Susie kept the house on schedule as she made calls to the packing company, 1-800-GOT-JUNK for a trash pickup, and a real estate agent who assured Gwen a house like this in Boulder would fly off the market. Two days after Gwen and Whitney were to start the drive to Dayton, there would be an estate sale. She was thankful she'd be out of Colorado by the time people in jorts and fanny packs traipsed across her lawn to manhandle her things.

Susie passed the phone number of a national moving company to Gwen while she ordered sandwiches from the Yellow Deli for lunch. Looking at the scrap of paper, Gwen realized she had always felt inferior to Susie, who had demanded a seat on TeckPocket's board from the beginning. She'd been taking scraps of paper from the woman for a decade, and it gave her a jolt of confidence to think how Nicola had repositioned her skills as assets on her résumé, to show the worth in all she'd done. It was another way she hoped Dayton might be a fresh start.

Gwen dialed the number of the moving company, pushed the buttons for customer service, and explained what she needed and when.

"What's the delivery address?" asked the woman at the moving company.

"Dayton, Ohio."

"I know that," the woman said impatiently, "but *where* in Dayton?" and at the sound of her harsh voice, Gwen's confidence scattered. It was only eleven in the morning, and already she had cried twice that day. She still needed to arrange a storage unit, never mind find a more permanent place to live. She'd looked at facilities that morning and the sheer number of options—24-hour, drive-up, climate-controlled—had her so overwhelmed she'd slammed the laptop shut. Plus, she didn't know where they'd end up living, what would be closest. Shouldn't she get the apartment before the storage unit? What if she needed a down payment? And shouldn't she have an estate sale *before* she rented the unit so she'd know how much stuff she was storing? Also, were people supposed to just know how to organize an estate sale? *How?*

She felt tears burn against her lids again as she took in a deep breath, counted to three, and let it out.

"Ma'am? Are you there?"

"Can't you just head that way and I'll let you know when you're closer?" Gwen said.

"So you don't have an address?" the woman clarified.

"I mean, I do," she said, but if her mother had been less than hospitable about two family members showing up, she couldn't imagine how she might react to a fifty-three-foot moving truck full of their stuff.

"We can't complete the order without an address," the woman said again, and so Gwen gave her Jeri's information, making sure she could change it as the date got closer.

"You can," the woman said, "but there's a charge."

"Of course there is," Gwen said. It seemed everything had a charge. Susie passed her a company credit card, and Gwen read off the number. TeckPocket hadn't been able to offer any kind of compensation after Todd's death, but as a courtesy had agreed to pay her moving expenses. And good thing, Gwen thought, because there wasn't much left on her own credit cards, never mind in the bank.

That afternoon, as Gwen wrapped the last of Todd's highball glasses in newspaper, she ran her finger along the rim of one, hoping to produce a sound from the vibration, but the kitchen was silent. It had been an old party trick of Todd's, and last Christmas he had played "Silent Night" on the cups convincingly enough that he received a round of applause at the TeckPocket holiday party. She shut the top of the box and straddled it on both sides with her knees as she taped the flaps down, tears tracking her cheeks.

Thankfully, her phone dinged to distract her: Nicola texting to ask how things were going. She'd asked Gwen to let her know when she landed in Denver last week, and it had struck Gwen as thoughtful. She liked the idea that someone was still worried about her whereabouts in the world.

Since then, they'd been in contact every few hours. Gwen sent what she hoped were amusing texts about packing and her day, including a photo of an overly cramped linen closet with the caption, how many towels does one person need???? And a picture of Weed's penis growth with the caption #dickpic. That one earned her an lolololol and she thought, maybe Nicola isn't so intimidating after all. Maybe we'll grow to be friends. She remembered how jealous she'd been back in the intern days that Nicola preferred Missy so much to her. *What does she have that I don't?* Gwen remembered thinking.

That evening, before Susie and Weed went home, Susie handed Gwen a list of chores for the morning on a pad of paper with a bee stenciled at the top with "Queen" written above it. That made Gwen the worker bee, she assumed, and sighed as she ordered a plain cheese pizza for herself and Whitney, cataloguing the millionth thing she missed now that Todd was gone: adult pizza toppings.

Nicola texted, time to chat?

Worried it might be about the job, Gwen texted back, of course!

Her phone rang a few seconds later, and Gwen left Whitney in front of the iPad with *Moana* as she skulked into the kitchen where most of her clutter had been packed, the cabinets now empty, the oven blasting heat behind her on self-clean for the open house. Two months ago, she and Todd had leaned over this counter eating thin crust with banana peppers.

"So how's it going?" Nicola asked when she answered. "Did you box up your life yet?"

"Hardly," Gwen said, but she didn't want to let on how over her head it all was. She liked this dick-pic-sending version of herself that Nicola thought was funny, so instead she told her how she'd be crammed into her childhood home temporarily, her daughter sleeping in the bed with her. She tried to spin it—pathetic, but make it funny!—but Nicola didn't bite.

"So you're staying with your mother?" Nicola audibly shuddered. "I'd rather die."

"You two don't get along?" Gwen asked.

"We do now," Nicola said. "She's dead."

Gwen started at Nicola's bluntness. As crazy as her mother drove her, she'd be a wreck if Jeri died. Sure, they had their differences, but there was love as a foundation. She felt bad for Jeri who, at seventy, had been diagnosed with diabetes, all that weight over the years catching up with her. Now rather than enjoying her golden years she was losing her mobility, the pain in her feet a constant. Because Gwen hadn't been home, she wasn't sure if that was Jeri's regular exaggeration—Jeri-fication, her dad used to call it—or if she really was having trouble.

"What about your dad?" Gwen asked.

"Basically a sperm donor. My stepdad raised me, but now he's dead too."

Gwen felt a pang about her own dad's death, but it seemed gauche to steal the spotlight. "How old were you?"

"I think my mom killed him," Nicola said, avoiding the question. She said it as if reading off a grocery list.

"Oh." Gwen had no idea what to say to that and let the silence rest over the phone line between them.

"Drunk driving accident, and supposedly he was driving, but I think now she was. They were both tanked, but Mom had the killer instincts. She would have climbed over him and shoved him in the driver's seat to let him take the heat. I mean, no skin off his nose, right? He died on impact."

Gwen was uneasy about such big confessions, but maybe this was how Nicola dealt with things: matter-of-factly. Maybe these reveals showed how much she trusted Gwen. How much she, too, needed a friend. "Any siblings?" Gwen asked awkwardly, having no idea what to say.

"Only child," Nicola said. "What about you?"

"Same. My folks had me when they were pretty old, a later-in-life surprise." That's what her mother had always said, but a welcome one, she was sure to add.

"I think that's why we get along so well," Nicola said. "Maybe we're like the sister the other never had." The clinking of ice against glass rang through the phone line. "But enough about families. Let's talk about what really matters." She asked what Gwen was looking for in a place, and Gwen took the hint to change the subject.

"It's not like I'm picky," she said. Looking around at the one-slab white granite countertop and the customized lemon-yellow backsplash, she knew that wasn't exactly true. But what did she need, really? If it came down to it, she could rent a two-bedroom apartment with one bathroom in a good public school district. All that mattered was that she be safe and with her daughter.

"But what's your dream list?" Nicola prodded. "I mean, you've got to start with something." Gwen told her what she'd really like, including two and a half baths and an outside seating area. What the hell, it was a wish list.

"Close to downtown?" Nicola added.

"That'd be good."

"And a shopping district?"

"Why not." Gwen laughed. "Maybe a spot for a garden."

"That's the way," Nicola said. "Think big. What are you willing to pay for rent?"

"I'll need to speak with my finance person," Gwen said, hoping that sounded sensible. She had no financial person; it had only been Todd, who swore he had it under control. It was like saying she was going to speak with the Hamburglar. Such a person did not exist.

"Clearly I know your salary so I can help you come up with a number too," Nicola offered, and took another sip of whatever she was drinking. "Who are you using for movers?" Gwen told her the name of the company. "They're good," Nicola said. "I used them when Derek and I moved in."

Even this slight praise from a new, cool friend warmed Gwen's heart. She wondered if she and Nicola would continue to grow closer when she moved to Dayton and hoped so. It would be hard moving home after all this time, back under her mother's roof, and while she knew there were high school friends who'd stayed put in Dayton and made lives for themselves, she couldn't imagine reaching out. She wouldn't be able to handle their sympathetic looks over Todd's passing, a nerve that was still too raw. She also couldn't imagine explaining why she was back living with her mom, figuring they'd smell her financial ruin like a bad stink.

With Nicola, it wasn't like that. She already knew about Todd and not only did she not prod for details, she seemed nearly indifferent. It was odd in a way, but also exhilarating.

"But in the meantime," Gwen said, "I guess I'm thankful my mom will take us in."

"You know," Nicola said, drawing out the word. "You could stay with me."

Gwen paused. That offer was weird, right? She barely knew Nicola.

"I mean, you already stayed *one* night," Nicola added, and Gwen remembered the pulse of humiliation, waking in a room she didn't recognize. Nicola was right. It wasn't like Gwen was being so good about the boundaries either.

"That's so sweet," Gwen said, "but trust me, the last thing you want is an eight-year-old grubbing her way around your house. Those smudge-free windows would be a thing of the past."

"Well, couldn't you stay with me and Whitney stay with your mom?"

Okay, Gwen *knew* that was weird. She wasn't about to be separated from her child, especially right after she'd lost her father. But she reminded herself: Nicola doesn't have kids. She doesn't understand that bond. And clearly her relationship with her own family had been strained. "Seriously, that is so sweet of you to offer," she said again, "especially because your place is so great. The sunlight, the hardwood floors. Did you guys hire a decorator?" she asked, hoping to move the conversation away from the awkward offer.

Nicola took the bait, or maybe realized her suggestion was strange and was anxious to move on. "They've got a great design team connected to the HOA," she explained. "They're built in to the buyer's fee," and with that Gwen breathed a sigh of relief.

This was it: the start of her new life.

RULE #2: KNOW YOUR FRIENDS

Chapter Thirteen

GWEN

August 2022

After three days on the road, Gwen pulled into her mother's driveway at dusk and cranked her tired, thirty-two-year-old bones out of the driver's seat, her daughter hopping out effortlessly from the back seat. Gwen was glad to see her bounce out, feeling hopeful it was a sign she'd made the right choice moving to Dayton.

The night before they'd fallen asleep at the hotel, tucked together like spoons, and a few hours later, Gwen had woken to a sharp, immediate pain in her stomach from a kick. Whitney's throat had rippled with a piercing scream as she snatched out an arm, her tiny fingernails digging two welts into the thin skin near her mother's eye.

Gwen had thrown a leg over her daughter and straddled her, dropping a portion of her weight on top of her. The pediatrician had said not to wake Whitney up during a nightmare, that most children would get through it on their own, and that the parent's job was to keep them safe from harming themselves. Gwen had tried that in the beginning, but quickly found Whitney felt most soothed by a steadying weight and, at the hotel, Gwen cursed herself for packing the weighted blanket in the moving van.

When Whitney had woken up a moment later, her eyes were no more than six inches away from her mother's, panic straining their lids. Each of them had stared back, their breaths locking and steadying until Whitney's lids began to droop back into the safety of sleep. What Gwen wouldn't give to be able to take those terrors on herself, to help her daughter sleep through the night, but instead she was powerless, her heart outside her body. One positive of staying at her mom's would be Gwen and Whitney in her old double bed together, sliding toward the dent in the middle of the mattress, drawn closer to each other out of need and gravity.

At Jeri's house, Gwen reached into the car to grab her purse as the front door slammed. She turned to see Jeri descend the two porch stairs, one hand blocking the setting sun from her eyes, the other in a death grip on the railing. Gwen gaped. Her mother must have put on fifty pounds since she'd last seen her. Jeri was only seventy-two, but Gwen was shocked at how old she looked. Her hair was white and thinning and sweat was popping at her temples from thirty seconds in the heat, although it was still styled in stiff peaks, and she had on a full face.

"I know. I got fat," Jeri said, and then added, "Fatter."

"Mom, let me help," Gwen said, and raced forward, slinging her shoulder into her mother's damp armpit. "Are you okay?"

"Just glad to see you," her mom said, and smacked her hands together twice to get Whitney's attention. "Let Grandma get a look at you."

Whitney came forward for the obligatory hug. This sweaty old woman was practically a stranger, and Gwen felt a stab of guilt she'd kept them apart so long. It's just that Todd's family was so much more available, always up for a weekend getaway. They were cosmopolitan and athletic and still in their late fifties, not to mention they often offered to pay. But where had they been the last few weeks? Europe.

After the funeral, they'd abandoned the country, saying everything reminded them of Todd.

Really? The whole country?

Jeri was the one who called every day at 2:00 p.m., a rhythm Gwen had grown to count on, steady as the tick of a metronome.

Gwen had told Whitney on the drive that one of the bright spots of the move would be how much time she'd get to spend with her grandma. But as she helped her mother back up the steps, watching one foot fall and settle into balance before she'd move the second, Gwen felt an impending dread. This was supposedly who would take care of her kid? Her mother seemed not like a caregiver but in need of one.

Inside, Gwen realized how much her mother's house had changed in the last few years. Jeri'd kept it immaculate when Gwen was growing up, but now there was dirt ground into the linoleum, stains on the carpet. And that was the flooring she could see. Every surface was crowded with magazines and newspapers, and three laundry baskets of clothes overflowed next to the sofa. "Are these clean?" she asked her mom as they walked through the living room, and Jeri's cheeks burned a bright pink.

"I don't get up and down the basement stairs so well anymore," Jeri said by way of explanation. Gwen ducked her head in the kitchen and found rows of canned and boxed food covering all the counters, the table buried under stacks of mail, empty grocery sacks, an extra-large weekly pill dispenser. In one corner there was an overflowing garbage can and three bags of garbage beside it. The stench of old coffee filters and stale chips filled the room. The smell reminded her of her dorm room in college. She used to change her sanitary pads in the room and then leave them in the trash for the week, too embarrassed still at eighteen to change them in a public toilet. Her roommate had to tell her they stank.

"Mom, what's happened?" Gwen said softly when she came back into the living room.

"Lockdown was tough," Jeri said. "I lost some ground." She took a sip from the glass of Diet Pepsi that had been at her side as long as Gwen could remember. She still drank it out of the thick amber-gold glasses of Gwen's childhood, the ones with circular indents that everyone in lower-class America seemed to own.

"Lost ground how?" Gwen pushed.

"I spent all day inside and didn't get any exercise, and then I had a little spill in the kitchen so I don't get on the stepladder anymore. When I couldn't do laundry, I just ordered more clothes. I'm fine, Gwennie," she insisted, but Gwen didn't think so. In the beginning of the pandemic there'd been regular calls and FaceTimes, most of which were Whitney filling up the screen looking up her own nose and laughing, but still genuine connection. Todd, the extrovert, had found a way to keep up his connections through Zoom happy hours and work calls, but slowly Gwen and Whitney had retreated into their introverted ways, a pod of two. Whitney had been so young when the pandemic started, she didn't know children outside of Gwen's mom circle and the occasional kindergarten playdate, so no best friends to keep in touch with. It was just Gwen and Whitney playing games and baking, or sitting in front of screens or reading. Even contact with Jeri had dropped away, a life beyond their walls unimaginable. Just how long had it been since she'd talked to Jeri on the phone before Todd's death? She was ashamed to realize how little she'd thought about her mother, locked in a house by herself.

Whitney went upstairs to see where they'd be sleeping, and Jeri asked how she was doing since her dad's death. Gwen thought about how tough it had been, her own father dying, and that had been when she was grown. "Not great," she admitted. She gave her a rundown of the night terrors, and how the pediatrician had said they were a common enough side effect to trauma. But that was the problem: her daughter had suffered trauma.

"Mom, how long—" Gwen started, but there was a knock at the door. Did her mother have a home health care worker?

"I'm not expecting anyone," Jeri volunteered, huffing to move a pillow to the floor and collapsing onto the couch, clearly expecting Gwen to answer the door. There was no way Gwen would trust her mother to watch Whitney for long, and she realized quickly there was another list to make of what Jeri needed. A home nurse? A house cleaner? An exterminator? And did her mom have any money to pay for these services?

Gwen answered the door, shocked to see Nicola on the welcome mat.

Chapter Fourteen

GWEN

November 2015

When Todd missed the turnoff for Home Depot, Gwen didn't want to say anything. She knew he took those kinds of comments as criticisms, and instead she sat back, hopeful they'd still make their 11:00 a.m. consultation. It was rare for Todd to take the initiative with something home related, but he'd insisted on making the appointment to pick out the new HVAC system. The AC had grumbled on through the summer but was clearly on its last legs, and with winter coming, they couldn't risk losing heat. It was one of those house expenses she hated—$15,000 to maintain the status quo—and was thankful once again they could afford it with little more than a blip.

Todd slapped on his turn signal for the Boulder Turnpike heading farther away from Home Depot. Gwen recalculated along with the GPS. She tried to keep some teasing in her voice when she said, "What do you have planned?" He loved surprises, big and small, and she thought maybe he'd told her the appointment was at 11:00 a.m. but it was really at 12:00 p.m. and he had made a lunch reservation for them—a day date while Whitney was with Gwen's mother-in-law.

"You'll see," he said, waggling his eyebrows.

Gwen felt just the tiniest prick of irritation. She had never been a big fan of surprises, although she'd done her best to adjust since she and Todd had been together. It was hard to believe it had been almost seven years since that night in the library. In the intervening years, she'd endured surprise birthday parties both at restaurants and at home, an unexpected guest from Todd's childhood who stayed for a week in the spare room.

Her girlfriends insisted Gwen's husband was romantic, sponta-neous, that Gwen was so lucky. But they didn't know about the $100 bourbon-of-the-month club he'd signed up for on a whim, a Mercedes leased without so much as a call to ask her opinion, an investment in a time-share that cost them their shirts. That one at least she'd spoken up about, raising her voice, which she hardly ever did. She'd been so mad she'd thrown her shoe. Not at him, but against the wall, and then for some reason she'd been reluctant to clean the scuff. Whenever she saw the black smudge she'd feel a pinch of shame that she'd lost her temper, but also pride that she'd spoken up. After that, he didn't talk to her about the finances, and when she asked, he assured her the sale of the time-share had brought a profit after all.

"Where are we going?" she asked, her heart sinking when he took the Northwest Parkway toward the Denver airport. It had to be a coin-cidence, right?

"Happy anniversary," Todd said, and stared at her as he curved onto the interstate, his eyes wide, smirk activated. She gripped the dashboard. *Watch the road!*

"Anniversary? That was months ago."

"I know, but . . ." A semi drove by, airhorn blaring. "Don't you want to celebrate our love year-round?" He always had been able to lay on the charm, riding that line between over-the-top and sincere.

"Todd Maner, what'd you do?"

He threw back his head and laughed, a sound she loved. "Jamaica, baby!"

"Jamaica?" she echoed.

"The bags are packed and in the trunk."

"Bags?" She turned as if she might be able to see them, but instead her eyes settled on her daughter's car seat, still rear facing since she was so young. "What about Whitney?" she asked.

"My folks are keeping her."

Gwen kept from wrinkling her nose. She knew his mother, Mary, would be delighted to get the time with her granddaughter, but how had it not occurred to him that it would be hard for Gwen to leave her? "How long will we be gone?"

"Seven days, six nights."

"A *week*?" Gwen hadn't spent more than a night away from Whitney since she was born, and even then, she'd woken in a panic every few hours at the hotel, her breasts swollen and painful as she'd pumped in the dark in the bathroom so as not to wake Todd. She'd quit breast-feeding by now but still felt a physical tether to Whitney whenever they were apart, as if their connection extended beyond space and time. But from Jamaica to Boulder, and for seven days?

"Don't worry, I packed for both of us." He winked at her. "Nothing but two-pieces for you."

"Two-pieces?" She could not stop echoing his words back to him. She hadn't worn a two-piece since Whitney was born when she'd traded them in for sturdy straps and a built-in bra so she wouldn't have to worry about anything popping out in Mommy and Me swim class.

"Maybe we can find a topless beach," Todd said, and reached over to tweak her thigh.

"And we're leaving *now*?"

He glanced at her slack face and a flutter of irritation crossed his. "I'm trying to do something romantic here, Gwennie." She watched his fingers flex against the steering wheel.

"It's just . . ." Her mind scrambled as she thought about the planner on the breakfast bar back home. Granted, she didn't have a job, but did he think that meant she had nothing to do? She had a handyman coming tomorrow to winterize the house; she had an assessment later this afternoon with a tree-care service for the oak dying in their yard; and what about their houseplants? Whitney's first dentist appointment was scheduled for Thursday, and while it was of course possible her grandmother could take her, Gwen wanted to be there for this monumental first.

"I need to text Susie," she said, and pulled her phone from her bag. She sent a quick text explaining she was going out of town with Todd—a surprise trip—and asked her if she could take care of the plants. The dots appeared almost immediately and Gwen held her breath, hoping Susie might support her and say, *But don't you have a child? Don't you have responsibilities?*

How romantic!!!!!! Susie texted back, along with numerous heart emojis, a sun emoji, and a bikini emoji. Gwen's heart sank.

I know!!! Gwen texted back, along with the heart-eyes emoji, because honestly, what kind of a shrew complained about a vacation to Jamaica? What stick-in-the-mud would rather go to the dentist than lay out on a beach? She smiled weakly at Todd with tears in her eyes she hoped he'd think were gratitude.

"There's my girl," he said.

"I'm sorry I wasn't more excited right away," she said, and he smiled at her again.

"It's fine," he said, apology accepted. "I know it takes you a bit to get on board. Grumpy Gwennie and her set plans." She hated when he called her that.

At the airport, all went smoothly, and at the resort, they were greeted by the hotel staff with plastic hurricane glasses they could take to the pool. It rained most of the week because it was the off-season, and when the skies were clear, Gwen folded herself into a lounger at the pool, a self-conscious arm flung over her stomach. She missed Whitney, and even though they FaceTimed every night, she could feel the tether stretching and thinning.

When it was finally time to go home, Gwen woke early, her bags already packed, while Todd grumbled through one more hangover and prodded for morning sex.

They landed in Denver to sharp winds, with the car thermometer at thirty-one degrees, and Gwen, the cardigan girl, blew hot air on her hands to warm them.

In Boulder, she unlocked the house and was hit with another wall of cold air.

The HVAC had officially died.

Chapter Fifteen

GWEN

August 2022

Nicola held two bags from Whole Foods in her arms, and Gwen blinked away her surprise at seeing her new boss on her mother's stoop. It was like seeing a UFO in a dirt field—shiny and wholly out of place.

"Hey!" Nicola said, holding up the two bags. "I figured you guys might not want to go out for dinner tonight after all that driving, and certainly you wouldn't want to cook, so I brought you some stuff from the food bar."

Gwen opened her arms to take the two bags—one warm, one cool—and could smell ground beef and the tang of salt and onions. She looked in the top package with a clear lid and her mouth began to water: empanadas. She hadn't even begun to think about what they might do for dinner, but all of a sudden, the thought of one more fast-food chicken sandwich made her want to throw up.

"Oh god, thank you," she said, and wanted to weep at the kindness.

She turned to show her mother the dinner and found Whitney crowded behind her. She wasn't sure how Nicola would do around kids when she was so adamantly childless, but she was already pointing at

Whitney, her daughter's travel-weary eyes staring back. "I know who you are," Nicola said. "Wendy Darling?" Whitney shook her head. "Dame Judi Dench? Ruth Bader Ginsburg? The blonde one from *Frozen*?" Whitney finally cracked a smile.

"I'm Whitney."

Nicola shook her head. "Nope. That's not it." She winked at Gwen.

Whitney leaned forward to get Nicola's attention back from her mother. "What did you think my name was?"

"Marlo Thomas? Taylor Swift?" Whitney giggled—giggled! Gwen marveled; her daughter was not the giggling type.

"Who are you?" Whitney asked, catching up to the game. "Hermione Granger?" Gwen knew this was high praise. Whitney ranked Hermione echelons higher than Harry because it was brains, not birthright, that got her where she was.

"Nice to meet you," Nicola said in a spot-on Oxfordshire accent. "Perhaps we'll have tea later?"

"I'd love that," Whitney said, holding an invisible skirt out in a deep curtsy, and that quickly, Nicola had won her over. Gwen couldn't remember when her daughter had taken so easily to a stranger, but once again, Nicola had made something look effortless. For the first time in weeks, Gwen felt the pressure in her chest ease. Maybe Dayton wasn't a last resort but a good idea.

As they unloaded dinner in the kitchen, Jeri shuffled in slowly, offering to help, and Gwen introduced the two women. Gwen could tell it would take her three times longer with her mother there, a hand always grasping the counter's edge for balance as she pulled one glass at a time from the cupboard. She told her mother to take a seat; she could handle it.

"I'm not used to being waited on in my own house," Jeri grumbled, but sat at the kitchen table.

"Well, don't get used to it," Nicola said, and Gwen felt her mother prickle. She did as well, attuned as she'd always been to the slightest vibration of conflict.

"What's that supposed to mean?" Jeri asked.

"It means," Nicola said, taking the lid off the empanadas as well as a tray of bean dip, "that Gwen is here for your help, not the other way around."

Jeri's eyes widened. "I know that."

"Well, good," Nicola said, and opened a cupboard, then another, until she found the plates. Jeri stiffened, and Gwen could see the mess inside those cupboards—plastic gas station glasses, to-go containers, Ball canning jars without the lids. Her mother was embarrassed but Nicola seemed to not notice as she plucked a plate from the cupboard and passed it to a surprised Jeri. "Then we won't have a problem."

They ate at the kitchen table, the old Formica one where Gwen used to do her homework. Afterward, Nicola asked for a tour of her childhood home, including her old bedroom where there was a *Princess Diaries* poster still taped to the wall. Nicola probably only had framed art as a child.

After dinner, Gwen and Nicola settled on the porch swing, each with a bottle of Dos Equis. Gwen felt another burn of shame looking out at the shabby lawn, imagining what Nicola thought about the dead patches of grass, the rusted swing, the ugly gnomes Gwen had painted in a ceramics class as a child. How many days had she spent on this porch in grade school, middle school, high school? Reading Magic Tree House books and then Stephen King, hoping the neighborhood kids would ask her to join them in a game of tag, or later, that the boy she liked might walk by?

"Is it strange being back?" Nicola asked.

Gwen nodded. "It's strange knowing I'm back for good. But it's not like I'm stuck in this house for the rest of my life." Still, it seemed like if she laid her head down tonight that was it; she was trapped here now. It seemed more final than the drive across the country, or cleaning out the house, or even burying Todd, which still felt like a surreal dream. A part of her wanted to say this aloud to Nicola—tell her how much she feared getting sucked into her old childhood life—but she sensed Nicola wouldn't have time for this kind of foolishness, that she was not a woman who looked back.

Instead, Gwen tried to make a joke of it, pointing to her old bedroom window. "My room is exactly the same. Same sheets, same comforter. My mom gave me a house key and put it on a chain like I used to wear in middle school." She pulled it out from the collar of her shirt. "It's like she still thinks I'm thirteen."

Nicola laughed, and Gwen saw the ridiculousness of it and laughed too. "A latchkey kid," Nicola said.

"Right?" She pointed at the obviously plastic stone in her mother's flower bed. "And she put out the spare, too, because she still thinks I'll lose it."

Nicola clinked her beer bottle against Gwen's. "Mothers are truly the worst, but don't let her ruin this for you." That hadn't been exactly what Gwen meant. Sure, it was infantilizing having Jeri loop the key around her neck, but it also felt like someone taking care of her. "And remember, you've got a lot of awesome stuff coming up too. Are you ready for work tomorrow?"

"I think so," Gwen said, but even as she tried to imbue her voice with some confidence, she felt her exhaustion creep deeper.

"I wish we could push it back," Nicola said, "but trust me: you don't want to get off on the wrong foot. You need to let the top know you're serious about the job."

"I am," Gwen promised, and she was. Or serious at least about seeming serious. She still didn't quite understand what the job *was*, but assumed that would become clear in the next few days. Right? She remembered Melanie Griffith at the end of *Working Girl*, strolling in with her big shoulder pads, and how the first thing she did was look out the big window and make a personal call. Certainly Gwen could handle that.

"Thanks so much for all of this," Gwen said again, meaning the job, the dinner, the whole second chance.

"It's what friends do," Nicola said. "And listen, I know this might be a lot, me showing up with dinner on your first night, but I wanted to let you know you're not alone. You can lean on me if you need to."

One thing was niggling at Gwen. "How'd you know my mom's address?"

"I dropped you off here years ago," Nicola explained. "Back during the internship."

Gwen was shocked. "Really?" Her mother lived in one of those pockets of suburban sprawl where all the houses looked the same street after street—tri-levels built in the late sixties and sided in shades of tan and gray. Why would Nicola have remembered that for all those years, but more oddly, if she hadn't, why would she lie about it?

Nicola looked at her and rolled her eyes. "No, psycho. It was on your résumé, remember?"

Gwen released a breathy laugh. "Oh yeah."

"What? Did you think I've been carrying a torch for you all these years, driving by your mom's house with my headlights off like we're in high school?"

"No, of course not."

Nicola took a long drink of her beer. "Because I've barely ever done that."

Gwen laughed more genuinely this time. "Well, good. And thank you too." It hadn't just been kind of Nicola to show up, not just above and beyond, but it'd been *fun*, both for her and her daughter. At dinner, Nicola had handed Whitney a full can of Coke and a silly straw, which basically put her at superstar status in the girl's eyes. "I—I didn't expect you to show up with a dinner, or anything. It was really nice of you." Gwen found herself unexpectedly choked up. It was customary in her circle of friends in Boulder to send a DoorDash gift certificate if anyone had a hardship, and while it was certainly appreciated, it wasn't personal. It wasn't standing at the hot-food bar at Whole Foods loading empanadas in a tray.

Nicola looked at her, sympathy frowning her face. "Has it occurred to you that maybe you've been expecting too little from your friends?" She pointed a thumb at the front door. "No offense, but it doesn't seem like your mom put much effort into getting ready for your visit. Maybe you've grown to think you don't deserve as good as you do."

Gwen sank into the words like a warm bath. She liked that: the idea she deserved better, especially after the rotten turns of her life the past six weeks. She'd always thought Todd had treated her so well, giving her better than she maybe deserved, but had he really? He'd planned secret trips when what she'd wanted was security. Rather than trust she could handle their financial situation, he'd simply kept it from her, never giving her the chance to prove she could.

Nicola put a hand over Gwen's. "I grew up with a shit mom too," she said, and continued before Gwen could interrupt and say that wasn't exactly how she'd qualify Jeri. "She put herself first in everything, absolutely everything. I didn't grow up knowing I deserved help, or have a role model for helping others, so I had to forge my own way. I don't want you to have to do that, Gwen. It took me a long time to realize it's okay to ask for things. It's okay to expect other people to help you. All you have to do is say the word."

"Thank you," Gwen said. "It's been a lot. And you're right: I do need help. I'm so overwhelmed, I don't even know what to ask for."

Nicola nodded. "I get that. Just show up for work tomorrow, and I'll be there." She gave Gwen's hand a squeeze, then stood up. "Ugh, how after-school special of us," she said, grimacing when she turned to see streaks of dust on the back of her pants. She smacked it away. "Don't you clean this," she said, pointing at the swing. "That's not why you're here."

"Gotcha," Gwen said, although until her mother's health had deteriorated, there wasn't a surface in Jeri's orbit that had been safe from dirt or dust.

They took their bottles back in and Nicola announced she was leaving, Whitney scrambling from the couch to say goodbye. Gwen was amazed again that Whitney seemed to like Nicola so much, and as her daughter opened her arms for a hug, Gwen felt a ping of jealousy.

"Goodbye, Ms. Nicola," Whitney said. "I hope we'll see you again soon."

"Ms. Nicola," Nicola chided. "So formal. Why don't you call me Auntie Nic."

"Oh, I don't—" Gwen started, but Whitney grinned with pleasure.

"I don't have an aunt!" she said. This wasn't true; Todd had a sister, but where was she now? Switzerland with Gwen's in-laws. And when Gwen had texted to say she was moving to Dayton, she'd sent her a Target gift card to help her get settled.

"Well, now you do," Nicola said, and patted Whitney on the head. Gwen marveled that Nicola seemed to know exactly how to behave with Whitney, and while it struck her as a bit presumptuous to refer to herself as an aunt, who was she to rob her child of more family, even if by name only.

Later, putting the leftovers in the fridge, Jeri said, "I don't like her," and Gwen felt her pulse spike. Leave it to her mother to see the negative, to shit on the one friend Gwen had.

"You just met her."

"I remember her from before. She was that snooty girl you interned with, the one who always thought she was so special."

"Maybe she is," Gwen said.

Jeri scoffed. "That's your problem. You're always willing to believe other people are better than you."

Gwen crossed her arms, feeling like a teenager again. "Why don't you want me to have any friends?" She was being hyperbolic, and even as she realized it, she couldn't stop herself. It was how she used to fight with Todd and it drove him batty.

"I want you to have *better* friends," Jeri said, and that sent Gwen's blood to boil.

"What do you mean, 'better'?"

"Wasn't she the one who wouldn't let you sit with her at lunch? She seemed like a piece of work." That was Jeri's worst condemnation: a piece of work. Weren't they all pieces of work? Works in progress? Although not Jeri, apparently, who couldn't even access a third of her house. Instantly Gwen felt bad about the snide thought.

"We were in college back then," Gwen said, knowing if she showed her emotions more than she already had, Jeri would take on that pitying mom-voice of condescension.

"And whatever happened to that other girl?" Jeri continued. "The one she supposedly liked so much better?" As Jeri said this with an edge in her voice, Gwen remembered she used to sit in the kitchen with her mother and tell her about the work dynamic. How Nicola would make rude comments about the way Gwen stuffed envelopes, or ate soup from a can, or answered the phone with her voice two octaves higher than it was normally. Nicola would make these remarks and tears would sting Gwen's eyes, and she'd excuse herself for the restroom, not wanting to cry in front of coworkers. The familiar wet prickle started again now. Obviously it had hurt her enough to tell her mom, the same woman who had held the grudgy flame for Nicola all these years.

"It's just, I know how trusting you are," Jeri said as she folded the leftover bag of tortilla chips and clipped it.

"And that's a bad thing?"

"It can be." Gwen knew she was right, but didn't want to hear it.

Jeri turned toward the sofa, where Gwen wondered if her mother had been sleeping for months, buying new shirts online every few days, the boxes piled in the kitchen. Who was she to be giving life advice?

Chapter Sixteen

NIKKI

December 2004

"Nik? Is that you?" Celeste called down through the floor of the hayloft.

Nikki's stomach jumped, a splinter slipping into the palm of her hand from the rough wooden ladder. She'd thought for sure her sister had a shift at the Dairy Dream today and wouldn't be home. There wasn't a rule about bringing friends to the hayloft, but she had a feeling Celeste would disapprove all the same.

Celeste kicked a few errant pieces of straw through the hole in the ceiling as her figure eclipsed the wan light with shadow. "Who's that?" Celeste asked, nodding to the girl behind Nikki.

Nikki climbed through the hole in the ceiling and skulked past her sister as Shelley Mills continued her climb, a messenger bag slung across her chest. Oh, how Nikki coveted that bag! She'd wanted one for over a year, a cross between a briefcase and a large purse, and what all the cool girls carried. Only babies had backpacks.

"She's my partner for a project." Mrs. Weaver, the freshman social studies teacher, had assigned the groups the last day of school before Christmas break, and Nikki and Shelley wanted to get a jump on it, even though it wasn't due until the new year. The splinter in Nikki's hand throbbed.

At the top of the ladder, Shelley looked around the hayloft, her eyes widening. "This place is so cool." The place was shabby, but an impressive clubhouse for teenagers. Years ago, Nikki and Celeste had hauled up an old beanbag they'd found dumpster diving and a milk crate that served as a table. There were a few old granny-square afghans they'd foraged at Goodwill and washed, as well as a Ouija board and some magazines Celeste had slid under her shirt and swiped from the school library.

Nikki noticed a small plastic Christmas tree in a corner beneath the slanted roof, decorated with gold garland and a string of paper clips. There was a box underneath wrapped in shiny green paper, jolly Santas dancing end to end. Celeste's job at the Dairy Dream gave her some running-around money. She paid half of it to their mom for rent and blew the rest on Wet n Wild eyeshadow and beer, but she was generous too. The tree and present hadn't been there yesterday, and judging by the scowl on her sister's face, Nikki had ruined the surprise.

"What's she doing here?" Celeste asked, her skinny arms crossed.

Shelley's mouth dropped open, then closed again with a small popping noise. She was a timid girl and rarely raised her hand in class, even when, Nikki suspected, she knew the answer. "Nikki invited me—" Shelley started, but Celeste snorted.

"I was talking to my *sister*."

The hairs on the back of Nikki's neck shot up. She hated to disappoint Celeste; she hated it. Since her sister had walloped Keith Gorgenson at the start of first grade, Nikki knew her sister had her back and she never wanted to appear ungrateful. Sometimes she could still hear that ringing noise: Keith's skull reverberating against the metal slide.

Plus, she still needed Celeste's help with so much. This fall, when Nikki had signed up for school as a freshman, Onita had said, "No more free rides. Full stop," freeing herself from the responsibility of her daughters. Now Nikki had to cook all the meals, work the garden, get herself ready, and bike to school. She never would have been able to do it without her sister, who always put her first, and all Celeste asked in return was that Nikki reciprocate.

Yet what had she done? Brought someone else home to their secret hayloft, desperate to show off. People in town thought they were trash, and she'd wanted someone to see they had their treasures too.

"It's this stupid project," Nikki said quickly. "We're not even friends."

Shelley started. "I thought—"

"We're not," Nikki insisted, shaking her head. "We just didn't have anywhere else to work." She turned to Celeste, desperate for her to understand. "It's just a stupid project. I don't even like her that much." Nikki winced as she said the words.

"You said . . . ," Shelley started, and her voice hitched, thick in her throat. Since the incident with Keith, the reputation of the Kimmel girls had spread. Mess with one, you messed with the other. Over the years, if anyone forgot that, Celeste was sure to remind them, and Nikki walked the school hallways as if in a protective bubble, the force field of her sister's love a solace and a weapon. But Shelley was new at school, having moved with her parents just a month ago. From the minute she saw Shelley's cool pink puffy coat, Nikki hoped they could be friends.

"And now she's going to *cry*," Celeste said, stretching out the word. Nikki's heartbeat tumbled in her chest and Celeste crossed her arms. "Why would you go somewhere you're not wanted?" she asked the sniffling girl, looking at Shelley like she was genuinely curious. Nikki couldn't watch, and instead stared at her shoes. "Why?"

"I guess I'll go," Shelley said, and then there was an awful ripping noise as Shelley tumbled toward the hole in the floor. Her pink coat caught the worst of the fall at the jagged edge of the opening, ripping a four-inch tear in her sleeve and zippering a line of blood up her arm. She yanked her hand away and her head thwacked against the ninety-degree edge of the ladder.

Nikki's hand whipped out and grabbed Shelley's as fear splotched across the girl's face. She pulled the girl to safety and Shelley grasped the open wooden studs of the wall and held on so tight a fingernail bent back from the pressure with a snap.

Shelley took a step toward the ladder, her chin quivering. "I better go."

"How are you going to get home?" Celeste asked. "It's three miles into town."

Shelley slid her messenger bag to the back, and dared a quick look at Nikki, confusion and tears wetting her eyes. She *had* invited Shelley, and both she and Shelley knew it, but she couldn't admit that in front of Celeste. Nikki had made a mistake, and if the only hell to pay was a ripped jacket and a three-mile walk, then Shelley should thank her lucky stars she'd gotten off that easy.

Shelley descended one rung of the ladder after another, and a moment later, the front barn door shut.

"Should we make sure she finds her way home?" Celeste asked without waiting for Nikki to answer. She unclasped the large rusty hook that held the hay door in place and swung it open with a screech. It was five o'clock and already growing dark, but one thing this shit farm had to offer was beautiful sunsets.

Celeste held on to the side of the wall and knelt down, folding one leg out and then the other. The door, five feet by seven, was where Weldon Kimmel, Nikki's dad, used to swing bales into the barn from his tractor with a crane. Nikki's dad had died close to eleven years ago in a car accident. Onita had gotten off that same night with a few bruises and a broken leg, but Weldon hadn't made it. He was driving, supposedly, both of them well over the legal limit, but Celeste said she'd never believed the story. Nikki had been three at the time, too young to remember, but both girls had loved him, even though he wasn't Celeste's real father. It wasn't until after he died that Onita got mean.

Nikki looked down more than a two-story drop; the concrete, already crumbled, had been destroyed from the bottom up by tree roots. There were cracks wide enough to drive a bike through, rebar spikes poking up like death wishes. Shelley walked quickly down their lane, clutching her arm, her messenger bag smacking against her rump. Stupid bag. Nikki knelt down at the opposite side from her sister and slowly inched closer, sliding bit by bit until their thighs and hips touched.

"Why'd you invite that girl?" Celeste asked. "God, I've seen hay bales with more personality."

Nikki sidestepped the question. "She's not about to win any dance contests either, falling through the floor like that."

Celeste snarled her upper lip in a laugh, her yellow crooked teeth on display. Nikki hated to see Celeste smile like this. Onita had to pay out of pocket for dental visits so neither girl had ever gone, and while Celeste didn't seem to care, Nikki was self-conscious. She held a hand in front of her mouth when she talked to strangers. Rather than smile like she used to—a grin wide on her face—Nikki had trained that joy out of herself and only smiled with her mouth closed. It was so obvious they were *poor*.

Nikki looked at the floor, too embarrassed to look at Shelley after lying about not inviting her. She'd tripped, right? It occurred to Nikki she hadn't actually seen it happen, and she thought again about the sound, that metal clang, of Keith Gorgenson's head hitting the slide.

"I wanted to give you your gift in private," Celeste said. "I took double shifts to get it."

"Can I open it now?"

To the left was the farmhouse, a light in the kitchen shining through the tacky sheer curtains. It looked like the dilapidated house was wearing cheap lingerie, but overhead, the sky was shifting like raw silk in pinks and oranges, the clouds morphing from blue to indigo. Shelley was barely visible now, gobbled up by the darkening sky.

Celeste shrugged. "I mean, if you want to."

Nikki scrambled up and grabbed the wrapped box, tearing at the paper. She snuck a glance at her sister, who had a real grin on her face now.

She pulled the lid off the box, and as she suspected, nestled in the white tissue paper was a messenger bag. Thick army-green fabric with a brown leather strap. She opened it up and saw the Diesel logo inside, along with three slim pockets for pens. It wasn't a cheap Walmart knockoff, but one that, in poor-people dollars, cost a small fortune. "I love it," she said.

"You can take it to college someday."

Nikki already knew she was smarter than any of the other kids in her class, but wasn't sure yet if that meant smart for Harris, Ohio, or in a way that could matter in the world. Celeste had always believed in her. Celeste knew she'd get out of Harris after graduation, and it meant the world. Her mother might be worthless, but Nikki knew, based on Celeste's love, that she was not. She had to bite her lip to keep her own tears back. This must be what it meant to be family.

"What's wrong?" Celeste said, looking at the tears glimmering in her sister's eyes. "Did I get the wrong color?"

Nikki shook her head. The splinter in her palm pulsed and she knew she'd have to dig it out before the site became infected. Most likely she wouldn't have the stomach for it and would have to pass the tweezers to her sister, biting her tongue hard as Celeste scraped below the layers of flesh, replacing one pain with another.

"I love it," Nikki repeated. Shelley was gone now, lost to the night.

"Good," Celeste said, and looped her hand through Nikki's for the knuckle game—tap-tap-tap. Nikki imagined the splinter lodging farther with each press of her sister's finger, eventually slipping all the way to her heart.

Chapter Seventeen

GWEN

August 2022

Monday morning, Gwen changed her outfit three times before settling on navy pants and a floral blouse, and the solitaire diamond earrings Todd had given her for her thirtieth birthday. She changed from flats to heels to flats again, glad by the time she finally made it to the nineteenth floor that she'd made the right decision. She'd left Whitney at her mother's. Jeri said she had lots planned for them for the day and Gwen worried it would be chores and TV, but she could only take on so much in a day. She still needed to figure out what school district they'd be living in before she could enroll her daughter.

Meet me in my office, Nicola had texted, and Gwen knocked at the doorway with her elbow, two iced lattes in her hand.

"Ooh," Nicola said, shooting out from behind her desk. "Caffeine. My favorite." Gwen had been to Nicola's office before the interview, but now had a chance to take it in: the clean lines, chevron throw pillows on a saturated-blue couch. Everything, down to the teak pencil holder, seemed hand curated. It was like Nicola's home, impersonal yet aspirational. Only one item didn't quite fit: a homey cross-stitch on cream

Aida cloth in blues and greens that hung next to a bookcase. *The Rules* it read at the top. *#1 Don't Let Anyone Make You Feel Small.*

Gwen slapped a hand over her mouth in surprise. "Oh my goodness. I remember these!" They were the rules Nicola had espoused all through the internship.

Nicola walked over and stood beside her. "We were so young," she said. "It feels like a lifetime ago."

Gwen read further:

#2 Know Your Friends

#3 Trust Your Instincts

"I was pretty intense back then," Nicola admitted.

Gwen shook her head. "You were so right, though. I wish I'd listened to you more. I wish I had taken the internship more seriously." *#4 Never Look Back.* She traced the stitching behind the glass.

#5 Truth, Not Facts

Gwen tapped the glass. "You said number five to me when I came for my interview, do you remember?" She lowered her voice. "We were talking about my résumé."

"I'm not saying the rules weren't accurate," Nicola said, and laughed. "Just that I was a bit intense. I thought if I had a list of rules to follow, it'd be a road map, and I'd end up with the life I wanted."

"And didn't you?" Gwen said, indicating the swank office on the nineteenth floor.

Nicola reached out to touch the frame, straightening it a fraction of an inch. "Missy stitched this for me," she said. "She gave it to me the last day of our internship, when we were both notified we'd get full-time positions."

Gwen felt a pang of longing and regret. "I don't remember that." She hadn't exchanged gifts with the other two women, but instead snuck out an hour early to meet Todd for coffee. She would do better this time. Take it seriously.

"She always did have terrible taste," Nicola said. "Who makes a cross-stitch for an office colleague and expects to be taken seriously?"

"But you hung it," Gwen pointed out, and Nicola smiled. She looked sad to Gwen for the first time since they'd reconnected.

"I did. And even after she left, I couldn't bring myself to take it down." Nicola turned away from the list and clapped her hands once as if erasing the conversation. "Ready to see your new digs?"

Gwen's stomach hiccupped in excitement. "Yes, please!" She wasn't sure what to expect but had set her expectations on a cubicle. Even with the fancy title, it seemed most realistic, so when Nicola walked her three doors down the hallway to another door and dropped the keys in Gwen's palm, Gwen's fingers shook as she inserted the key and swung the door open.

The office was about half the size of Nicola's with an old metal desk docked in front of a narrow slice of floor-to-ceiling window. "I love it," Gwen said, her voice a little breathless. It reminded her of the studio apartment she'd rented for six months between living in her mother's house and marrying Todd. It had been four hundred square feet of *hers*, never mind the orange shag or the windows painted shut.

Gwen set her latte down and went behind the desk. She picked up the phone receiver, listened to the dial tone, and replaced it, then sat in the desk chair and spun around. "Seriously. It's perfect."

"I have a little office-warming gift for you," Nicola said, and pulled a bag from behind her back that Gwen hadn't noticed. She wondered for a second if it would be a cross-stitch, although Nicola hardly seemed the crafty type. She handed it over and Gwen dug around the tissue paper, pulling out a framed photo of the two of them along with Missy, one of the rare nights they'd all gone out. It was before cell phones had decent flashes, all of their eyes red and their bodies cast in shadow.

"Welcome back," Nicola said, and Gwen clutched the frame to her chest.

"I don't even know how to thank you for this. Really. You're like a fairy godmother."

Nicola leaned against the one empty bookshelf in the room. "Hardly. And I feel like I should disclose, kind of like a real estate agent when someone dies in the house, that this used to be Missy's office."

Gwen looked at the picture, their three wide smiles. "You miss her, don't you?" She was curious to hear more about Missy's sudden departure, but didn't want to be a gossip.

Nicola sat in the chair across from Gwen's new desk. "You two kind of remind me of each other."

"How so?"

"Tell me this," Nicola said. "How long does it take you to pick out deodorant at the store?"

Gwen puffed out a laugh. "What?" This was what she liked about Nicola: she always said something unexpected, while Gwen made the same benign comments as everyone else ("Looks like it's going to rain," etc., etc.). Nicola had a different way of approaching the world that always felt fresh. "I don't know," Gwen said. "Not that long?"

"Every time I went shopping with Missy, she would debate in the deodorant aisle. Secret or Degree? Powder fresh or shower scent? I would stand behind her tapping my foot until finally I couldn't stand it any longer and I'd throw one in the cart. You rub it in your armpits and go on with your day. We're not talking about an important decision."

Gwen knew if pressed she'd have to revise her answer, because the truth was that she did the same thing. "But what does that have to do with anything?"

"I'm saying that Missy was indecisive. She could never quite see what was best for her and never quite had the gumption to get it. I liked her, but it was difficult watching her vacillate, hedging her bets. I always pushed her to make better decisions, but instead she went along to get along. And her relationship with Jonas? Seriously, she fell in love like falling into a vat of stupid syrup. He controlled everything."

"Like what?" Gwen thought of Todd. "Finances?"

"More than that," Nicola said, and leaned back, a finger tapping against her lip. "Like, originally they were going to have this big wedding and I was going to be the maid of honor. But then Jonas starts pushing for a smaller affair, and so it went from a hundred and fifty people to fifty, and then to twenty-five, and then to a destination wedding with only family." She shook her head. "So tacky, I told her. I'm out. All those hillbillies on some beach somewhere with their toes in the sand." She smiled at Gwen knowingly. "It was just classic abusive behavior: isolating a woman from her closest friends, the ones who look out for her."

"Like you," Gwen said.

"Exactly."

Gwen sat with this for a second. She'd gotten the wedding of her dreams, but since then, had she rolled over with every decision Todd decreed? As much as she wanted to believe that wasn't the case, she knew the truth. "I don't want to be like that," she blurted out. "I don't want to be a doormat."

"And you don't have to be," Nicola said easily. "Rule #1: *Don't Let Anyone Make You Feel Small*. Trust me, you're going to kill it at this job."

"I hope so."

"No hope about it," Nicola reasoned. "You've got to do great so there's no reason for the board to go snooping into your résumé."

Gwen's pulse shot up. "Go snooping?"

"You know, if there's an issue with your performance? I told them there was no need to check your references, I've known you forever, but if things go badly . . ." She let the words hang there like a noose.

Gwen wobbled. "But . . . but you're the one who changed the résumé. You're the one who"—she lowered her voice—"lied."

In the whirlwind of the last week, Gwen had barely had a chance to think about the résumé, much less what this job would actually entail. She'd done some digging into the position at other companies and figured she'd be managing accounts, dealing directly with marketing managers about their media needs and brand management, handling corporate accounts worth hundreds of thousands of dollars. Intimidating, yes. But doable. Hadn't she already proven to herself how much more she could handle than she would have guessed?

Nicola put her hands on Gwen's shoulders. "This is moot, Gwen, and anyways, you should thank me." She gave her shoulders a pat. "You've got this job because I believe in you. After meeting your mom, I think you're not used to that. Would you rather I didn't believe in you? That I didn't help?"

"Of course not," Gwen said, and thought of the rule, *Know Your Friends.* If someone as wonderful as Nicola could believe in her, certainly she could believe in herself. *Maybe I should make my own list of rules,* Gwen thought. *#1: Fake It Till You Make It.*

"You're right," Gwen said, and drew in a shaky breath. "I can do this. Thank you. I don't know what I'd do without you."

"Well, don't you worry," Nicola said, smiling. "Play your cards right and you won't have to find out."

Chapter Eighteen

After showing her the office, Nicola escorted Gwen down to the seventeenth floor, their footsteps echoing in the cavernous cement staircase.

"We've grown a bit since the intern days," Nicola said, and went on to explain there were over a hundred employees, but many of them worked from home at least a few days a week. "But not the high-ranking men," she added. "They want to get away from their wives and kids and scurried back to the office the second they could. So you know who else comes in every day?"

"Who?"

Nicola pointed at her chest, and Gwen nodded, knowing this meant she should too. She'd be here every day at 8:30 a.m. on the dot.

As Nicola opened the door to the seventeenth floor, she lowered her voice. "And I just want to warn you, Bethany can be a bit . . . judgy." Bethany was the HR rep Gwen was meeting to go over paperwork and benefits.

"Judgy how?"

Nicola shook her head. "I probably shouldn't have said anything. You should get to know people on your own terms." She walked down a maze of corridors and knocked on Bethany's door. "New blood," she said, and Bethany smiled warmly.

"I'll have her back in about a half an hour," she said to Nicola, then turned to Gwen. "And you must be Gwen." Bethany smiled at her and pointed to Gwen's blazer. "Retro. I love it."

"I haven't had a chance to go shopping since I started," Gwen said as she took a seat. She knew her clothes were out of date, but that didn't mean people had to make fun of her. Nicola gave her a pointed look, then headed back to the staircase.

"What? No, I really love it," Bethany stammered. "You look great," she went on, and Gwen felt tears sting her eyes. Would she ever be enough? Every time she felt she was starting to get a sense of what it might be like to handle her new life, a small kick would set her back. Desperate to change the conversation, Gwen pointed and asked about the picture of two toddlers on the credenza behind Bethany.

"My twin girls," Bethany said, turning and touching the edge of the frame. "I miss them so much but am also so relieved to throw them at my husband in the morning. He's a baker and gets home in time to feed them breakfast while I get ready." She cocked her head to the side. "What about you? Any kids?"

"One," Gwen said, and told her about Whitney.

"How is she handling the move?" Bethany glanced at Gwen's driver's license, which she'd given her, along with her social security card for verification. "Ohio's pretty different from Colorado, right?"

"It is," Gwen agreed, and then the question she was dreading came.

"And do you have a partner? What do they do?"

Gwen swallowed as her hands started to shake.

"Oh god," Bethany said. "I'm sorry. And I'm in HR so should know better. I wasn't asking for business reasons, just to get to know you. You don't have to answer, of course." She grimaced.

"He died," Gwen said, and Bethany blushed, clearly mortified she'd asked.

"I'm so sorry. God, how awful."

The women looked uncomfortably at each other for a long beat, until finally Gwen nodded toward the paperwork and raised her eyebrows. All she wanted was to get the hell out of this room, back to Nicola where she didn't feel like she had to engage in petty conversation.

Bethany laid the paperwork across her desk, turning it toward Gwen. She tapped two lines she'd already initialed. "I've verified your social security number and driver's license, and need you to verify you gave them to me." Gwen signed *GM* next to Bethany's initials, and Bethany tapped the sheet lower on the form. "And your résumé."

Truth, not facts, Gwen told herself, and leaned forward and initialed.

◆　◆　◆

Nicola and Gwen ate lunch that day squirreled away in Nicola's office where she warned Gwen, "Women in business are a tricky thing."

"How so?"

Nicola took a bite of her chicken Caesar salad. She'd told Gwen she ate the same thing every day, and had ordered her the same. "Some women have a hard time leaving high school behind. There are a lot more politics than I would have guessed. A lot of backstabbing. I thought we'd all be Gloria Steinem trying to lift each other up, but rather than reaching a hand back to pull up the others, they're balling up a fist and punching down."

"Ouch," Gwen said.

"Not literally," Nicola said, laughing. "But you get the idea."

Gwen thought back to Bethany's comment about her out-of-date blazer. Todd had told her about all the politics in his office and had often said women were the worst about gossip, blaming everything on the "old boy's network" if they couldn't get ahead. "Did you hear what Bethany said about my outfit this morning?" she asked.

"She's one of the worst," Nicola confirmed, and Gwen felt her heart sink. Nicola speared a piece of lettuce with her fork. She kept a set of real flatware in her desk so she didn't have to use plastic silverware, and Gwen thought she'd do the same.

Gwen explained how Bethany had stopped by later that morning to say how glad she was that there was another mom on staff, and then Gwen had wondered if *that* was a crack, like Gwen was a mom first and would half-ass her job. As she spoke, Nicola nodded, and then said, "Typical Bethany."

Gwen's phone vibrated, and she looked down to see the number for her movers. "I should get this," she said, and slid the button to accept.

"Gwen Maner?" the woman asked, and went on to say the truck had broken down in Kansas, slight delay, they'd need a few extra days to replace it. No apology, just everything should be sorted by next Wednesday. It was supposed to arrive this Saturday. Tears welled in Gwen's eyes; it was becoming a Pavlovian response to any kind of news. If the truck came during the week, she'd need to take time off from her new job, the one where she already felt behind and had been warned to be visible in the office.

"That late?" she said to the woman on the phone, and Nicola whispered, "What's going on?"

Gwen put her hand over the speaker. "All my furniture is stranded in Kansas."

Nicola motioned for Gwen to pass the phone and interrupted the woman on the line midsentence. "This is Nicola Kimmel," she said, as if that name would mean anything to the woman, but by the way she said it, with utter confidence and authority, Gwen guessed it did make the woman sit up straighter. "And when will that be?" There was a long pause. "Unacceptable." She went back and forth a few times, nodding as the woman spoke. "Yes, that'll do. And no extra charge." There was another pause, and then Nicola rattled off her own phone number, directing the woman to use it from now on.

She hung up and passed the phone to Gwen. "Done and done. You'll have your stuff by Saturday. No weekend charges."

"Really?" Gwen's shoulders slumped with relief. "God, thank you. Really. I don't know what I would have done."

"Just takes some gumption," Nicola said, and forked another hunk of chicken. "I gave them my number, so if anything else comes up they'll have to deal with me."

"I don't want to be a bother," Gwen said, but she was torn. Part of her wanted someone to take care of her, and part of her wanted to handle this kind of issue herself. It would not have been that hard to speak firmly to a stranger, who she soon wouldn't have to talk to again, and yet she hadn't been able to do it. It left her feeling oddly hollow, but what did it matter? Right now that unknown person was calling around for another truck, Gwen's day restored and hers ruined.

Chapter Nineteen

Gwen had figured out by the end of her first week that most of the job would be drumming up new business for Dacks, so she spent a good amount of time making potential client lists and composing emails and figuring out what went into a pitch deck. A few times, armpits damp, she cold-called strangers, and to her surprise and delight, found the cliché of midwestern niceness still held, as three potential clients agreed to meet her for new-media meetings the following week.

She learned to use the copier and, after picking up *Excel for Dummies* from the library, could do all kinds of tricks in the software. The thrill of triumph when she finally figured out how to add rows was a little ridiculous, but how long had it been since she'd felt a sense of accomplishment that was only hers and not tied to her husband's success or her child?

Friday, Nicola appeared in the doorway and gave three quick raps on the frame. "You almost ready?" she asked. She'd volunteered to arrange a happy hour with some of the other women in the office so Gwen could get to know them, and Jeri had agreed to watch Whitney a few extra hours.

"I am," Gwen said, and looped her purse over her shoulder, surveying the office to make sure she hadn't missed anything. She'd brought a gray cardigan and draped it on the back of her chair for when the air-conditioning was too much, and it looked homey there, a personal touch. She still needed to bring in a framed picture of her daughter. The only photo on the shelf was the one of Gwen, Nicola, and Missy, and Gwen kind of liked that it was the only one, even if she felt a little guilty not displaying her family. It was as if she were looking at an alternate future and not the past, one where she'd stayed single in the workforce.

As they walked to the Century Bar, Gwen kept her blazer on. *Retro, my ass,* she thought, shame lighting her cheeks. She spoke with Nicola about her furniture, still hurtling its way toward Ohio, due to arrive the next day at an overpriced storage unit in the suburbs. Gwen complained about how she'd looked and looked for a suitable apartment to rent, but with the sale of her Boulder house still not finalized, she lacked the funds for the first month and deposit. She'd thought for a half second about asking Nicola for help, but quickly dismissed that as a terrible idea. They'd muddied the professional waters plenty already.

When Nicola opened the Century Bar door, a few people winced at the slice of late-afternoon light. The place was packed, bodies against bodies, the smell of cigarette smoke somehow in the air even though Dayton establishments had been smoke-free for nearly two decades.

Nicola looped an arm through Gwen's and dragged her forward through the crowd, stretching to see over the other patrons, an easy feat given her height and tall heels. Halfway to the back, she turned around and ducked to speak into Gwen's ear. "I don't see anyone yet, do you?" Gwen shook her head, Nicola's breath hot on her skin. "I'll get us drinks," Nicola added, and left for the bar.

Looking around, Gwen felt full with anticipation. That morning, while blow-drying her hair, she'd practiced her smile in the mirror, the engaged tilt of her head. She had made a list of conversation starters in her mind, from "Where did you get that cute blouse?" to "What do you think of the school systems?"

Nicola returned a few minutes later with two martinis, a drink Gwen didn't particularly love, but she did enjoy drinking because the glass made her feel fancy. They talked about work as Gwen surreptitiously strained to see every nook and cranny of the bar as well as the door, hoping for another face she'd recognize.

Finally, when they were on their second martini, Nicola put a hand on Gwen's arm. "I'm so sorry," she said, a commiserative look on her face. She'd been stood up. Gwen didn't think she could take Nicola's pity on top of everything else and tried to smile in return.

"Oh please," Gwen said with a weak smile. "It's no biggie. People have a lot going on. Families to see, dates. I get it."

"Still, it's rude," Nicola said. "I must have told six or seven people we were meeting here."

"Maybe they got the time wrong," Gwen suggested, throwing herself a life raft.

"All of them?"

Gwen shrugged. "Maybe."

"I think it's more of the bullshit we were talking about earlier in the week," Nicola said as the light from outside sliced through once again. Gwen squinted toward the door then pointed.

"It's Bethany!"

Nicola turned to the door. "So it is." She downed the rest of her drink and said she'd grab two more on her way to let Bethany know where they were.

Gwen was relieved, but also felt uneasy because she'd had so much trouble reading Bethany. She'd convinced herself the comment about her jacket was a burn, then a compliment, and then a burn again. What did it say about her if she couldn't even tell one way or the other?

Bethany followed Nicola back to their table, an easy smile on her face.

She wrapped one arm around Gwen's shoulders and gave her a little squeeze. "I see you found the local watering hole for the cool kids," she said, and once again Gwen felt uneasy. Was Bethany implying Gwen wasn't a cool kid, or was it an innocuous comment?

"I'm actually meeting my husband here before we head to a show at the Schuster Center," Bethany said. "Every six months we try to get a night away from the twins whether we need it or not." She laughed and Gwen felt her face fall a bit. Bethany hadn't come to her happy hour after all; it was dumb luck she'd shown up.

Nicola leaned forward and whispered something to Bethany, and Bethany's hand flew up to her mouth. "Oh, Gwen, I'm sorry. I didn't mean to say something so insensitive about a date with my husband."

Gwen smiled unevenly. "It's fine, really."

"No," Bethany said, insistent. "That was insensitive after . . ."

"It's no big deal," Gwen said, more of a bite in her voice than she'd meant. "I hope you have fun tonight. A date night sounds great." But what really sounded great was drinks with girlfriends.

Bethany's smile wavered, and she signaled to the front. "I should see if Stu's here yet. We really did just pop in for a quick throwback."

When she left, Nicola turned to Gwen. "She could have at least acted like she was trying to join you for your happy hour," she said.

"It's fine," Gwen said. She thought of how many times she'd blown off friends when she was with Todd, and couldn't help but defend Bethany. "I get it: she wants to spend the weekend with her husband."

Nicola swirled her martini in her hand. "I would *never* leave you to spend time with my husband. Even if I did like him." She shook her head. "Six years I've given that prick."

Gwen laughed. Her only impression was of sweaty Derek making a protein smoothie the morning she was hungover. "What's he really like?" she asked, anxious to move the conversation beyond Bethany.

"An asshole," Nicola said, and shrugged. "Too good looking for his own good." She put an olive in her mouth and pulled it from the plastic sword with her teeth. "Guys like that, they think they can get away with anything because they live in the bubble, but he underestimated me. He thought he could cheat and I wouldn't find out. He thought he could do whatever he wanted, but that's not what's going to happen."

"So you know for sure he cheated?"

Nicola nodded. "I found his Tinder."

"But it could be he just has an account," Gwen said. "Maybe he hasn't met up with anyone."

Nicola patted Gwen's cheek. "Oh, my sweet baby Gwen."

Gwen smiled to show she could take the joke but it was all so incredibly patronizing, and she couldn't believe how calm Nicola sounded about the possible affair. She would have set all of Todd's clothes on fire, and *she* was the timid one. "Why don't you leave him if he's so awful?" Gwen didn't mean to sound cavalier about such a huge decision, but she did wonder. Nicola had her own money; they didn't have any children. What was the first rule? *Don't Let Anyone Make You Feel Small?*

"Oh he'd love that, I'm sure," Nicola said. "But I'm not done with him yet. Too many men pull this shit and wiggle off the hook, then they go on to ruin some other woman's life. I don't think that's fair." She looked intently at Gwen. "I'm very big on fair, and the thing about the bubble? It just takes one little pinprick to burst it."

"Or one little prick," Gwen quipped.

Nicola threw her head back and laughed, full-throated. Gwen felt the laugh like a wave breaking over her. *I'm funny!*

"*Yes,* a little prick," Nicola repeated, laughing. "You're too much, Gwen." She slung an arm around Gwen's shoulders as Bethany had. "We could have been friends all this time," she said, shaking her head as she lifted her second—third?—martini to her mouth. "What a waste of a decade. Why weren't we closer?"

Nicola looked at her. Gwen wasn't the best at reading people as she'd begun to realize recently, but the look that seemed to be on Nicola's face was something both curious and desperate. The memory that came to mind was of her, Nicola, and Missy on a bar stage singing karaoke. Nicola had selected the duet "Islands in the Stream" for her and Missy, but Missy had pulled Gwen onstage by the elbow, insisting she sing along.

It had been so embarrassing, not only because Gwen was tone deaf and should not be singing into a microphone, but because Nicola had been determined that she and Missy would face each other as if they were the only two onstage, with Gwen crowded to the back. Eventually Gwen had slunk off the stage. It was a duet, after all. She thought of the picture Nicola had given her for her office. They looked like such good friends, all three of them, with their arms slung around each other's shoulders: the Three Musketeers.

"I wish I could have come back before Missy left," Gwen said, two martinis sluicing through her bloodstream and now making her feel sentimental. "The three of us would have had fun."

"She was another one," Nicola said, and Gwen wasn't sure what she meant. "The bubble," she clarified, and poked the surprisingly sharp plastic sword into Gwen's arm. "Pop."

The next morning, Gwen woke with another hangover, her second in two weeks, and she wondered briefly if it was becoming a problem. But no, it didn't feel like a problem. If anything, it felt like college, or the college she had imagined if she hadn't spent all of her time with Todd. Hanging out with a girlfriend too late, laughing so hard vodka shot out her nose. Around midnight, Nicola had dropped her off and Gwen had ordered Domino's, extra green olives and banana peppers, then ate it straight from the box on her mother's porch swing. She'd been cold out there, the summer nights starting to dip in the sixties, but she hadn't gone in for a sweater. It had felt like a small defiance, a step toward a tougher self.

Todd used to call her a "cardigan girl"—the type of girl who always carried a light sweater, even in the summer, because she couldn't stand to be cold. "Who likes to be cold?" she'd say back, laughing, but it wasn't about the sweater or the cold, not really. She was a woman who didn't like to be uncomfortable and her tolerance for discomfort was the difference between seventy-one and seventy-two degrees. Maybe Todd should have seen that the lesson wasn't that she couldn't stand to be even the smallest bit uncomfortable, but that she came prepared. Had he ever thought of that?

Her phone dinged, and she rolled over to the nightstand thinking it might be the alarm she'd set to remind her to meet the movers. Instead, it was a text from Nicola.

New plan. Meet me at my place at 9. Bring lattes

Gwen wrote back: Would love to but meeting movers this morning 😥.

She admitted to herself she felt a little disappointed that Nicola had forgotten about the movers, but it was too much to expect her new friend to remember every detail of her life. What did Nicola care if she was about to be reunited with her ten-year-old couch?

NEW PLAN, Nicola texted back, and sent a pic of what looked like the outside of her condo, although Gwen would have sworn the door was on the left not the right. But maybe it was backward in the picture? Or more likely, she'd run out of there so quickly the morning after the interview, hungover like a teenager the day after prom, that she was remembering it wrong in her scrambled brain.

She enlarged the picture. Was Nicola sending her some new landscaping she'd finished? Or had she painted her door? Maybe Nicola had finally had enough of Derek's bubble and somehow by this morning had found another place?

But Gwen didn't think any of those were the reasons for the picture, as a creeping feeling wound its way into her stomach, already soured from last night's alcohol.

Before she could reply, another text from Nicola dinged through. See you at 9!!

There were the three rotating dots, and then bring Whitney!

Chapter Twenty

Gwen swung her Land Rover into the parking spaces near Nicola's condo at 9:10 a.m., Whitney in the back seat and two skinny vanilla lattes in the cup holders.

Nicola stepped through her front door in boyfriend jeans and a French-tucked T-shirt, her hair in a messy bun. She scowled at Gwen. "You're late."

Gwen flinched and had the urge to say, "You're demanding," but it wasn't the tone she wanted to set for this mystery visit. "Sorry. Lots to do this morning with the movers coming."

"Don't I know it," Nicola said as they climbed out of the SUV, Whitney running over for a hug.

Gwen held out the latte, and Nicola took a sip, closing her eyes. "Bless you. Derek gave up caffeine so isn't picking mine up on his morning run anymore." She looked knowingly at Gwen. "It's another way he's proving how little he actually does to make me happy. Like, as long as it doesn't inconvenience *him* he'll pick it up." She held a hand out to Whitney, who eagerly clasped it. "But enough about me. I have a surprise for the two of you."

Nicola tugged Whitney forward and Gwen followed, walking past Nicola's own door as well as the next condo. The development was relatively new—Gwen would guess built in the last five years—and almost every door sported a fall wreath, now that they were quickly approaching the beginning of September. As she thought of the change of season, she was reminded that Whitney would be in school soon, and while she wouldn't admit it or be able to articulate it, Gwen knew she was nervous about making friends.

Three doors down from Nicola's condo, she pulled Whitney to a stop.

"Soooo," Nicola started. "Usually to get in this complex you need to buy—they've never rented before—but I met with the HOA and they're making an exception." She turned to Gwen, her face expectant, but Gwen didn't understand. Was Nicola renting a place now? Was this about Derek?

"Welcome home," Nicola said, and pulled a key from her pocket, dangling it on a gold ring in front of Gwen.

"Home?" She turned to the front door of the condo, the only door without a wreath, navy blue with a silver knocker.

"Wait, what?" Gwen's mind flitted through the debt she and Todd had racked up: the credit card bills maxed, the second mortgage she'd discovered after his death. Her job was the first step out of that, but she hadn't even gotten a paycheck yet. "You rented me a *house?*"

"A condo, and, well, I couldn't actually sign a lease for someone else, so the HOA had me put it in my name. I'm more like your slumlord." Nicola laughed. "But don't worry, I know you're good for it. And if not, I can garnish your wages." Gwen tripped over the words, trying to make sense. *She's rented us a house?* Nicola nudged Gwen. "Go on. Take a look."

"Mom?" Whitney asked. "Is this really our place?" Gwen looked at her daughter, whose cheeks were flush with hope.

Hand shaking, Gwen unlocked the front door, shiny and clean compared to the peeling paint of her mother's house. She didn't respond to Whitney, unsure of the answer. Condo? Slumlord? Garnished wages? She remembered the fourteen-foot ceilings and the wide, airy hallway at Nicola's place. God knows what this was going to cost, Gwen thought, but Nicola knew her salary. Certainly she wouldn't have gotten Gwen in over her head.

She pushed open the heavy navy door and walked across the narrow threshold. The walls were an eggshell white, unmarred and smooth, the wood floors a shiny pine that bounced sunlight from the sliding glass door toward the backyard. It was smaller than the house in Boulder by a long shot, but also cozier.

"Two bedrooms, not four like mine," Nicola said from behind Gwen as Whitney pushed past, scurrying up the stairs to claim a room. "And I talked to the movers. They should be here around ten."

"The movers?" Gwen set her latte on the countertop, a white marble, just like her old kitchen in Boulder. "How are you talking to my movers?"

Nicola looked at her, confused. "I gave them my number when I talked to them. You gave me the phone?"

The memory scurried through Gwen's brain. "You changed the address? What about the storage unit?"

Nicola jiggled her hands like, *ta-da*! "I canceled it. Aren't you the one who's been telling me how overwhelmed you are trying to start a new job, and deal with your mom, and find a place? And who said she didn't want to pay storage fees?"

"You're right. I'm just . . ." She looked at Nicola's face, clouded now with exasperation. "I'm sorry, Nicola. You're right. This is all so generous. You shouldn't have." Gwen wanted to cry for so many reasons. Because she didn't feel worthy of such a gesture. Because someone had stepped up and taken care of her in a way, if she was honest, Todd hadn't the past few years, so consumed with work and the pandemic. She felt a quick stab of guilt for even thinking that, followed quickly by a new sadness: he wouldn't be here to make this house a home.

She looked around the airy, bright condo again and saw a laundry basket in the corner, a nine-pack of Charmin peeking out the top. "What's that?" she asked. One more kindness might break her. Gwen peered inside and saw, in addition to the toilet paper, a small bottle of Dawn dish soap, two hand sanitizers she recognized as the Target brand, a roll of paper towels, coffee filters, two toothbrushes, and a tube of Crest. She breathed a sigh of relief that, while these things did add up to thirty or so dollars, it wasn't a small fortune. She'd been afraid for a beat she'd look in and see a savings bond or a wad of cash. Nicola had leased her a *house*.

"Thank you," Gwen said, whirling around. She should be grateful, right? But at the same time, she thought of one of her mother's truisms: there's no such thing as a free lunch. If a free lunch required payback, what about a condo? How much did she owe Nicola?

Nicola held up a finger. "One more tiny surprise."

Gwen's stomach flipped. *Another one?*

She followed Nicola out the sliding door to the backyard, a smallish lot but enough for a few chairs and maybe a garden: the outdoor space she wanted.

Gwen looked down, and toddling toward her was a fat-tummied, curly-haired apricot puppy with a cowlick on his forehead. He couldn't weigh much more than three or four pounds and looked like something that ended in "doodle"—a Cavapoo, Nicola confirmed.

The puppy saw Gwen and gamboled toward her. He barked like a squeaky toy.

"A puppy?" Gwen asked, incredulous. She was trying to get her head around the situation. Why was there a dog in her backyard? Whitney had been begging her for weeks and she'd said no. "You got us a puppy?"

"I got myself a puppy," Nicola clarified, and she bent down and circled the dog's head with her hand until he began to chase it and then fell over.

"You got a dog?" Gwen asked. She tried to picture an animal in Nicola's spacious condo, with the small knickknacks made of brass and gold and nothing out of place. One of the reasons Gwen had resisted a dog was the mess one would make: ripped-up carpets, snacked-on shoes, accidents on the floor. She couldn't imagine Nicola putting up with that.

Whitney clamored down the stairs. "My room is blue!" she yelled, her favorite color. She raced out the open sliding door, saw the puppy, and gasped. Both hands slapped her cheeks as she dropped to her knees.

Nicola raised her voice an octave, the way people do when they talk to children but really to adults through them. "The dog is mine, but Whitney can play with him anytime."

"He's so cute!" Whitney yelled back. It took Gwen's breath away to see her daughter so happy, so lit up. She could have counted Whitney's teeth.

Gwen felt off center, like she had to sit down. What did this mean? Of course it was fine that Nicola adopted a dog—she had every right—but why now? Maybe she'd always wanted one? Maybe she had a dog pass away a month or two ago? She realized, as a cold chill swept through her, how little she really knew about Nicola's life. They had been friends for three weeks and she'd rented Gwen a *house*.

"What's his name?" Gwen said. It was the only question she could think to ask.

"He doesn't have one yet," Nicola said. "We need to get to know him." She looked at Whitney. "No use calling him Fred when he's clearly a George."

"Those aren't dog names!" Whitney said, and she and Nicola looked at each other and laughed. "Can I help name him?"

"Of course," Nicola said. "I'm going to need help walking him too."

"And feeding him, and teaching him tricks." Whitney held her hand out and the puppy licked it. "I could help with all of that."

Nicola was kneeling by the dog now, Whitney, too, and that's when it hit Gwen: she was on the outside of this tableau. They were the two aligned.

"And teaching him to go to the bathroom outside," Whitney said. "He'll need to learn that."

"True," Nicola said. "One accident and *sreeeech*." She pulled a finger across her neck like she was decapitating herself. Gwen winced but Whitney laughed. "You better train him well."

"I will," Whitney promised, clearly thrilled to be given such responsibility.

"She wouldn't really hurt the dog," Gwen said. But what did she really know about Nicola? She turned the thought away. This woman had been nothing but nice to her. Too nice? Was that a thing? She'd helped her get a job, a place to live; she'd made her daughter happy. Todd used to say to her, "Sometimes I think you look for the rain cloud." But he'd said this as she was wringing her hands over the new Mercedes, the pizza oven he'd installed after a deck redo, and she'd ultimately been proven right to worry.

Gwen bent down and the dog waddled toward her. Jesus, he was cute. A mop with feet and a button nose.

She held out her hand and he licked it, his tongue like supple, wet leather. Gwen tried to name the emotion tickling through her and realized it was jealousy. Not only because the dog had created a closeness between Nicola and Whitney, but because she had wanted to be the one to make her daughter this happy.

But would she have? She didn't want a dog, one more thing to feed and clean up after. Maybe she would have continued to put her own wants above her child's, unlike Nicola, who seemed to have selflessly gotten her a dog to play with without the slightest provocation.

Nicola seemed to pick up on Gwen's ambivalence and overwhelm. "Okay, I'm taking Fritz home now," she said. "Let you guys get settled."

"Fritz?" Whitney said. "No."

"You're right," Nicola said. "Let's keep trying." She bent down and scooped the dog into her arms, and Whitney ran over to give him more kisses before Nicola took him away.

"Can we come play with him later?" Whitney asked. "After we unpack?"

"I'm sure Nicola has other things to do today," Gwen said.

"Of course," Nicola said, talking over her. "You can come by. We'll see if he likes peanut butter and work on his name."

Whitney put her small, chubby hand under the dog's chin and kissed his nose. "You're not really going to get mad if he potties in the house, are you?"

Nicola bent down and whispered in Whitney's ear. "He wouldn't dare."

Gwen attempted to laugh. "She's kidding, honey."

"Of course I'm kidding," Nicola said, and smiled brightly. She looked at her iPhone screen. "Your movers should be here in about thirty minutes. Maybe I should stay. We can leave Whitney out here in the backyard with the puppy and you and I can arrange the furniture."

"Please, Mom," Whitney begged.

"You don't have to help—" Gwen started.

"I know I don't have to," Nicola said. "But I want to." She walked back in as if she owned the place, which in a way, she did.

Gwen didn't know how to tell Nicola she'd been looking forward to setting up the rooms on her own. Even when she thought it would be a crappy apartment with no natural light and not this palatial condo with perfect windows, she'd imagined putting her dishes away in the cupboard. Arranging her life as she wanted it to be, very Mary Tyler Moore. But how did you tell the person who had given you everything that you didn't want any more?

Nicola was motioning to the living room walls and saying a bright accent wall would work wonders, a nice sea-salt green would go well in the bathroom. Gwen tried to imagine what Todd would say and realized it was up to her. What did *she* want? She tried to imagine but couldn't. Was she really ready to be left to her own wits? She hadn't been able to find a job on her own, or pack up her old place, or even handle the movers.

The dog in the backyard growled and she heard Whitney laugh, a welcome sound. The dog let loose a string of barks that sounded about as threatening as a marshmallow. *Maybe this is for the best,* she thought to herself.

"Where do you think I should put the couch?" Gwen asked, and walked toward the left wall.

"No, here," Nicola said, pointing toward the right.

Moments later the movers arrived and the couch was one of the first things unloaded. When they asked Gwen where to put it, she motioned to the right, where Nicola had said it should go.

Chapter Twenty-One

GWEN

December 2022

Gwen hit play on her "Xmas Vibes" playlist and connected her phone to Bluetooth. She'd bought a tiny Sony speaker with her first paycheck so she and Whitney could listen to music while they made dinner, and she loved how music pumping through the condo made everything brighter.

Yesterday, the two of them had driven to the Christmas tree lot on Heritage Point and picked out a Douglas fir, the same type they always used to cut down in Boulder. All of the literature Gwen had read on grief warned her that firsts were the hardest: first birthday, first anniversary, first Christmas. She understood why.

In the kitchen, Nicola leaned over the phone and hit "Skip" on the song. "Dean Martin is a perv," she said by way of explanation, as Alvin and the Chipmunks rang through the speakers, a sound like knuckles on a cheese grater.

"You think this is better?" Gwen joked, and Nicola looked at her darkly.

"Better than drugging a woman and forcing her to stay the night? Yes. I do."

"You're in a mood," Gwen said, meaning it as a criticism though also hoping it wouldn't be taken that way. She'd felt a little unsettled in their conversations lately, like there was the smallest pebble in her shoe. Nicola jabbing when Gwen had been joking, saying she was joking when Gwen felt she was jabbing. Gwen had to cut Nicola some slack, though. Things with Derek had gotten worse. Gwen wasn't quite sure what had happened, but Nicola had told her, "Karma finds a way."

"Gwennie, can you bring me a hot cocoa," Jeri called from the living room.

"Be right there, Mom," Gwen said as she slammed the teakettle on the stove.

"Queen Jeri," Nicola snorted. The two women were a constant rub. Gwen did her best to keep them separated, but they'd both wanted to decorate the Christmas tree. Nicola had told Gwen over dinner one night, "Your mom isn't doing you any favors," and Gwen knew she had a point. Jeri babysat Whitney for free after school, and usually they just sat on the sofa and watched *Wheel of Fortune* or *Let's Make A Deal*. It was hardly educational, and in exchange, Gwen spent at least one weekend day over at Jeri's, packing the fridge with meals, washing her clothes, scrubbing her sink.

She was exhausted from working sixty hours a week and helping her mother, although the job was a thrill. She loved the small rituals of putting on earrings every day and pouring her coffee in a travel mug— the signs she had somewhere to be. She spent her days making pitch decks for clients, tweaking their media needs, visiting video shoots, and learning tricks for photographing everything from pears to plastic bolts. There were also budget meetings, and leadership meetings, and team meetings, as well as the obligatory birthday-cake celebrations in the conference room, but even these were exciting. Each time, Gwen would arrive with her notebook, a fresh pen in hand. She felt accomplished at the end of each workday, and knew she owed that all to Nicola.

"I can make the hot cocoa," Nicola said by way of apology for her prickliness. She hip-checked Gwen from in front of the stove, shaking a pack of Swiss Miss back and forth before ripping it open. She really could be a great friend. She knew the best places to shop, had a caustic and cutting wit, was always up for a Target run, and frankly, was the only friend Gwen had in Dayton, her old high school and college friends having grown into their own lives without Gwen. Yes, sometimes Nicola was a bit of a forceful personality—like when she told Gwen to quit burning vanilla candles at home because the sweet smell made her sick. Or that her bath mat was so dingy it was a disgrace, and bought her one to replace it. Or insisting they eat lunch together every day at work, even though Bethany had asked Gwen to join her three times early on.

Nicola poured the hot water over the cocoa mix, stirred it with a spoon, and brought it to Jeri in the living room. Gwen trailed behind. Whitney was on the sofa untangling the old Christmas lights, Maxx asleep at her hip.

After weeks of debate, Whitney and Nicola had decided on the puppy's name. In the beginning, every time one of them would say it, the other would yell, "Take it to the Maxx!" and they'd both dissolve in a fit of giggles.

"What does that mean?" Gwen would ask, but that just made Nicola and Whitney laugh harder, and finally Gwen got so irritated she stopped asking. *Let them have their inside joke,* she'd thought, but still, it bothered her. She wanted to be the one to have inside jokes with Whitney, although she knew she should be happy Whitney had them with anyone. She still hadn't requested a playdate with a new friend, or talked about anyone in her class except Mr. TopHat, the class budgie, a light-green bird with black markings on his head who loved sweet potatoes, grated carrots, and scratches. He had had a neck goiter due to an iodine deficiency, but Mr. TopHat didn't let that get him down.

"Are those colored lights?" Nicola asked, scrunching her nose. "I don't think the HOA approves them for outside."

Gwen smiled tightly. She was ever grateful that Nicola had found her this house, and that she didn't have to mow the lawn herself, but she was not built for condo living. She'd rather hire a high school kid to mow and put up whatever tacky lights she wanted. But for now, she'd do what she had to do. Her lease was only for a year—eight more months and then she could look for a new place, although how she'd ever tell Nicola she didn't know.

"I'll get white for outside," she said. It was easier that way, to defer to Nicola, although it made Gwen wonder how much capitulating she'd done with Todd in their marriage. Agreeing to Christmas with his parents instead of her mom. A Land Rover versus a more practical Honda. At the Crowded Plate the night he'd died, he'd asked her to get the pork special so he could try it, instead of the ravioli she'd wanted.

But with Nicola, each time Gwen tried to pull back, even a little, Nicola would grab on tighter. Nicola was there, in every part of her life. Her job, a friend to get a drink with on Fridays, someone close by to watch Whitney when she needed to run a quick errand. Plus, Whitney loved her, with the added bonus of Maxx, who was so cute he made Gwen's teeth ache.

Thank god for Maxx, Gwen thought, as the dog stared intently at the lights as Whitney unwound them. The rule to not let the puppy on the furniture had lasted about fifteen minutes, although Nicola swore he didn't jump up at home. She wondered if Nicola had ever had a dog before. When she first brought Maxx home, she seemed to think she could leave an eight-week-old puppy in a travel kennel all day while she was at work, so Gwen had volunteered to come and let him out.

"I mean, if you want to," Nicola had said, and Gwen had made it seem like, yes, she wanted to take another half hour from her workday to go home and let her boss's dog out, but she couldn't express that to Nicola. It was the least she could do given all Nicola had done for her. What mattered, Gwen had told herself, was that the dog was cared for, because she loved that dog and so did her kid.

Whitney laughed as Maxx pounced on the light string. She'd always been an animal lover. Each child in the third grade was allowed to take Mr. TopHat home for a weekend during the school year, and Whitney had copied the schedule and stuck it on the fridge. She complained every Friday that February 10, her date, was so far away, but her teacher had announced last week she'd pick one of the students to take the bird home for holiday break since she'd be going to Michigan with her family. Each student would be judged on their school SPIRIT—Success, Persistence, Integrity, Regard, Immersion, and Teamwork—as well as an essay. Whitney was an introverted child but a self-aware one, and knew that SPIRIT might not get her far, so she'd been working on her argument each night. Every evening while Gwen cooked one-pot spaghetti or tore apart a rotisserie chicken, and soft rock sang from the speaker, Whitney scratched her number-two pencil against a wide-rule Composition notebook, her letters fat and wobbly and determined.

Jeri took a sip and grimaced. "Did you even stir this?" she accused, holding up the cup of cocoa, and Gwen took a deep breath before turning around.

"Of course," Nicola said.

"Maybe you need to whisk it," Jeri said, still holding the cup up, now with a fresh kiss of red lipstick on the rim.

"Maybe *you* do," Nicola said pointedly, and while Gwen appreciated Nicola making the hot cocoa, the tension between her friend and her mom was more than she could take tonight.

"You try walking on these," Jeri said, pointing to her bloated and bruised ankles, so swollen with fluid they looked like they'd stretch open and leak. The cane she'd started using a month ago leaned against her hip. Gwen knew she needed to get her mother to physical therapy. It was yet another thing that she wrote on her to-do list for the week every Monday, but where to start? Jeri said she'd had a falling-out with her GP over her weight gain and she'd need a referral for insurance to consider paying for PT, but Jeri's lists of demands—female doctor, over the age of fifty, Ohio native—was too big of a mountain for Gwen to climb.

"I'll get it," Gwen said about the whisk, and smiled brightly at both of them to let them know *I don't mind!* Both glowered in return.

In the kitchen, she opened three different drawers trying to find the whisk. Nicola had insisted she organize her kitchen a certain way, swearing it was intuitive, but even after all these months, Gwen rarely found something on the first try.

Voices erupted from the living room, and Gwen rounded the corner to find the cup of hot cocoa upside down and seeping into the rug she'd brought from Colorado. "What happened?" she asked.

"I held it out!" Jeri said as Nicola yelled over her.

"You let it go before I had a grip!"

Nicola turned to Gwen, exasperated. "Did you see?"

"I—" she started, but Nicola didn't stop to listen.

"Jesus, Jeri, it's bad enough you come over here and demand to be waited on, but now you're making a mess too?"

"This isn't your house!" Jeri yelled back, and the screech of her voice reminded Gwen of all the times her parents had fought in front of her as a child. She hated it, absolutely hated it.

"Stop it, both of you," Gwen said, but the women ignored her.

"I don't care what happened," Gwen said. "It's just a stupid rug." It wasn't, actually. Todd had given it to her for their sixth anniversary after she fell in love with it in a shop in Denver specializing in bespoke, one-of-a-kind items, but she couldn't think of that now—the rug or Todd. He was gone; the rug was ruined. If she told these two what the rug actually meant to her it would be another problem, another confrontation, and Gwen couldn't handle that right now. All she wanted was the issue behind her.

Nicola and Jeri both opened their mouths to protest.

"It's *fine*," Gwen growled, and both women looked at her, surprise on their faces. It was almost humorous to see them twinned that way. "We are going to enjoy this tree decorating no matter what," Gwen said. "No exceptions." She pointed a finger at Whitney and winked to show her they were on to fun and games. "Now, be merry."

Nicola and Jeri, begrudgingly at best, returned to what they'd been doing—Jeri stringing popcorn and Nicola unpacking Gwen's collection of nutcrackers.

She smiled at her daughter and opened the door to the garage. Her hands were shaking as she turned on the light, but she'd done it. She'd told Jeri and Nicola to be quiet and they'd listened. It was like a small flame ignited in her chest. She moved aside a bike pump and an old cooler and found a box marked "rags." Someone had to clean up the mess.

Chapter Twenty-Two

NIKKI

July 2008

In the hayloft, Nikki and her sister spread afghans across the bales they'd fashioned into a sofa and leaned back to read, the sun streaming in and bathing their bare arms through the hayloft door.

Nikki had slept fitfully the night before, waking every hour without realizing she'd fallen asleep. Her mother had been released the day before, after a three-month sentence for possession with intent to sell. Nikki expected at any moment to hear her car spit gravel up the drive. Where had she gone last night rather than coming home?

With Onita out of the house, Celeste had moved out of their double bed and now slept in their mother's room. In the morning when she emerged to make sure Nikki was ready for school, it was like seeing the ghost of their mother appear. Celeste's body was too thin, her hair like the straw Nikki now leaned against. A sore, so much like one of Mom's, had bloomed on the corner of her sister's mouth, and she scratched at it while they watched TV at night, blood always under her nails.

One morning, about a month after their mother went to jail, Nikki had come into the kitchen and found a strange man in Wranglers. He was bare chested, his belly creased over the waistband of his jeans as if it had been attached haphazardly to his skinny body. He was too old to be Celeste's boyfriend, too ugly, and Nikki choked to think her sister had started the picture game, that despised pastime of their mother's when they were young girls.

In the months she'd been gone, Onita had missed Nikki's high school graduation, Celeste's promotion to assistant manager at the Dairy Dream, and Nikki's acceptance letter to Glenn State. Now on the milk crate between them in the hayloft sat Nikki's thick packet from the college. A full ride. Celeste had taken to calling the packet Glenn, as if it were Nikki's boyfriend, which never failed to make Nikki laugh, giddy with anticipation.

Nikki had kept up those As like she'd promised, and while Celeste soaked her feet in Epsom salts every night at the age of twenty, Nikki had her hands on a future. When Glenn first arrived, Celeste's eyes had filled with tears—"I'm so, so proud of you, Nik"—but there'd been a hollowness behind them. High school was four years in the rearview mirror for her sister, yet Celeste still drank beer in the middle school parking lot between working a full forty at the Dairy Dream. Her promotion meant a dollar fifty more an hour and key privileges, but the shit schedule of closing.

Nikki flipped to the next chapter in *Jane Eyre*—Celeste had insisted she email and request her syllabi for fall to get a jump; this was for British lit—when she heard the low rumble of a dying muffler slow and then pick up speed again. A car had turned down the lane.

Celeste turned to Nikki. "Oh goody," she said wryly. "Mommy Dearest is home."

The car stopped with a spit of gravel, and Nikki pieced together Onita's movements: the metal-on-metal clang of the rusted car door shutting, the slap of the screen door as she went in the house, a muffled call as Onita said their names as questions, and then the slap of the screen again.

A long moment later, she heard the barn door screech and the shuffle of Onita's flip-flops across the concrete, sweeping away errant stalks of hay. "Nikki? Cel? You up there?"

Nikki locked eyes with her sister but neither answered. Her heart banged in her chest. A moment later, there was a sharp groan of wood as Onita climbed the rickety ladder with her slight, hundred-pound frame.

It was obvious from the moment Onita stuck her head through the hole in the floor that she was high, and Nikki felt her stomach sink. Onita's blonde hair was greasy at the dark roots, the rest of it dry as kindling. Her face was mottled with sores and acne scars from her teen years when, despite the pimples, she'd been beautiful.

"Avon calling!" Onita said, and threw back her head to laugh, catching herself from throwing her weight off balance. Her mother's mouth was open, and Nikki could see a rock to the side of her tongue. Onita sucked them when she was trying to quit a bad habit, a worry rock for her mouth. As far as Nikki could tell, they'd never helped, but Onita said it was better than sugar and wouldn't make her fat. She peered at her girls now, one eye winked shut and the other wild, the pupil a black hole.

"How was prison?" Celeste asked conversationally. "Make any new friends?"

"Yes. We bonded over our smart-mouthed daughters."

Nikki hated when Mom and Celeste got like this. All she wanted was one night for them to be a family, and rather than be angry at her mother, she felt a flare of irritation that Celeste would poke her like this. Why couldn't her sister at least pretend like they all got along?

Their mom held Celeste's eyes with her own as she climbed the rest of the way into the loft. Nikki wondered how she could even see, the blackness of those pupils so vast. "Funny thing," Onita said, keeping up the light tone. "My nightstand is empty."

"Who's been sleeping in *my* bed?" Celeste mocked in a deep voice, and Nikki's stomach clutched.

"Where is it?" Mom said, and kicked at Celeste's foot. Celeste snatched her leg back so fast it was like she'd been bitten.

"I threw it out."

Mom shook her head. "You're not that stupid."

"Fine, I sold it."

Mom nodded. "That tracks. Where's the money?"

"Gone."

Nikki's heart sputtered. *Jesus, Celeste, just give it to her,* but even as she thought it, she knew the money really was gone. Celeste had taken her shopping in Cleveland last week and told her the clothes were for both of them since they wore the same size, but the clothes they bought were not ones Celeste would wear: sensible jeans, cardigans, even a sweater vest. Nikki knew these clothes were for her future self, strolling Glenn's campus as the leaves began to turn. Celeste had insisted on buying her an overpriced pair of burgundy clogs, convinced this was what college girls wore, while she herself slid further into Onita's footsteps. The other night, Nikki had heard Celeste's worn flip-flops shuffle across the floor and felt a wave of sadness crash through her body.

"You," Mom said, and pointed at Nikki. "Stand up."

She leaned forward to follow her mother's command when Celeste held out a hand. "Don't do it, Nikki," she said, but it was too late. Nikki was a rule follower. Mom moved quicker than Nikki would have thought possible and stood behind her, an arm around her daughter's neck and the other around her waist. Nikki felt it suddenly, the cool flat of a knife against her stomach through her T-shirt.

"I want the money," Onita said, and Celeste stood slowly, her hands out as if that had ever defused a situation; Nikki felt the knife turn, pulling down her skin. "Now."

"I'll get it for you," Celeste said, her eyes rattling from Nikki's to their mother's. "It's in the house. Let's go in the house."

Mom shook her head. Nikki could feel the heat of her mother against her, Onita's body like a solar panel as the knife pressed tighter.

Nikki felt a sharp and acute sliver of pain and looked down to see a thin red line soak her shirt. "It's not in the house. I looked."

"Fine, I need to get it," Celeste said. "Give me a day."

"How—" Mom started.

"I'll get it from the Dairy."

Nikki thought of the keys clipped to the red polyester vest her sister wore to work, the worn edges at the pocket where the fabric had frayed. She didn't want this for her sister. Since they were kids, Celeste had done everything she could so Nikki would have a better life no matter the uphill slog, the clawing they both had to do to get ahead.

"Let her go," Celeste said. Her voice was calm but fierce. Nikki knew that was the thing about Celeste; Nikki might have the brains, but her sister had the backbone.

"Why should I?" Mom asked. She pushed Nikki forward and lightning sliced across Nikki's stomach. She had no choice but to inch forward to the open hayloft door.

"She's your daughter? Isn't that reason enough?" Celeste argued.

"She's my insurance policy," Mom said, and when it got down to it, that was the truth. Nikki knew she and Celeste hadn't mattered to their mother for a long time, once the meth started tearing away at her, bite by gasping bite.

"Let her go," Celeste said, and locked eyes with her sister.

Tap-tap-tap rang in Nikki's head, and she only hoped her sister would remain in rhythm with her. Before she could think through the consequences, run the analysis of what could go wrong, Nikki slammed her head backward, pain radiating through her skull from the crash. She caught Onita on the chin and reached for the knife in the same swoop.

Fire blasted her hand. She'd hoped for the handle but caught the blade instead.

Nikki's palm pulsed and she opened her fist. Onita bent low and cratered her shoulder into her daughter's middle. The knife clattered to the floor.

Nikki stumbled, once, twice. The gaping maw of the door was in front of her, and then somehow above her, along with the sky. Celeste stretched a hand to catch her and Nikki reached back, her eyes on her sister's hand as it grew smaller and smaller—the desperate fingers, the worn knuckles.

Tap-tap-tap.

Chapter Twenty-Three

GWEN

December 2022

The day after decorating the Christmas tree, Gwen turned into Nicola's driveway over her lunch hour, surprised to see Derek's Dodge Charger parked there. She came home most afternoons, cutting twenty minutes out of her lunch hour, to make sure Maxx had water and a chance to pee. It still struck Gwen as odd that Nicola had adopted the puppy when she so clearly seemed not to be a dog person. She complained about the muddy tracks in the house, the cost of vaccines, even the smell of the puppy's breath, while Gwen would have ranked it as one of her top five scents.

She paused with her finger on the ignition button. Why would Derek be home? And if he was, did she need to stay? Certainly that would mean he let Maxx out for a quick leg up. She debated texting Nicola to ask her but remembered she had a meeting over the lunch hour. She was about to reverse and head back to work when it occurred to her Derek might have seen her and then *leaving* would look weird.

Channel your inner Nicola, she thought to herself. Go to the door and knock like any other person with a link of vertebrae.

From the porch, she could hear heavy metal music screeching through the all-over speaker system, the thunderous guitars vibrating the door. She still did not understand how they worked as a couple. He listened to this music and Nicola to the headliners from Lilith Fair. He drove a muscle car, she a Prius.

Gwen knocked but there was no answer, so she tried again. The music volume lowered and Derek appeared a moment later, his face an angry red, sweat rivulets running down his forehead.

"Are you okay?" she asked.

"Do I look okay?" he spat back. She hated being confronted with male anger and aggression, and it was coming off him in waves. He huffed out a breath. "I'm sorry. Shit day. I got fired."

"Fired?"

"Yeah, as in lost my job? Now unemployed? Let go?" He started to walk back in the house, and she felt the only thing to do was to follow him. Maxx came scurrying out from the kitchen, a tether toy in his mouth that Whitney had bought with her own savings. It had been such a sweet thing for her daughter to do given that she no longer received an allowance while Gwen pinched every penny she could to rebuild their savings.

Derek flopped down on the couch and Maxx scurried up next to him. Gwen remembered the morning she'd woken up in this house, hungover on the same yellow couch. The surprise of seeing his hulking, sweaty body as he entered the house after his run. It seemed both years ago and like yesterday. She'd of course seen Derek a few times in the months since, but it was surprising how rarely their paths crossed. And if she was honest, she wasn't bummed about it. Nicola was right: her husband was a jerk, not that Gwen would ever say that aloud.

Nicola said that when she met him, she was attracted to the bad-boy aspects. "Nothing too crazy," she had clarified, laughing. "Sex in public, dine and dash, that kind of thing." Gwen had worked to keep her eyes from bugging—for her that was crazy. My god, had she and

Todd really been that boring? But then Nicola had admitted, "That kind of bad-boy thing I was attracted to? It was really him being an asshole. There was no heart of gold lurking."

"You want a drink or anything?" Derek asked Gwen now, and it was then she noticed the bottle of scotch on the coffee table next to the half-full glass. It was shortly after noon. She looked back at Derek, recognizing the somewhat glazed eyes, the looseness in his joints, the laxness in his mouth. His face wasn't quite so red anymore, just a shiny pink, and she wondered if he'd been exercising in the condo. She could tell he wasn't drunk but on his way, though that seemed a reasonable response to getting sacked.

"I've been hoping I'd get a chance to talk to you," Derek said, scooching forward and picking up his drink. Maxx leaned his slight weight against Derek's hip, and Gwen looked at Derek cautiously.

"Why are you here every day?" he asked.

"Oh." She let out a surprised puff of laughter, realizing how nervous she'd been about what he'd say. "I stop by to take out Maxx."

"I know that, but *why*? Why not Nicola? Isn't she the one who wanted a dog?"

"I volunteered," Gwen said, which was true.

He shook his head. "She's a taker, Gwen. Through and through. And she's so good at it, she's got you thinking it was your idea."

"That's not true," Gwen said defensively, and he took another swig of his drink. She didn't want to talk to him about Nicola. She had a sneaking suspicion that would be seen as a betrayal, but all the same, she took a seat across the room from him, curious.

"She is," he insisted. "She's a taker with a jealous streak. Talk to Missy about that." He poked a finger in the air as if just remembering something. "Oh wait," he said, and let the words linger.

Why was he bringing up Missy? She knew Derek had gone out for dinner on a couples' date with them, but what did that have to do with a jealous streak? What was he implying Nicola had taken? "What are you saying?" Gwen asked.

"All I'm saying is, I was accused of sexual harassment, but I didn't do it." He held up his hand again. "I know, I know, it's like how everyone in prison claims they're innocent and no one believes them, but I swear, I've always been professional at work. I'm sure Nicola's told you I've dogged around," he said, and Gwen did her best to keep her face neutral. *You prick,* she thought. Last she knew, Nicola knew about his Tinder account but hadn't confirmed anything. It made Gwen's heart ache to think Nicola might have found out for sure but didn't think she could confide in her.

And he was right: she didn't believe him about work. His flat denial was suspicious, but also she knew that many men didn't even recognize how awful, creepy, and predatory their behavior was. An investor in Todd's company had been accused of telling a woman if she didn't sleep with him, she'd never get ahead. When the allegations were made public, he'd said, "Well, yeah, I said *that,* but I wasn't serious."

"It's true," Derek continued. "It was like someone was out to get me."

"So you're the victim?" Gwen said, disgusted. She stood up to leave, and Derek shook his head.

"Sorry, bad choice of words. I'm not the victim, but no single woman was either." He leaned forward and waited for her to sit back down. Gwen was willing to hear him out *only* because he was Nicola's husband. "There wasn't a specific person making the accusation, but like, a lot of them."

"And that's a good thing?" Gwen said as Maxx trotted to Gwen for a pet. Since when did multiple accusers lighten an accusation?

"No, I mean there wasn't a name attached. Just a lot of speculation and rumors swirling around from different accounts. Just a lot of 'she said, she said,' but no actual *she.*"

"I don't understand," Gwen said, and pulled Maxx into her lap.

"What I mean is that no one actually stepped forward and said, 'I'm making the accusation.' It was a lot of speculation online, anonymous tips but no formal statement."

"A lot of women don't feel safe—" Gwen started, and he cut her off, which did not work in his favor.

"I get that, and I certainly wouldn't blame them if it was *true*. But because it was anonymous, I don't have anyone to talk to, to try to figure out who was saying what."

"You shouldn't approach the wom—"

"I know that too," he said, with what passed as drunk patience. "But what I'm saying is, even if I wanted to, there's no name. Like, if I was to hire a lawyer and say, this person or these people are accusing me, there are *no names*."

"Then how did this come about?"

He snapped his fingers and Maxx flew off Gwen's lap and back to the sofa, circling Derek's hip and flopping down. She watched the way his hand instinctually, almost unconsciously, petted the dog from the top of his head to his tail, with a stop at the neck for a scratch. He couldn't be all bad. Dogs could sense that kind of thing.

"It blew up on this whistleblower website," Derek said. "One that started like a Google Doc where women could make whatever warnings they wanted about men, saying this guy was grabby or tried to get colleagues back to his hotel room or worse. Whatever. But it was more of a warning system than an accusation, so it didn't have to be fact." Gwen opened her mouth to protest, and he held up his hand. "And I agree, these women shouldn't have the burden of proof. I see something like that as doing a service, and I support it. But then it became a website, one where they were publicizing these men's names."

This didn't make sense to her. "But to fire you? Surely they had to have *some* proof."

"They didn't have proof so much as quantity." She looked at him skeptically. "I work for a private company and signed a morality clause when they hired me that said they could basically fire me for anything they saw as unfit. I play my radio too loud in the morning, whatever they want."

"But why would they believe it if you're such a good guy?"

"Well, I'm not an angel," he said, grinning. He was on the smarmy side for her, but she could see how others might fall for his charm. It surprised her, though, that Nicola had been one of them.

"So a website," she said, and he continued.

"But it was like the website organized a campaign against me. They got more and more women to post about me, and then they started calling my company, really letting it rip. They'd tell whoever answered the phone that I was a rapist . . . a monster. They sent letters to the CEO and CFO's *wives* saying to never be alone in a room with me. It was awful. It finally got so it was so disruptive they let me go. With a good severance package, but it was immediate. No warning, no nothing."

"So it was targeted," Gwen said, and Derek nodded. "But who would hate you enough to do something like that?" She crossed her arms. "You clearly have an enemy for *some* reason."

Derek leaned forward. "There's only one person who hates me that much." As if on cue, his phone dinged and he flipped it over. "Speak of the devil." He began typing back, waited a moment, and set the phone back down. "She wants you to text her."

Gwen reached for her phone and saw Nicola was texting her right then. She waited a moment for the words to pop through. God knows what he's telling you. The three dots rotated. He's a pig. I'll see you tonight.

See you then xo. She had never signed a text to Nicola with "xo" before, but it seemed appropriate. She wanted Nicola to know she was on her side, even if she was sometimes irritated with her. Like Nicola said, that was part of friendship, of sisterhood. Gwen felt a pang of regret that she hadn't realized how much her friend had been hurting—and a little ping of something else. It felt suspiciously like relief someone else's life was falling apart, not just hers.

Gwen stood up. "So you expect me to believe your own wife would get you fired from your job? Would obliterate half the household income for no reason?"

"Like I said, I'm no angel, but there's a big difference between having a reasonable conversation about shit and what's happened. Even if she'd posted on that website as a way to warn other women, like a Yelp for Assholes, that would have been one thing. But to try to ruin my career? That's some next-level shit."

Her phone dinged. Thank you, Nicola texted. I'm so lucky to have you in my life.

Yes, Gwen thought. I am a good friend. She hearted the message and walked to the door. "Good luck with your job search," she said bitingly.

"Yeah, well, good luck with your friendship," he replied.

Chapter Twenty-Four

Gwen's phone dinged at 9:04 that night with a text from Nicola. On my way.

See you soon! Gwen texted back, and waited for Nicola at the curb after she pulled the large recycling and garbage bins to the end of the driveway. Most nights Nicola came over for a drink after Whitney was in bed, a routine Gwen had grown to love.

"Well, what did that asshole say?" Nicola asked, following her back up through the garage. Gwen slapped the button and the garage door cranked down as Nicola grabbed a raspberry White Claw from Gwen's fridge and flopped on her beige couch.

"He told me why he was fired."

Nicola looked at her suspiciously. "And why was that? I mean, I *know* why, but how did he spin it?"

"He said that he was accused of sexual harassment but that the allegations weren't attached to a single person, and that he was never able to verify that someone actually said anything."

Nicola took a loud slurp from her can. "I do not think those words mean what he thinks they mean," she said, paraphrasing *The Princess Bride*. "He honestly thinks not having one person but many is a positive thing?"

Gwen shook her head somewhere between yes and no. "I get it if he's saying that there isn't an actual victim coming forward—" she started, and Nicola rolled her eyes. "Do you think it's possible he was set up?" Gwen asked.

"Oh please," Nicola said. "Do you know how I found out he was cheating on me this time?" Gwen shook her head. "His phone. One night we're watching TV and he gets up to go to the bathroom, and I see a text pop up on his screen and look over—instinct, you know?—and there it is: some text from someone named 'J' talking about how she wants to suck his dick. It was such a cliché, and like, so insulting. He wasn't even trying to hide it." Nicola snorted like she was trying not to cry, and an honest-to-goodness snot bubble flapped out of her nose and then back in again. That vulnerability made Gwen want to believe her friend. "As if any woman really wants to do that," Nicola said. "God, we'll say anything. I confronted him and there wasn't much he could do to deny it. I mean, it's not a text you can misinterpret like 'Can't wait to see you later.'"

"Autocorrect?" Gwen suggested as his excuse, and Nicola nodded.

"He tried that, but please. I'm not an idiot." As if expecting Gwen's next question, she said, "That was a few months ago, and then all the stuff started circulating online about him at work on the website. I found out about it because I'm the kind of woman that list is made for: someone in business who needs the sisterhood looking out for her." Gwen nodded. "And I know things like that aren't always about sex, they're about dominance. They're about proving you can. And that is Derek to a tee."

"Did you confront him when you first saw the website?"

Nicola shook her head. "I figured, he made his bed, let him lie in it."

Maybe Nicola was right to let Derek get what he deserved. She hated how all those public-figure wives were forced to stand by their men when they screwed up. She'd always wondered what would happen if instead one of them stepped back and pointed to the podium to say, *Have at it. See how well things go when I'm not willing to sop up your messes.* When Gwen found out Todd had screwed up their finances, it had been mixed with all the grief over his death. A part of her thought it must feel wonderful to just be ruthlessly *mad*.

She asked if Nicola had any ideas about who the women could be, or if she had her suspicions.

Nicola drank the rest of her White Claw and dented the can. "I'm sure he's made a pass at all of them. Even the ugly ones."

"But maybe one in particular you could talk to?" Gwen pushed, and Nicola turned to her, anger apparent on her face.

"Why are you asking?" Nicola demanded.

Gwen opened her mouth to speak, then closed it again. Why *was* she asking? "Aren't you curious to hear what they have to say?" she asked, but that wasn't all of it. A part of her believed that prick over her friend. Why?

"Gwen?" Nicola pressed. "Are you taking his side?"

"No, of course not," she sputtered. "It doesn't have anything to do with sides."

Nicola laughed without humor. "Oh my god, do you really believe that? It is *all* about taking sides. Either you're with me or you're against me." She leaned forward and Gwen could smell something dank on her breath, like old vegetables caught deep in her teeth.

"I'm not saying—"

"He has a temper, and god knows I do too," Nicola said, a self-owning hand to her chest. "But not like him. I get mad and I might take it out on things, but never people."

Gwen's mind scrambled at the thought of Derek's temper. Todd had been a yeller, but not once had Gwen felt in physical danger with her husband. "Wait, has he hurt you?" Why hadn't Nicola told her sooner? Gwen understood it was complicated to disclose domestic violence, but something about this felt off. Why was Nicola telling her *now*?

Nicola wobbled her hand in the air: yes and no. "He's grabbed my arm here and there, or maybe shoved me, but it seemed kind of like an accident. It could have been my fault for provoking him."

Gwen put a hand on Nicola's. "It's not your fault."

"I'm not victim blaming, but I know I can be a lot." Nicola stuttered a laugh. "I mean, you have to admit, right?"

"Not at all," Gwen said. "You're just the right amount." Even in the moment, she wondered how she'd gone from doubting Nicola to reassuring her.

"Promise me," Nicola said. "If Derek does anything to you or says anything about me that you'll tell me."

"What would he do to me?" Gwen tried her best to understand the moment. Was Nicola really concerned about her safety, or did she not want her around Derek? And if the latter, why? What did she think Derek might say?

"Hit on you, or—" She paused. "Or worse. I don't know. Don't be alone with him, okay? Don't trust him or anything he says."

"Are you sure you're okay?"

"I mean, I *think* so," Nicola said. "But like, where would I go?"

Nicola looked at Gwen, who felt caught in the high beams. She knew she had to make the offer, but something felt off about this. She wasn't following the full thread of the conversation. She thought of all Nicola had done for her, but she hadn't asked for it. Had she? The silence stretched between them until finally Gwen couldn't take it any longer.

"You don't want to stay here, do you?"

Nicola flinched. "Wow," she said, standing, snatching the can from the coffee table as she took a large step over Gwen's feet, careful not to touch her as she slammed her way into the kitchen and threw the can in recycling. "Just wow." She shook her head, and Gwen ran after her down the hall.

"Nicola, it's just that Whitney's finally starting to sleep through more nights, and my mom is still so unstable. I feel like, until I get her all sorted at home and the health care set, I can't be giving up a room. But if you need a night, and don't mind the couch—"

"The couch!" Nicola said, sarcasm clear in her voice. "Why thank you, Queen Gwen. I would have been happy with the floor. I didn't expect you to be so generous."

"I, it's just—"

"I got it," Nicola said, and turned to Gwen, her eyes glassy with rage. "Family first. I guess I wouldn't know what that's like. Must be nice to have all those people to count on." Maybe it wasn't rage in her eyes, but true hurt. Gwen felt her chest cave.

"Nic—"

Nicola held up a hand. "No, I get it. I was thinking we were friends who could count on each other, but I guess not." She stalked down the short hallway to the foyer, where she yanked open the front door. "I don't want to be an inconvenience."

"You're not—" Gwen started, but Nicola slammed the door behind her.

Gwen stood there a long moment, straining to hear Nicola's footfalls but the night was silent. Was Nicola right? Was Gwen a terrible friend?

Gwen clicked the steel-bolt lock, although what was the point? She'd already given Nicola a key.

RULE #3: TRUST YOUR INSTINCTS

Chapter Twenty-Five

NICOLA

August 2008

Nicola stepped into Glenn State's student union. The air-conditioning slapped her damp skin, her oxford shirt stuck at the small of her back. A young woman in low-slung khaki pants and an orange polo asked if she was here for student orientation, and she nodded. "Name?"

"Nicola Kimmel." She was leaving Nikki and the farm behind.

The woman flipped through the open envelope box labeled *K*, her short nails painted with black polish. "Here you are!" she said enthusiastically. She handed Nicola a white envelope full of paper, and Nicola could feel two metal keys at the bottom.

"Those'll get you into the dorm and into your room." The woman pointed at the building behind her. "You can get your ID pic in the basement. The lighting sucks but it's not like anyone has ever had a cute ID." Nicola could tell the woman had already said it a hundred times that day, and there was something so sweet about her ability to still say it like she meant it.

In the past three months, Nicola had repeated her new name to herself until she could say it like she believed it. Nikki was the gangly straight-A girl from Harris, Ohio, but Nicola, this new version, would take on the world.

That awful July night at the farm when her family had shattered, a hole opened in Nikki's heart that would never be filled. In the hours after, Celeste had snuck into the Dairy Dream with her assistant manager key and emptied the cash register and safe. The next morning, when two cops drove a cruiser down the long lane to their farmhouse, Nicola and Onita said that Celeste had disappeared, not mentioning the money she'd left behind, every penny of it intended for Nicola to start a new life. She was determined to see her sister's sacrifice for the opportunity it was: a chance to claim her future and break ties with her mother for good.

After Celeste's disappearance, Nicola moved to Dayton to attend Glenn State on scholarship. Nicola made it clear to Onita that if she contacted her for any reason, then Nicola would tell the police her mother had tried to kill her. Onita agreed readily enough, finally blessed with the life she'd always wanted: one without daughters.

As she sat in the university basement, waiting for her name to be called, Nicola flipped through the paperwork the woman had given her. There was a flier for the student health center complete with mental wellness counseling. Coed intramurals. A rec center boasting fifteen treadmills. There was a list of colleges and majors on slick cardstock, with photos of students smiling around a table. She already knew she'd go into business, one of the tracks that promised financial security. She ran her tongue over her new teeth. Like the name, she was still getting used to them. When she'd arrived in Dayton, she visited a dentist for the first time in her life, paying cash from the Dairy Dream. The whirl and heat of the drill, the stretch of her mouth: it felt like a penance and a promise. She started her college life smiling in every mirror she passed.

The last sheet listed internship opportunities, available senior year. The headline at the top read IT's NEVER TOO SOON TO BE PLANNING FOR YOUR FUTURE!

"Nicola Kimmel," a cheery volunteer read from a clipboard.

The future, Nicola thought, and stood up to take her place in line.

Chapter Twenty-Six

Gwen

December 2022

Gwen tossed most of the night, alternating between body sweats and too few covers, finally succumbing to sleep after four. She dreamed of the fight with Nicola and the sound of a slamming door, of Mr. TopHat in flight, all of it blending together in nonsensical and ominous ways.

When she finally bolted from bed at seven fifteen, the morning was pure chaos. Whitney threw a tantrum over the shirt Gwen picked out, then Gwen swiped her mascara wand down her own blouse and had to change. When they were finally ready to leave, Gwen opened the door from the kitchen to the garage and found the garage door up.

What the hell?

Gwen instinctively put a hand on Whitney's chest, then pressed her daughter against her. Whitney's small heft was like a weighted blanket.

Had there been an intruder?

Gwen's eyebrows pulled together. She remembered clearly closing the door when she came in from putting out the garbage the night before. Right? Or maybe she'd left it open when she took the bins to the street? But no, she remembered watching the door crank down as Nicola waltzed into her kitchen.

A quick scan of the garage showed everything in place, so Gwen was hopeful they hadn't been burglarized. She must have just been scatter-brained. She told Whitney to climb in her seat—"Go, go"—then locked the door to the condo and slid in the Rover.

She pulled the shift lever to reverse and looked in the back-up cam, surprised to see the bird's-eye view off kilter. As she tapped the gas, the car tilted to the back right, as if she'd run into a pothole in her own garage.

"What happened?" Whitney asked.

Gwen threw the car back into park and did a quick check of the clock. She had fourteen minutes to get Whitney to school with a ten-minute drive. "Let me check."

She circled the front of the car and saw nothing, although admittedly she had no idea what she was looking for. She came around the rear fender, and there it was: a flat tire. "Shit."

She glanced around the garage as if that would do anything—*What, am I going to inflate it with a bike pump?* "Shit, shit." Tears stung her eyes. God, she was so sick of crying. It seemed like all she did anymore was cry no matter the situation. She was so damn emotional, and when presented with a problem that Todd would have solved in her old life, it about did her in.

"What's wrong?" Whitney said, and Gwen pulled herself together.

"Flat tire," she said, wiping the tears from her cheeks. "No biggie."

"No biggie?" Whitney echoed back incredulously. "Won't we be late for school?"

"Yes, but it's not a huge deal, Whit."

"But I've got roll first thing! My teacher told us how important attendance is. That's one of the things she's tracking to see who's responsible enough to get Mr. TopHat at the holidays!"

A headache started behind Gwen's eye, a pounding throb. That stupid bird was all she heard about. "Whitney," she said, doing her best to keep the warble out of her voice. "It's fine. Parent trumps teacher."

It was a joke between her and Todd about the hierarchy of final words—parent trumps teacher; Mom trumps Dad. And there it was, the gut punch after the tears. There was no Dad, only her, doing the best she could.

A quick honk startled her, and she looked up from the tire and saw Nicola in her Prius, the window descending. "Everything okay?" she said in her bright voice.

"We have a flat tire!" Whitney said, unbuckling herself and climbing out of the back seat. Gwen pointed to the offensive flat.

"That's no good," Nicola said, easing her car behind Gwen's in the driveway, boxing her in. For a split second, Gwen's heart slapped against her chest—a fight-or-flight reaction to being trapped.

"Do you need some help?"

Gwen paused. Of course this would happen right after she'd been a crap friend to Nicola, but she needed help and she needed it now. "That would be amazing."

Nicola tugged Whitney's ponytail. "Grab your backpack, kiddo. I'll get you to school and we can call AAA and have them deal with the flat."

"Mom might have left the garage door open last night," Whitney supplied.

Nicola looked at Gwen, her eyebrows raised. "It's a safe neighborhood, Gwen, but there's no need to court danger."

"I thought I closed it," Gwen insisted, and again, it was like a ghost memory she could pull up and replay: hitting the button on her way into the house, watching the door descend.

"You should be more careful," Nicola said, and then dropped her voice. "It's not like you've got Todd here to protect you now. You've got to keep an eye on things."

"I know," Gwen said, tears sprouting once again. "You're right." It was just so much to handle all on her own, and she was thankful once again to have Nicola looking out for her, ready to help when Gwen dropped the ball.

They loaded Whitney into the back seat along with their bags and were quickly on the road. Gwen knew they'd be late to school, but only by a few minutes. Still, Whitney reminded her if she was late even once she couldn't get a certificate for perfect attendance at the end of the school year.

"Only the dorks get those," Nicola piped in.

"What do you mean?" Whitney asked.

Nicola turned from the front seat. "Who wants a perfect record as a goody-goody?"

"Me," Whitney said sincerely.

"Boring," Nicola said. "You know what happens if you always play by the rules?"

"What?"

"You get a participant's medal. You know what happens when you break the rules?"

"What?" Whitney asked, and Gwen held her breath, waiting for Nicola's answer.

"You *win*."

"Win what?"

"At life."

Whitney sat back, satisfied, and Gwen could tell she liked that idea: winning at life. *But at what cost and to whom?*

"Well, the rules are in place—" Gwen started, but Nicola broke in.

"Bah. You want to win, full stop."

Whitney laughed, and Gwen's chest filled with pressure. "Not bah," she insisted, but Whitney was looking out the window and not listening, content now with being late. Gwen promised herself she'd talk to her daughter after school about regulations and boundaries. The idea of Nicola parenting Whitney left her with a hollowness in her stomach.

Nicola waited in the car while Gwen shepherded her daughter into the grade school, reminding herself this wasn't a big deal. Don't blow this out of proportion. It was third grade; what did she think Whitney was going to miss? Quantum physics? This was not life or death.

In the school office, Gwen told Mary, the woman at the front desk in gel nails and a perm, that they'd had a flat tire and she needed to sign her daughter in late. She made a point of not apologizing, embarrassed how much her heart hammered in her chest because of it. She was used to apologizing for everything—wasn't that what women did?—but Nicola was right: this wasn't a big deal.

The woman turned a sheet of paper on a clipboard toward Gwen and pointed to the first empty line. "Kid's name, grade, teacher, and your signature." She indicated each empty block in the row.

"That's it?" Gwen asked.

"That's it," she confirmed.

Gwen filled in the form, then turned and gave Whitney a kiss on the forehead, double-checking she had her lunch. Her kid had sustenance; all was fine with the world.

But was it?

The thought tickled the back of her throat. She would bet money (if she had any) that she'd closed that garage door the night before. She could remember standing on the cold concrete step into the house, Nicola already inside and helping herself to the contents of Gwen's fridge. Gwen seemed to remember a short, quick burst of irritation. Gwen didn't even like White Claw, but Nicola had told her to pick some up at the store, sick of having to carry her own over every night. Originally Gwen had bought strawberry, but Nicola told her that was disgusting: only raspberry or lime.

Gwen was 90 percent sure she'd shut the garage, maybe 95. Did that mean she'd just run over a nail earlier yesterday? Certainly that must be it.

Outside, Gwen hunched her shoulders against the cold and climbed into Nicola's car.

"Everything work out?" Nicola asked as Gwen pulled her seat belt over her waist.

"I think so," she said, but she actually didn't think that at all.

"Good," Nicola said as she pressed the button to start the car. "I'm glad I was there to help."

Chapter Twenty-Seven

Gwen and Nicola parted ways at the Dacks elevator. Nicola was back to her cheery, chatty self, and the fight the night before was behind them. But once alone in her office, Gwen tried to sort through the situation. Something about the sequence of events didn't sit right, and it felt like more than just the garage door she may or may not have left open. Again, she replayed the night before, her hand slapping the garage button. She knew with certainty she'd shut the door, and that, Gwen realized, was as close to the definition of faith as she could get. Tears blurred her eyes as she looked down at her desk. That was what felt so unfamiliar. She had faith in herself.

Gwen sat down at her desk and turned on her computer. She had dozens of new messages in her inbox, and she was happy to lose herself in work. At first she'd been surprised to find how much she loved this job. Each morning, she would make her to-do list at her desk and label the first one to four tasks to complete, get those done, and label the next four. By the time she'd look up, it was nearly noon. Was this what Todd had referred to as "flow"? He'd made it sound magical, almost mystical, but was it simply concentration? For too long she'd believed she didn't belong in the office world. But she was delighted to find out, not only did she belong, she was *good* at the work.

Gwen focused on her list and the day flew by. Right before leaving, she stopped by the bathroom and after washing her hands, looked at herself in the full-length mirror. How was it she could look so much the same, and yet feel unrecognizable to herself? Her life was nothing like what she'd imagined six months ago, and yet, she felt like she was coming into her own. When she'd first moved, any pride over her accomplishments had been quickly shadowed by grief, and while that was still there, she'd begun to see the good as well. She was tougher than she'd realized. She was good at her job. She was learning to trust the way she saw the world. Sure, she needed her bangs trimmed and highlights touched up, but her daughter knew she was loved. She turned to look at her butt in the mirror over her shoulder. She'd put on a few pounds since moving, but who gave a shit? She was also kissing her kid good night each night and earning a paycheck. She was *proud* of herself.

The bathroom door creaked open as she was looking at her own butt. Gwen told Bethany the first excuse that came to mind, that she'd sat in something.

Bethany, to Gwen's mortification, said, "Here, let me take a look." She bent her knees and did a quick scan of Gwen's hiney and declared, "All good."

As Bethany stood back up, Gwen looked for judgment on her face, about her out-of-style pants, the size of her ass, but there was nothing but warm kindness. Gwen thought about how Nicola had warned her Bethany was a backstabber and a gossip, but had that been the jealous streak Derek spoke about? She couldn't stand Derek but also wondered if he knew a side to Nicola that she hadn't seen yet. One of the best things Nicola had taught her was to trust her instincts.

"Can I ask you something?" Gwen said.

"Shoot."

"Do you remember when I first started?" Bethany nodded. "Nicola and I ran into you at the Century Bar that Friday. You were there with your husband."

Bethany's eyes brightened in recognition. "That's right. We were going to a play."

"Did you know anything about a happy hour that night? Nicola sent out an invitation, a meet and greet for me to get to know the women in the office."

Bethany shook her head. "Nope. Didn't happen."

Gwen felt sucker-punched. "You're sure? Maybe you forgot that you received the invite?"

"I would have remembered. Nicola has never asked other women out to happy hour, only Missy." She paused. "And now you."

Gwen felt uneasy being aligned with Missy, the tether between them Nicola. "Did you know Missy well?" Gwen asked.

Bethany squinched her mouth to the side. "Not really. I liked her, we'd say hi in the halls, but she pretty much spent time exclusively with Nicola." She seemed to think about it for a second. "It was like Nicola kept her on a short leash."

"What do you mean?" Gwen asked, but she thought she understood something about that leash. How Nicola wanted to dictate what they ate for lunch, how Gwen decorated her condo, what drinks she kept on hand, or even what kind of toilet paper she used. Anytime she'd tried to tug away she'd feel the pressure on her windpipe, the straining of her breath.

Bethany leaned her hip against the wet countertop. "One time, a bunch of us had to go to Columbus for training a few years ago—this was pre-COVID—and at the last second, my husband's engine light came on and he had to take my car for the day, so I asked Missy if I could ride with her. She seemed hesitant to accept and said she'd have to talk to Nicola first."

"Was Nicola driving?"

Bethany shook her head. "Missy was, but she needed to get permission anyway, it seemed. I rode in the back seat and Nicola was in charge of the temperature, the music, the route. Everything. And she seemed to keep the music just loud enough I couldn't really hear what was going on in the front, so I read on my phone." She waved a hand. "Anyway, that's not the point. Or it's a point but not the one I was thinking of. Afterward, the three of us went out for lunch, and it wasn't like Nicola could ask me to sit at another table, although my guess is she wanted to. But when the bread basket came, here's the weird part: Nicola told Missy not to butter her bread."

Gwen almost laughed. "That's it?" It seemed pretty benign.

Bethany grimaced. "It's nothing, but also something. A tip of the iceberg, maybe. Missy reached out her butter knife, and Nicola picked up her own and clashed against it like they were two swords. She reminded Missy she was on a diet and said she shouldn't eat the bread, much less the butter." Her eyes grew wide. "Weird, right? Like, sure, maybe a friend is looking out for you, but it struck me as so controlling."

"Did she eat it?"

Bethany nodded, a satisfied look on her face. "Three pieces. I remember thinking, that's a relationship I'm glad to be outside of."

"I get it," Gwen said, "but isn't that pretty harmless?"

Bethany seemed to think about it. "Yes and no. After lockdown, things were different. Dacks went to a hybrid model where half the staff worked from home on alternating days, and Nicola insisted she be on the same office schedule as Missy because of certain projects. But between you and me, Missy had told me not to put her on the same days as Nicola." She shook her head. "I shouldn't even be telling you that, but . . ." She shrugged. "I had to sync their schedules since Missy's was more of a personal, not a professional request, but when I told her they'd be working together, it was like she deflated. She did *not* want to be around Nicola anymore."

"Did you know her fiancé?" Gwen asked, thinking how Nicola had called him controlling. Maybe that was why.

"Jonas? I met him once or twice in the office when we all came back from quarantine. He seemed like a nice guy, but no, I didn't really know him." She paused. "But I was surprised when Missy left so suddenly. It seemed odd. She'd been so excited to get married, she'd already started the paperwork to change her name to Missy Hansen. It didn't seem like someone that excited about the future would just disappear." Gwen thought about Derek's snide comment about not being able to talk to Missy about Nicola. Did someone else not want people talking to Missy? Bethany shrugged. "But like I said, I didn't know him well."

She turned to the mirror one more time and pulled a lipstick out of her front pocket, smoothing it over her mouth. "It was good to chat with you, Gwen," she said.

"Likewise," Gwen said. Maybe she and Bethany would get lunch someday after all.

◆ ◆ ◆

Walking back to her office, Gwen heard her cell phone ringing and jogged the last few feet, answering when she saw the number she'd programmed for the garage. "Gwen Maner," she said, her voice high in her darkened office. She'd turned her light out when she was leaving for the bathroom, something she did instinctively whenever she left a room after years of hounding her daughter.

"Ms. Maner, yeah, it's Ted from SC Garage. Your car's ready to go."

"Oh, excellent." She glanced at her watch. It was already four thirty; maybe she could ask Nicola to leave a little early and drop her at the garage before she had to get Whitney at five fifteen.

"I found a screw," Ted said as Gwen reached under the desk and pulled up her purse. "Too close to the rim to patch so you'll need a new tire, but we've got one in stock." He told her the price and Gwen felt a surge of self-sufficiency that she had enough to cover it in her bank account. "Funny thing, though," Ted continued. "Not sure how you could have driven over that screw."

Gwen stilled, her planner in her hand hovered over her purse. "How so?"

"Well, a couple of things. I can show you when you get here. Ask for Ted."

They said their pleasantries and hung up, and as Gwen was reaching down to change into her snow shoes, she heard the confident click of Nicola's heels on the laminate hallway.

Gwen's desk was one of the few metal behemoths left over from the last office redo, and it was closed in the front. She liked that she could take her shoes off without anyone seeing. When she heard Nicola's heels clicking louder and louder, closer and closer, the sound pushed out all rational thought and she slipped under the desk, tightened herself into a ball.

She gripped her knees, the knuckles of her hands turning white.

Chapter Twenty-Eight

Gwen held her breath as the silence swelled around her.

She was confused by what she'd just done. What the hell? Who hid from their best friend *underneath a desk at work*? Nicola paused at the doorway—could she see Gwen's reflection in the window? Jesus, please no. Her heart thumped, and Gwen was convinced she'd telltale-heart herself into giving away her hiding place.

Eventually, slowly, she heard Nicola's heels start moving and recede into the distance.

Gwen paused under the desk, trying to remember the second when she had darted to the floor and what she was thinking, but she hadn't been thinking. It had been radio silence in her head, or more accurately, radio static. She didn't think, she just *moved*; some base part of her had known she didn't want to ride with Nicola, that whatever the mechanic had to say shouldn't be said in front of her.

She stayed there until her heart slowed at least to a cardio rate, then climbed out, looking over the desk to make sure no one was in her doorway. Empty.

◆ ◆ ◆

Gwen waited until she was in her Lyft before sending a text to Nicola. Car's done and I'm heading to garage. She knew Nicola would stop by before leaving for the day, expecting Gwen would need a ride.

Her phone dinged within seconds. I would have taken you.

Gwen stared at the words, trying to parse their tone. Was Nicola being helpful, reassuring Gwen that it wasn't a bother, or reproachful? You're the best, but hate to bother you with everything! she replied, followed by the zany-face emoji.

Nicola thumbs-upped the text.

Her driver dropped her at the front door of the garage. Gwen pulled open the heavy door and took in the comforting smell of motor oil so similar to the workbench in her father's garage, a TV bolted to the wall blaring a game show in the corner. A woman shuffled in from the back in a blue sweatshirt with the letters of the garage embroidered above the right breast, a pair of worn bootleg jeans underneath. "What's the car, sweetie?" she asked, even though they were approximately the same age, and Gwen told her.

"Ah yes. Let me get Sherlock Holmes out of the back."

A few minutes later, a man in his fifties lumbered forward on a bad hip, his T-shirt neatly tucked into his blue jeans. "You're Gwen?" he asked, and she nodded. He motioned for her to follow him into the garage, AC/DC blaring through tinny speakers, two cars on lifts in the air.

"Here it is," he said, and raised her flattened tire from where it rested against the wall. He rotated it until she could see where the screw was. "A couple of things. See this?" He pointed at the screw and she nodded. "The head's not worn or scuffed." He looked at her expectantly, but she remained blank. "If you'd driven on this screw after running it over, that would surely have happened."

He rotated the tire a bit more so they were looking at the screw on an angle. "Once I noticed how new the screw looked, a few other things stood out. See this?" He pointed to the millimeters of space between the tire and the screw head. "The screw's sticking out a ways and the shaft is still straight, which is also unlikely if it'd been driven on. Finally"—he pointed at the rubber of the tire—"if you'd run over the screw, the force would have dimpled the rubber in, but as is, it's pooched outward, a likely sign someone screwed it in rather than you running it over."

Gwen's stomach dropped. "So you're saying someone flattened my tire on purpose?"

"Sure looks like it." Ted pulled up his ball cap and set it back down on his balding head. "Could all be coincidences, but it's an awful lot in a row." Gwen thought about the garage door, her holding a boundary with Nicola the night before, the flattened tire in front of her. The way she'd scurried under her desk, heart pounding.

Could it be?

At the counter, the woman in the sweatshirt swiped Gwen's card. She nodded toward the garage. "Ted's been talking about that tire all day. Man watches *Forensic Files* like it's his paying job. You'd think he'd cracked the code to the Bermuda Triangle."

Gwen smiled wanly. "I appreciate him paying such close attention." Even as she said it, there was a part of her that resented it. She wanted to go back to feeling safe, even if that feeling was an illusion, but there was no way she could dismiss the mounting evidence: someone had sabotaged her tire.

The woman held out Gwen's card and when Gwen went to tug it away, the woman kept it in her grip, her eyes locked on Gwen's. "You sure you're okay, sweetie?"

Gwen swallowed thickly and nodded. What was there to say?

The woman released the card, and Gwen felt her eyes on her as she slid it in her wallet. The woman lowered her voice. "You keep yourself safe, hear? A man who'll send a message like that isn't going to stop until it's loud and clear."

But was it a man? She thought of Nicola's insistence that Derek would do what he had to do to come between them. Did he assume she'd blame Nicola? Was she falling under the sway of another man, this one not even her husband? Or had Nicola done this herself? Gwen wasn't sure, but she was determined to find out. She thought about her conversation with Bethany. *Nicola has never asked other women out to happy hour, only Missy. And now you.* And what had she said Jonas's last name was? Hansen?

"Thanks," Gwen said, and placed her wallet in her purse. "I'll keep that in mind."

In the parking lot, she climbed into the driver's seat. The seat was too far back, the rearview mirror pointed toward the ceiling. Her feet rested on a sheet of white paper with the garage's logo. Gwen had the unsteady feeling she'd slid into a new life, one that wasn't quite hers. She pulled up the seat until her feet touched the pedals and repositioned the mirror.

That night, Gwen typed "Jonas Hansen" into Google and narrowed the search down to three guys in their thirties who lived close to Dayton, all with available emails online. She sent messages to all three introducing herself, saying she'd known Missy in college and now worked at Dacks with Nicola Kimmel, and if this was the right Jonas Hansen, wondered if he'd have a chance to get a coffee.

Chapter Twenty-Nine

NICOLA

April 2012

Nicola strode into the interns' office with a stack of financial documents in her arms.

"How'd it go?" Missy asked, and Nicola grinned. "That good?"

"Better," she said. Nicola had been reviewing tax documents for 2011 and noticed an error in the audit that would save Dacks upward of $100,000 in billing. Their in-house accountants had missed it, overworked and focused only on the April 15 deadline. Nicola had double-checked her numbers and printed off the materials, and then presented them herself to Mr. Donovan, the CEO, that morning. At first, he'd seemed annoyed that a lowly intern had dared to enter his office, but she was tall and good looking and aware that opened doors. By the time she left, he'd put his hand warmly on her back and said she had a bright future at the company.

You're damn right I do, she'd thought, and told him she wanted a starting number in writing for negotiations. She also knew men like that appreciated moxie. Donovan had laughed and said he'd have his assistant write something up. "And a job for Missy too," she'd added.

"Congrats," Gwen said half-heartedly, looking up from the Cobb salad she was eating at her desk. She had two pictures of her and Todd pinned to the bulletin board next to her, while Missy had decorated her board with a collage of family, friends, and pets, spun on pink ribbon with tiny clothespins. Nicola had gone the professional route, with a sleek metal pen holder and a three-stack of files, decor that would eventually work in a solo office. Next to the folding rack was a white ceramic elephant from a high-end store she couldn't afford, its sole purpose to demonstrate she had money to burn.

Nicola was about to tell Missy that she'd put a word in for her, too, when there was a ruckus outside their small office. "You can't go back there—" said Amy, the floor administrative assistant, her voice raised. Nicola glanced toward the door, along with Missy and Gwen.

A woman walked past the doorway. She had scraggly, long blonde hair, and was hunched in a shiny, purple polyester coat with grime ground into it. Gwen gasped at the sight. Nicola couldn't see the woman's face, but she could tell by the curve of the woman's back and the cramp of her stomach it was Onita.

Her mother turned around, and out of the corner of her eye, Nicola saw Missy flinch. Onita's skin was etched with lines and dotted with age spots well beyond her forty-some years. She looked as if she'd died and come back.

"Long time, no see," Onita said, and then leaned over and coughed into her cupped bare hands, violently expelling a hack of wet air. She stood back up, a half-inch rock in her hand. The white film coating her tongue was visible as she tucked it back in her cheek.

Nicola knew that rock; it meant Onita was trying to quit a bad habit—smoking, drinking, drugs—but there wasn't a boulder big enough to keep all the wanting from her mouth. "What are you doing here?" she asked her mother evenly. Her mind focused to a pinprick, assessing. Of first importance: get Onita alone before she could say anything damning. All through college, she'd stuck to the story that her mother had died. It simplified things.

Onita smiled at her grimly before losing herself to another chest-rattling cough. "Nice office you've got here, Nikki," Onita croaked.

"Nikki?" Missy echoed.

"I don't go by that anymore," she said. "It's Nicola."

Missy looked from Nicola to Onita and back again as if to say, *Who is this woman?* Gwen folded her arms around herself as if afraid the woman was contagious, and to her deep surprise, Nicola felt an unexpected rush of empathy on her mother's behalf. She's still a *person*, she wanted to say to Gwen.

"You must be Nikki's coworkers," Onita said to Gwen and Missy, sneering at her daughter, and that quickly, the empathy melted away.

"How do you two know each other?" Missy asked.

"We—" Nicola started, as Onita said, "I'm her—" and both women stopped and locked eyes.

Missy looked again at the ragged woman in front of her. Even stooped as her spine was, it was clear the woman was tall, noticeably so, just like Nicola. She could not let them see the resemblance. Nicola turned abruptly, grabbing Onita by the elbow and pulling her into the hallway, past the bank of elevators, and into the cold stairwell.

"Why are you here?" Nicola demanded. "The rule was no contact."

Onita crossed her arms, the rub of cheap polyester making a shushing noise. To Nicola's ears, it sounded like poverty and desperation.

Onita rolled the rock to the other cheek. "Those were the rules back when I still had something to lose."

A half hour later, Nicola and Onita sat across from each other at Bob Evans, cups of coffee warming their hands and a stack of buttermilk pancakes in front of Onita. To the side of her plate sat the rock she'd pulled from her mouth, still wet with saliva. The smell of syrup, thick and cloying, hung in the air, and Nicola had to put her hand under her nose to stop from smelling it.

She'd hustled her mother out of Dacks as soon as she could. Had Missy and Gwen noticed the family resemblance? The hollow cheeks. The straight, angry mouths. She hoped it was hidden behind the lives they now lived: Onita's burned down by drugs and bad decisions, and Nicola's full of raw vegetables and promise and drive.

"You look like shit," she said to her mother, and Onita plowed a forkful of pancake into her mouth.

"Yeah, well, I feel like shit. I'm sick." She went on to tell Nicola that Walmart had kept her just under full-time, just low enough to avoid benefits, and now she'd missed so much work, they'd fired her. "I haven't worked in months," she said. "I'm about to lose the farm."

"Is that why you're here? You think I care about that shithole?" Nicola watched as a thick bead of syrup rolled slowly down her mother's chin. "Or you?"

Onita grinned, her lips shiny, pancake caulked to her gums. Her teeth had been yellow and crooked for as long as Nicola could remember, but the last four years had taken a further toll. She ran her tongue over her straight white teeth. She would not have guessed she and her sister had kept their mother in line, but there had been a precipitous decline since they left. Every third tooth or so had been worn back in Onita's mouth, disintegrated to nubs, blackness like mold rolling through and taking root sporadically. "I raised you," she pointed out. "I think I know you a little better than that."

Nicola could feel her anger burn off the top of her scalp. "So what do you want?"

Onita shoved another bite of pancake into her mouth after slopping it through the melted butter and syrup. "Money."

"No."

Onita slurped her coffee and held up her cup until the waitress came back and filled it from a fresh pot. "That looked like a pretty fancy office back there," she said, referring to Dacks. "You must make pretty good money."

"I don't make any money," she said, which was the truth, but she knew after her meeting with Donovan today that a job would be waiting in the mid five figures. It might not be a fortune to some, but as a starting point for someone out of Harris, Ohio, it was a big deal. "And even if I did, I wouldn't give you any. I owe you nothing. No contact: that was the deal."

"It was, but . . ." Onita wiped her mouth with her paper napkin. "When we struck that deal, I had a way to support myself. I could afford taxes on the farm. Not anymore." She leaned forward. "Now I've got nothing to lose. You on the other hand . . ." She let the words trail off before erupting in a series of coughs that seemed to start at her feet, cycloning between a harsh, dry sound and a wet slurp. "All I want is enough to keep the farm, a small amount for my troubles." Onita grinned. "Maybe enough to have a little fun every now and again."

This is what mothers did: take, take, take.

Nicola looked at her mother and saw her true self reflected back. Not the life she'd created, but the future that would have awaited her in Harris: one of loneliness and despair. Of complete isolation. She wanted to go back to the beginning before everything had gone so terribly wrong. She could fix this, she told herself.

"I'll buy the farm," Nicola said. "I'll buy it from you." As soon as her job started, she'd scrape together what was needed for back taxes and a down payment. There was no way she'd give Onita actual cash, but she also couldn't afford to have her default on the farm. It held too many memories, too many secrets.

"That's not what I'm asking," Onita said.

"Well, it's what I'm offering. I'll buy the farm and you can live there." She leaned forward. "But hear me out," she said between tight teeth, her molars ground together. Onita popped her rock back in her mouth. "If you ever come to Dayton again, I'll kill you. You hear me?"

Onita seemed to weigh the truth in that statement, resting it in her palm like a fragile egg.

Nicola looked her mother in the eye and said, "You're not the only one who knows what it's like to have nothing to lose."

Chapter Thirty

GWEN

December 2022

Gwen knew that Derek ran every morning. Nicola used to complain that he insisted on getting up at five thirty, even on weekends, so he could do his daily three miles before the rest of the world was awake. According to Nicola, when he got up, he'd slam the closet door and clatter around the bathroom. She described how he somehow made chugging water an audible experience through the pillow over her head. Then, as soon as he was back from the run, he'd fire up the Vitamix like a small plane landing in the kitchen. Nicola insisted it wasn't so much because he was an early bird, but because he loved to piss her off.

The day after she spoke with the mechanic, Gwen was out on the porch by six, tucked in the wicker chair next to her small, potted fir tree. She held a fresh cup of coffee and had a flannel quilt over her lap.

Across the street, two of the condos twinkled with colored lights. Were those decorations really outlawed by the HOA, or was that another lie Nicola had told her to get what she wanted?

Gwen was nearly to the bottom of her coffee mug when Derek rounded the corner into the condo complex in a zip-up and shorts despite temps in the twenties. His eyes were pointed at the road, and she recognized that particular exhaustion from when she'd run in college. Rather than looking at how far you had to go, you watched your feet, one then the other. She'd done that especially on hills, counting breaths like pennies.

She waved her hand to get his attention to no avail, threw off the quilt, and scurried to the edge of her street. He looked up as she drew closer, started, and then slowed down. When she waved, he did the same, tapping his AirPods to stop whatever was playing.

"Hey," he said, his breath hitching.

"Hey."

He jogged in place, a body still in motion. "Did you want to speak with me?"

"I do." She thumbed toward her house. "You have time to talk for a sec?"

He eventually slowed and stopped. "Sure. I guess." His eyes narrowed. "Did Nicola put you up to this?"

Gwen looked toward their condo, and almost convinced herself she saw a curtain move before remembering that Nicola had blinds. When Gwen had hung her own, Nicola said they often hid mites and were unsanitary. "Plus," she'd said, "a little tacky." And where were Gwen's curtains now? In a crawl space in the attic.

"No," Gwen said. "She doesn't know anything about this."

He followed her into her condo, and in the kitchen, took a spin at her paper towels, ripping off four or five to pat the sweat on his forehead and neck. His actions seemed presumptuous, like he had a right to her things. She really did not like this guy. What had Nicola ever seen in him?

"Why did you bring up Missy the other day?" Gwen asked. He looked at her, confused. "When we were talking about you getting fired. You said to ask Missy something about Nicola's jealous streak, knowing I couldn't do that because she's gone. Why?"

He crumpled the damp paper towels and looked right to left; Gwen pointed under the sink to indicate the garbage.

"They were really close, you know," he said, opening the cupboard and pitching the wad inside. "I used to joke that I didn't know why Nicola married me instead of Missy."

"Are you saying you thought they were more than friends?"

"No, nothing like that, or at least I don't think so." She was glad he didn't make a tasteless joke about the two women together, a possible threesome; it made her hate him a little less. "But there was something about their friendship that was off." He asked her for a glass of water and she pointed toward the cupboard. A small victory: she would not wait on him. Derek took a long gulp after filling his glass at the sink, then leaned against the counter. "When I was a kid, we adopted a dog from a shelter. They told us when we got him they didn't know about his life before, but to avoid loud noises, other dogs in the house. Missy reminded me of that dog. Always cowering, waiting for the smack." He was lost in thought for a moment. "Still, I don't think she was the type to up and run."

"Do you think she was happy? I know Nicola didn't."

Derek laughed. "Seriously, Gwen, you can't trust a word that woman says. I mean, there's gullible"—he held up a hand as if to set the level, then dropped it six or so inches—"and then there's you." God, he was such a jerk. "Missy was happy with her fiancé. And not like the love of a good man is all that can save a woman, but they seemed good together. Good for each other. Nicola dragged me to a dinner with that dolt, and he adored her. Totally whipped. She'd been between two entrées and he'd said"—here he raised his voice as if imitating a girl—"order both and I'll eat whichever one you don't like." He rolled his eyes.

Jonas sounded like the opposite of Todd, who had ordered for the both of them ever since he'd introduced himself as an excellent burger-orderer at the library. It had been both charming—he was so excited for her to try what he loved—and infantilizing. Still, being reminded so casually of Todd, for good and bad, she was caught off guard, breathless, at how she could suddenly miss him, like missing a vital organ. The intimacy of sharing bites from the same fork, how he'd put an arm around her shoulders when she sat too close to an air vent. Would she ever be through her grief?

Gwen lowered her voice. "So what do you think happened to Missy? Surely if there'd been foul play, the police would have looked into it."

"They did, briefly, but Missy left a note in her phone." Gwen's eyes widened. This was the first she'd heard about police involvement. "She said she'd figured out in quarantine she wanted a new start, plus there was no actual evidence of a crime. They didn't have anything to go on." He shook his head again. "Either way, I'm done."

"With what?"

"All of it. I'm out of there any day," he said, flipping a thumb over his shoulder to Nicola and his condo. "The marriage experience was not for me, and honestly? I'm surprised we made it the six years we did. I've got to cross some t's with my accountant and lawyer first. And you're right, I'm a prick, but that woman is a psycho bitch."

Gwen rolled her eyes. "That's what everyone always says about their ex. It says more about you than it does about her."

"Maybe, but it says plenty about her too." Derek set his glass on the counter next to the sink. "Thanks for the water," he said, and she followed him to the door, wanting nothing as much as him out of her house. Although she had a sinking feeling she'd spend the day thinking about what he'd said about Missy.

On the porch, Gwen looked at the small fir, decorated with red wooden beads and pine cones. When she and Nicola had been running errands at Target, Nicola had spotted the small trees and clapped her hands. "I'll get one for each of us," she'd said, and heaved one of the heavy buckets into her cart. Gwen had pointed to the one sprayed with fake snow, a bright sunny star on the top, knowing Whitney would like that one better, but Nicola insisted they have matchies.

Gwen had imagined people driving past Nicola's condo and then her own, seeing her as a pale impersonation. She didn't want to be a match to Nicola. She wanted to be herself. When she said she wanted the other one, even saying she'd pay for it herself, Nicola had reached toward the one with red garland. "Nope," she'd said, and plopped the bucket in her cart, wiped any dirt off her hands, and pushed it forward without looking back.

She could imagine it wasn't easy being married to Nicola. It wasn't even easy being her friend. Gwen stared at the fir tree. She had a call to make, just to find out about her options.

She dumped the rest of her own coffee in the fir pot, hoping as she did that the bitterness might kill it.

Chapter Thirty-One

Back in the condo, Gwen called the police department. She pressed through the automated system and was eventually connected to a woman with a curt voice that brooked no nonsense. Gwen asked what her options would be if she was being harassed by someone.

"A husband or partner?" the woman asked. "A domestic dispute?" Gwen wanted to explain that Todd would never have harassed her, but she pushed through and concentrated on the task at hand.

"A friend . . . I guess that would be closest."

"So someone you know well?"

Gwen confirmed and heard the clicking of a keyboard.

"The actual legal definition of domestic violence," the woman said, keys still clattering, "extends only to a family or household member or someone you're dating. Would that qualify?" Gwen told her no. "Has she or he stalked you? Or committed an aggravated trespass?" Hardly, Gwen thought; I gave her a key. "Or committed any act of abuse to a child?"

Gwen pictured Whitney walking Maxx, one of the few joys in her young life, and felt herself deflate. "No, nothing like that."

The woman's fingers stilled. "Okay," she said, drawing out the word. "Can you describe the harassment to me?"

Gwen's cheeks began to heat. What was there to say? The woman in question may or may not have flattened my tire and had something to do with the disappearance of a coworker? She'd watched enough *Law & Order* over the years to know that wasn't even close to evidence that could be seen as circumstantial. *Gossipy* would be the word for it. Maybe *paranoid*.

"Well, it's not so much what she's done, as the tone," Gwen said.

"Ma'am," the woman said, and her voice was so kind Gwen felt even worse. "Is there something you're not telling me?" Gwen realized then that the woman didn't believe her, but not in the way she had expected. The woman thought Gwen was lying—protecting an abusive man and not yet ready to name him. She assured the woman she wasn't. "Then maybe we should go over what steps you might take if the threat were to become more than tonal."

The woman went on to explain how restraining orders worked in Ohio. Gwen would need to fill out the appropriate forms, which she could find on the government website, then name the respondent and list out the most recent acts of violence. The woman was either reading straight from the website, or she had an amazing memory. Most likely, Gwen sadly realized, she had to recite these lines a number of times every day: "Acts of violence may include slapping, hitting, grabbing, threatening, etc.," none of which applied. From there, a judge would decide whether the application warranted an ex parte hearing, which would only involve Gwen, and then afterward, they'd serve Nicola papers for a full hearing. Already, Gwen was shaking her head.

There was no way she had enough evidence for a restraining order, and the thought of taking the stand in a courtroom to say Nicola was guilty of finding her a job and a place to live left her nauseated.

"Thank you," she said, cutting the woman off. "I think I overreacted."

"Are you sure?"

"I'm sure."

"Okay," she said, "but a lot of times when women call, they're trusting their gut. Listen to that, even if you're not ready to go the legal route yet. My name's Melinda Willis. Let me give you my number in case things escalate."

Gwen wrote down her information and tucked the slip of paper in her wallet.

◆ ◆ ◆

That evening, Gwen checked her email. There was a response from a Jonas Hansen who didn't know about Dacks or a Nicola Kimmel, and Gwen apologized for bothering him. Two Jonases had yet to respond, so she held out hope. Gwen had seen photos of Nicola on social media, but she'd never googled her, and she wondered what she might find. A quick search for Nicola Kimmel brought up articles about her as a woman's leader in Dayton, a merger she'd spearheaded at Dacks, and a few conferences on new media where she'd presented. There was a licensed nurse with the same name in Florida, and an aesthetician in Delaware. It wasn't until the fourth page that Gwen found a link for a graduating high school class in Harris, Ohio, with a Nicola Kimmel as valedictorian. A click through showed the page listed her name and no other information.

Gwen entered Harris into Google Maps; it was just over two and a half hours away. She toggled to the town's website for local details: population, 1,100; median income: *yikes*. This wasn't one of those rich suburbs of a larger midwestern city, but one that had been mowed over by supposed progress. She dug deeper and it appeared to be a farming community that had lost most of its land and livestock to Big Farm. The biggest local employer was a Walmart that had gone up in the early aughts. She guessed from the median income, the lucky ones were those who could still afford to shop there.

She clicked through to the town's weekly newspaper. Presumably, Nicola would have graduated high school the same year as Gwen. She couldn't find a record of Nicola by name in the paper, but a reunion page on Facebook linked to photos from the yearbook. She marveled at how small the graduating class was that year—eighteen—but it made searching through the pictures less of a chore.

The photos were low quality; most likely they'd been photographed with a phone. Some of them had slashes of white from the flash's reflection and others had creases where the pages had folded. From what Gwen could see, the images were achingly similar to her own pics from that time—the near desperation in the smiles of the hormonal teenagers, the anxiousness about who they would become.

She was through the seventeenth page of pictures when she caught a glimpse of a girl who could be Nicola. She was on the cheerleading squad. The girls stood posed with their arms crossed in Xs, all of them in short skirts and sweaters that looked like they'd lasted a few seasons too long—waistbands saggy, necks stretched. The familiar girl was second to the left, her clear eyes locked on the camera.

She had the same large nose as Nicola, but her hair was darker with bangs curled under, her skin blotchy. Her cheeks were full, not severe like Nicola's. Most notable were her crooked teeth. How many times had Gwen looked at Nicola's perfect smile and thought, *That's what it's like to come from money*. She must have had her teeth fixed after high school. They were something Nicola had obviously changed and wanted to leave in the past, and seeing them in their original form was like looking at someone naked without their permission, and Gwen wondered if she should stop digging. What was Rule #4? *Never Look Back*? She had a feeling the teeth were related to what Nicola wanted left behind, and the betrayal of her digging seemed clear. But Rule #2 flitted through her head as well: *Know Your Friends*. Did that imply *and your enemies*?

Gwen squinted at the photo again. The caption with names of the people was at the bottom, and there it was: Nikki Kimmel. Gwen would have thought Nicola was taller than the girl in the picture, but she was also used to seeing her in heels and not next to other corn-fed girls.

Gwen searched all the combinations she could think of based on the town, the high school, family names, other girls on the cheer team, and so on. She found a few hits for Nicola on Google, mainly about the football team for which she must have cheered, and an article even further back from when she was confirmed in the Lutheran church, this one without a picture. Then Gwen found a newspaper article on the high school's Facebook page about Nicola's full-ride scholarship to Glenn State, though she was referred to as Nikki, not Nicola. Was that another example of leaving her past behind? This article was accompanied by a picture of her with her hair tucked under her graduation cap and her ragged mouth in an open smile. This one was even less conclusive: a photo of a photo of newspaper print.

She clicked through a few more pages of Google links and eventually landed on an article about the disappearance of Celeste Clark, sister to recent valedictorian Nikki Kimmel. Her heart rate increased as she scanned the article for more information about the robbery of the Dairy Dream where Celeste was an assistant manager, police pleading for any leads into her whereabouts. She did a search for Celeste Clark and found an obituary for Gary Clark: entered fully into the presence of the Lord on February 16, 1987 . . . farming accident . . . Survived by his wife, Onita Clark, and daughter, Celeste.

Then Gwen searched for Onita Clark, no results, but then tried Onita Kimmel. There were a few articles here and there about arrests and at least one court date from 2019. Further digging for Onita Kimmel found a marriage license to Weldon Kimmel, as well as his death certificate from 1993. He'd died in a car accident, survived by his wife, Onita Kimmel; daughter, Nicola; and stepdaughter, Celeste. Nicola had said her mother was dead, but there was no death certificate for either Onita Clark or Kimmel.

Gwen remembered a woman showing up at Dacks all those years ago during the internship and how Nicola had shuffled her out of their office. Missy and Gwen had talked about the encounter after they left, eyes wide, wondering who *was* that woman? She certainly hadn't looked like someone they would have imagined from Nicola's past.

Gwen called Information to see if, on the off chance, a landline was still connected to Onita Kimmel's name, and was patched through.

She was about to hang up after five rings when a gruff female voice answered. Gwen could hear decades of cigarettes through the phone as the woman said hello.

"Hi, can I speak with Onita Kimmel, please?" Gwen asked.

"Who's this?"

"I work with Nicola Kimmel—"

"Wrong number," the woman croaked.

She seemed like the type to hang up and Gwen said, "Wait!"

The woman paused. "Are you a cop?"

What an odd question, Gwen thought. "No, I promise. I believe I work with your daughter." Her heart thudded, and she half hoped she had it wrong, that Nicola hadn't been lying about her mother all these years.

"I don't have a daughter named Nicola Kimmel," the woman said, and there was a long inhaling sound; Gwen was certain now she was right about the cigarettes, if nothing else.

"You're not Nicola's mother?" Gwen asked.

"I'm nobody's mother," she said, and hung up. Even though she'd denied it, Gwen had the sinking feeling she *was* Nicola's mother, but then why had Nicola lied and said her mother was dead? And what exactly had happened to Nicola's sister, Celeste?

Gwen's email dinged and she flipped to Outlook.

She had a message from the right Jonas.

Chapter Thirty-Two

GWEN

January 2021

Gwen stood in front of the cash box full of quarters, dimes, and ones with Whitney at her side. A parent crossed the gymnasium with a stack of books.

"You remember how much each book is?" Gwen asked her daughter.

"A dollar a hardback, fifty cents for the others," Whitney parroted back.

"And how many cents in a dollar?" she asked as the other mom approached, and Whitney answered correctly.

"That's pretty good," the woman said, handing the stack over to Whitney. "I was hoping to pull a fast one on you."

Whitney smiled behind her mask, or Gwen thought she did. Whitney was over halfway through first grade, and it had looked nothing like Gwen had imagined. Whitney had been so excited for school, but the first semester had been entirely online, and every morning, Gwen would have to drag her daughter from bed, tired and crabby, to spend three hours in front of a computer. They'd moved to in-person in January, but now Whitney was shy and unsteady, raised the last year in a panic-stricken world.

"I'm Gwen," she said to the other mother.

"Alpana," she said, and handed the stack of books to Whitney. She had long black hair loose and curled around her shoulders, a large expensive purse in the crook of her elbow. She pulled a water bottle from her bag and pinched down her mask to take a long drink. It was weird now seeing glimpses of other people's faces with so much visible skin.

"How many kids do you have here?" Gwen asked. Like Whitney, she felt she'd lost her sea legs when it came to socializing. She had realized over the last year just how superficial many of her friendships had been and that she hadn't been top tier enough to make the cut during quarantine.

"Four," Alpana said. "First, third, and twins in fifth. You?"

Whitney counted the books, tallying the cost on a sheet of paper. "Just the one," Gwen said. "First grade."

"I can only imagine how hard it's been having your child start during all this," Alpana said, waving a hand to indicate their face masks, the social distancing, the pandemic, and Gwen felt a loosening in her chest: someone understood.

"It has," she agreed.

Alpana reached a hand out, and touched Gwen's forearm. "Listen, I know every in and out of this school. You need any help, you just let me know, okay?"

Gwen's eyes suddenly filled with tears, and she was surprised to hear her voice catch, her throat thick with emotion. "I will, thanks—"

There was a squeak of steps as more moms moseyed into the gymnasium in athleisure gear and new tennis shoes, Starbucks cups in their hands.

"Alps?" one of the women yelped.

Alpana turned, recognition dawning on her face. "Erika?" She rushed forward and hugged the other woman only at the shoulders, their hips still a foot apart.

"I barely recognized you real-size and not in a bitty square on my computer," Erika said.

"I barely recognized you without a chardonnay in your hand," Alpana said in return, and Erika laughed, turning to introduce Alpana to the other two women.

"Four fifty," Whitney said loudly, her voice an echo in the cavernous room. Whitney wore a small bottle of hand sanitizer around her neck at all times now, like a bulky amulet warding off evil spirits.

The women stopped chatting and turned. "What's that, sweetie?" Alpana asked.

Whitney held up the stack of books, and Gwen felt her neck warm. Her daughter wasn't reading the cues that she was interrupting. Gwen had been telling herself for a long time that Whitney would be fine after the pandemic, they'd figure it out when the time came, but what kind of role model was Gwen? She had no daily friends, no career, no direction.

"Four fifty," Whitney repeated, and moved the pile of books an inch closer to Alpana.

"Oh, that's right!" she said, and dug in her oversize status purse for her wallet. She flipped through the bills and pulled out a ten. "Here you go. Keep the change."

She held it out and Whitney looked at it. "Keep the change?"

"A donation," Alpana clarified.

"But—" Whitney started, and Gwen took the money from between Alpana's fingers.

"Thank you."

"Thank *you*," Alpana said, and smiled at Gwen. "Call me if you need anything, seriously," she said, and started toward the hallway with the other women.

"Your number," Gwen started, and Alpana turned to wave good-bye, her eyes never leaving Erika as she relayed a story, all four women bursting into laughter as they rounded the corner.

Whitney turned to her mom and plucked the ten from her, shoving it unceremoniously into the change box. "That's not the way it works," she said, crossing her arms after clattering the lid shut with a bang. "I'm supposed to give change." She glanced up at her mom, desperate tears already filling her eyes. "The count's going to be off. I'm going to get in trouble."

"We can still separate it," Gwen started, but Whitney huffed.

"It's ruined."

"It's not ruined," Gwen insisted, but who knew? Maybe it was.

Chapter Thirty-Three

GWEN

December 2022

Gwen loaded Whitney into the car to spend the day at Grandma's. They were going to clean out the kitchen pantry and stock it with a few ready-made items her mom could throw together herself. Plus, Gwen didn't want to be a sitting duck in her house, waiting for Nicola to drop by.

Last night Gwen had gone to bed early to read, about the same time as Whitney, and when Nicola texted she was heading over, Gwen had ignored it. She knew that wasn't a long-term solution, but it was all she could muster at the end of a long day. She'd also emailed Jonas and asked about getting together for coffee. He was busy all weekend, but they settled on late Monday afternoon.

Jeri now sat at the kitchen table and Gwen at the counter, every available surface covered with cans and boxes of food. They were weeding out by expiration dates, and so far the winner was 2013. Gwen had held up the can of sliced peaches and thought, *This has been on the earth longer than my daughter.* As she opened another jar to dump and recycle, Gwen told her mom about finding the flat tire in her garage. "It's weird," she said, trying to pass it off nonchalantly to get her mother's read, "but the mechanic said it was possible the puncture was deliberate."

Jeri paused, a box of Bisquick in her hand. She was seated at the Formica table in one of the brown plaid pleather chairs with metal legs that she'd had for thirty-plus years. "What do you mean, 'deliberate'?"

"He couldn't say a hundred percent, but he thought maybe someone had put a screw in on pur—"

"Nicola," Jeri said definitively.

To hear it spoken out loud was a relief, but still, Gwen couldn't fully accept it. She leaned forward. "But *why*? She's been nothing but nice to me. She got me a job, found me a place to live."

Jeri nodded along. "It's too much. Friends should help you, but not take over. You act like she's giving you this big life, but she's actually making it smaller." She bent down and put the Bisquick in a half-full box. "A job in media? What's that got to do with you?"

"But, Mom, I'm not qualified for anything else!"

"Says who?"

Gwen looked at Jeri incredulously. "Employers."

"Which ones? Did you actually talk to any of them, or did you assume you couldn't find a job?" Gwen looked away. "Exactly. You have some social grace. You're a quick learner. You've got a college degree thanks to your father's insistence. Certainly you could have found something." Gwen thought back to her English classes and how much she had loved them, even though Todd had chided her that no one actually read books for a living. Was that really what he thought an English degree was, or had it been another way to chip at her confidence?

"And while I know this place isn't a palace," Jeri continued, "you were welcome to stay here as long as you needed."

Gwen rolled her eyes at that. "Certainly didn't seem like it."

"Well, that's on me. I admit, I was embarrassed."

Gwen was surprised to hear her mother say this, to admit to a chink in her armor. "Why?" she asked, and Jeri looked at her like, *Don't patronize me.* "I should have been checking on you more, seeing how you were doing," Gwen admitted. She looked around at the piles of food, the cluster of empty Country Crock containers Jeri had saved for years, a precarious slope of *Better Homes & Gardens*. "I didn't realize it had gotten quite this bad."

Jeri reached over and gripped Gwen's hand, an uncharacteristic move. They had never been a physically affectionate family, something Gwen had worked to change with her own daughter. "Listen, Gwennie, I know a thing or two about life getting smaller. Don't let her do it. Even if she's not behind the tire and it was a one-in-a-hundred shot, take it as a wake-up call. I want you to keep your eye on her."

Gwen nodded. "I will," she said, but an hour later when the doorbell rang, her stomach dropped.

Jeri snorted. "Well, go get it."

Nicola was waiting impatiently on the porch with bags of groceries in her arms, and Gwen had to keep herself from grimacing. The last thing she needed was more groceries in the house. "You don't look happy to see me," Nicola said, and walked in past Gwen, who still had a bundle of magazines to throw in the recycling in her arms. Nicola set the bags on the kitchen counter and turned around, irritation clear on her face. "I thought you wanted me to come."

Gwen scurried through her mind trying to piece together why Nicola would have thought that. She remembered telling Nicola earlier in the week about her plans at Jeri's and how she wasn't looking forward to it. What was it she had said? "It's one of those awful jobs—cleaning out Mom's place—where I wish I had Todd here to help me." Had Nicola thought that was an invitation? Gwen remembered the night she moved to Dayton, Nicola showing up unexpectedly with two Whole Foods bags. It had been so nice to have someone looking out for her, but even then, there was the niggling question of why. If she were to ask, she could hear Nicola's response: *The very asking of the question shows how little you believe in your own worth,* Nicola would say. *This is how real friends behave.* How long had she felt a little off around Nicola?

"I thought it would be nice to prepare a few meals for the freezer so Jeri doesn't have to worry about menus every night and won't assume you'll come feed her." In the kitchen, Nicola reached into a grocery bag and pulled out a can of diced tomatoes.

"What's she doing here?" Jeri asked, and Gwen rolled her eyes at her rudeness.

"Mom."

"What? I don't need her food," Jeri said. "She's here to be a buttinsky."

Nicola pursed her lips in a tight, white line. "I didn't realize I was such a bother. I came because Gwen so obviously needs help setting boundaries with you."

"Oh please," Jeri said. "You can help by leaving."

"Mom!" Gwen said.

"What? I can say what I want in my own house."

"I can see when I'm not wanted," Nicola said stoically, and Jeri shot back, "It's hard to tell since you're still standing in my kitchen."

"This is what I was talking about," Nicola said to Gwen. "She's controlling."

Jeri guffawed with no humor in her voice. "Me? Jesus Christ, are you kidding me right now? What about what happened with the tire?"

Nicola visibly flinched and looked at Gwen. "The tire?"

"It's nothing," Gwen said, wiping a hand through the air as if to erase what her mother had said. "The mechanic. He thought maybe . . ."

"Maybe what?" Nicola demanded.

"Maybe someone had flattened it on purpose."

Nicola's eyes widened. "And you thought *me*? The one who rescued you the next morning and got your kid to school and you to work? Oh my god, what do you think of me?"

"It was my mom," Gwen said. "She's the one who thought maybe you—"

Nicola turned on Jeri, her nostrils flaring. "What about *you*? Maybe you hauled your fat ass across town and did it."

Gwen felt a rush of heat consume her, a rash clawing its way up her neck.

"I wasn't the only one who thought it," Jeri spat back. "Tell her," she demanded of Gwen. "Tell her you thought she did it too." All Gwen could do was shake her head to rid herself of the conflict. All she wanted was to be home and away from this, curled on her sofa in sweatpants with Whitney, watching a Disney movie with a bowl of popcorn in her lap. What she wanted was to go home.

Home.

That was now her condo in Dayton.

That was now her life without Todd.

"Whitney and I are leaving," Gwen said, and threw the armful of old magazines in the recycling bin. "I'm not going to listen to you two fight." Nicola scowled as Gwen yelled for her daughter to pack up her stuff.

"Thank god," Whitney huffed. "Can I walk Maxx when we get home?"

"Nope." Let Nicola deal with her dog.

"But—" Whitney started, and Gwen had to steel herself against the begging. She'd never been great about saying no to her daughter, but since Todd's death, every time she did it felt like she was denying Whitney the one thing that might fill the hole in her heart. A dog, a make-believe aunt, a Frosty from Wendy's.

"Fine," Nicola said. "If you think you can handle all"—she waved a hand to indicate Jeri, the house, all of it—"*this* on your own, be my guest. I'm done." She grabbed her purse and stormed out.

Gwen wanted to leave in a huff but needed to repack the bag of cleaning supplies she'd brought over so she could take them home to clean her own damn house. They still needed to finish the pantry, and next up would be the big redo of her dad's office so they could move Jeri's bedroom to the main floor, the stairs becoming more and more precarious. All of it exhausted Gwen further, but she'd face it another day.

She heard Jeri's cane scrape into the living room as she threw a canister of Pledge into the old grocery bag. "I don't care if you're mad at me for going," she said to her mother, which they both knew was a lie.

"I'm not, actually."

"Well, that's a first."

"I'll give you this," Jeri said, leaning more of her weight on the cane. "She's helping you speak your mind."

"And that's a good thing, right?" Gwen said, and realized she wasn't actually asking. It *was* a good thing.

Jeri rubbed a supportive hand across Gwen's back. "I want to be sure you're speaking your mind, not hers."

In the car, Whitney crossed her arms and harrumphed, then did it again when her mother didn't react.

"What?" Gwen asked. She had thought many times about how inextricably her own life had woven into Nicola's, and one of the ways was her daughter. Whitney loved not only her auntie Nic but Maxx, and walked him faithfully almost every night.

"You can miss one walk," she reasoned with her daughter. *But what about the nights to come?* Gwen wondered. Would she really let Whitney near Nicola, given what she suspected?

"Yeah, well. I guess I'm out five bucks," Whitney grumbled, and leaned back, crossing her arms.

"What do you mean?" Gwen asked, catching her daughter's eye in the rearview mirror. Only then did Whitney seem to understand what she'd said. "Wait, has Nicola been paying you?"

Whitney stiffened. "I don't know."

"Yes, you do," Gwen insisted. "And what, five bucks a walk?" That was a ridiculous amount of money. Not for a professional walker, but for a child? She did a quick calculation; that was like $150 a month! She remembered how proud she'd been of Whitney selflessly spending her savings on a toy for Maxx, and puckered her mouth as a trill of anger and unease crawled up her spine. What was Nicola thinking employing her eight-year-old daughter without her permission? Even as she thought it, she could imagine Nicola's response. *What's the big deal? It's only five dollars. I'm teaching her responsibility, something she's sorely lacking.* It would be out of the Nicola playbook: the minimizing of Gwen's concerns, the slap down of Gwen's parenting. She'd probably add something like, *I can't believe you're overreacting like this!* as if she should be the one to label Gwen's reactions as appropriate or not. Was Nicola deliberately driving a wedge between her and her daughter?

And when had Nicola become one of the voices in Gwen's head, telling her she was wrong, stupid, overreacting? Those spots had always belonged to Jeri and then Todd, although deep down Gwen knew it was the voice of herself.

She thought about Whitney and Nicola saying "to the Maxx!" when they said the dog's name, how sullen it had made Gwen feel to be on the outside. Sullen was one thing, but this was another.

Gwen turned the car onto a side street and put it in park so she could turn around and lock eyes with her daughter. "What other secrets do you two have?"

"None," Whitney insisted. "Promise."

Gwen scanned her daughter's face. She looked older than she had when they'd moved here five months ago. Her limbs lengthening, her teeth too big for her mouth. It surprised Gwen she couldn't tell if Whitney was telling the truth. When had that happened? "You need to tell me if you do, Whitney. This isn't fun and games."

"What is it then?" Whitney asked, and Gwen stared at her daughter, unsure how to answer. She didn't want to scare her, but at the same time, she needed her daughter to be on alert.

"You need to tell Mommy if something's going on. If Nicola has made you feel uncomfortable."

"She hasn't," Whitney said. "Okay? *You* do that. Dragging me to Grandma's when I don't want to go, making me hang out there after school every day. She smells weird and her place is gross."

"But she's family," Gwen said lamely.

"Who cares?" Whitney said. "I'd rather hang out with Auntie Nic and Maxx. They're fun and don't make me watch game shows." She looked darkly at her mother. "I'd rather hang out with them than *you*."

Gwen felt a flame of anger shoot through her. After everything she'd done to get the two of them back on their feet. After picking up the rubble of their lives after Todd's death and mismanagement of their finances. What about what *she* wanted? In Boulder, her biggest problem had been what to make for dinner, and now her entire life was a problem.

"Yeah, well," Gwen said, turning around. She threw the car back in drive and hit the gas so hard her head reared back and smacked the headrest. "Looks like you can't always get what you want."

Whitney ignored her the rest of the night, turning right as her mother was going to kiss her on the forehead, Gwen's lips landing at the hairline. She still wasn't used to it: being the only parent to kiss her child good night.

With Whitney in bed, Gwen sat at the dining table and made a list of all she had to do. It was so achingly similar to the one she'd made after Todd's death, it made her breath catch, but this one was how to extricate herself from Nicola.

First, she needed to find a new job, and second, a new place to live. Or maybe not second but simultaneously. She remembered a friend in Boulder who had contemplated leaving her husband for years, saying she could never quite figure out the sequence: Do you tell him and then live together awkwardly for a few weeks while you look for a place, or do you find the place in secret? If you stay, who sleeps on the sofa? It had all seemed so overwhelming it took her forever to actually get up the courage, and in the end, it hadn't been a well-planned-out execution but a flailing, screaming fight where she declared she was going.

It shocked Gwen how much this friendship felt like an abusive marriage. She'd always assumed only romantic relationships could have these kinds of ties, but her life was as woven into Nicola's as if they were a couple. She remembered what Nicola had said early on, about how one person couldn't be everything to another.

But Gwen also reminded herself that she had been strong enough to move across the country on her own and to build a life after Todd. She could do it again. She was smarter now, more independent, and despite what Nicola had apparently intended, she'd inspired Gwen.

A soft glow still coming from the hallway, Gwen climbed into her bed. She pulled up the text chain with Nicola and began typing.

I appreciate all you've done for me since I moved to dayton but need to concentrate on my family now. I'll pay you back for the condo deposit as soon as I can and will set up with bank. It was inevitable they'd see each other at work—no getting around that—but she had to minimize the contact as much as she could. I think it is best if we take a little break.

She sent the text and watched as the three dots appeared then went away. Appeared and disappeared. Gwen tightened her grip on the phone, realizing how nervous she was to hear Nicola's response. Would she be furious? Try to talk her out of it? Something else?

A text dinged through and she looked at the screen.

Understood.

Gwen flooded with relief. But behind that, there was an emptiness, which made no sense. Hadn't she wanted Nicola out of her hair? But maybe it was the realization she, Gwen, was so easy to let go.

Chapter Thirty-Four

Gwen sat anxiously at her desk Monday morning, one ear cocked toward the doorway for the cadence of Nicola's heels. She'd received a text while drying her hair that morning from Jeri asking if everything was okay with Nicola, and Gwen had texted back saying she'd asked for some space, and that Nicola's "understood" had left her uneasy. It sounds like she's respecting your wishes, Jeri replied, and that had put Gwen further on edge. Since when did Jeri defend Nicola?

Morning turned into late morning, sunlight streaming in through her narrow office window. Gwen's stomach was grumbling by one, but she refused to stop for lunch. It would be one thing to work through lunch—the meal she and Nicola always ate together—and another thing entirely to go to the deli and buy a sandwich on her own.

Nicola kept passing by Gwen's door throughout the day, her eyes pointed forward and not looking in. She frequently talked to Helene at the front desk and laughed brightly, seeming to make a point to show how little it bothered her not to be hanging out with Gwen. As the day ticked on, Gwen found herself more anxious, not less so, as she waited for the other shoe to drop.

Around four, her cell phone rang. She looked down at the screen to see the name every parent dreads, her child's elementary school, and felt a quick flick of fear.

Before she could imagine the worst, she answered halfway through the second ring. "Everything's fine," Mary, the school secretary assured her, which was how these calls always started. Mary was well versed in minimizing panic, but even so, Gwen's heart rate spiked.

"What happened?"

"Everything's fine," Mary repeated, "but your mom didn't pick up Whitney after school today so she's in after-school now, unauthorized, and we're wondering how soon you can come get her."

"Jeri's not there?" Gwen asked. She felt another jolt of panic, but reminded herself not to worry. Her mother might have fallen asleep in front of the TV, or run out of gas, or lost track of time at the grocery store. There were a million innocuous reasons why her mother wouldn't have made it to the school on time, although a handful of bad ones too.

"I'm on my way," Gwen said to Mary, scanning her desk to see what she needed to throw into her purse: keys, wallet, phone in hand. "I'll be there just as soon as I can."

"Thanks a bunch, Gwen," Mary said, and they relayed their good-byes, a perfectly fine conversation, but Gwen was already turning off her computer and texting her mother. There were no rotating dots in response. She slung her purse quickly over her shoulder, and the weight of it made her lurch into the door, bumping her shoulder. At the elevator, she stabbed the down button repeatedly, already dialing her mother. The number rang and rang, so even and slow, she hung up and tried it again, smacking now at the elevator button with her open palm.

"What's that racket?" Nicola said irritably, coming out of her office. "Gwen? Where are you going?"

"School," she said, surprised to find herself breathless. She reminded herself: Whitney is safe. Whitney is fine. But was her mother?

"What for? Didn't Jeri pick up Whitney?"

Gwen shook her head, surprised to feel tears on her cheeks.

"Gwen, honey, calm down." Nicola approached her swiftly and put her cool hands on Gwen's hot wrists. "Are you going to the school?" Gwen nodded. "And then what? Your mom's?" She nodded again.

"Gwen, you can't bring Whitney there. You don't know what you'll find." So Gwen wasn't the only one jumping to horrible conclusions. It comforted her, but also ratcheted up her fears. She flashed back to Nicola walking by throughout the day, her loud conversations with Helene. Given the travel time to Jeri's, there was no way she could have left and done anything.

The elevator opened and Gwen turned to look at it, but Nicola put a hand on her chin and pulled her back. Their eyes locked. "What do you need?" Nicola asked, but Gwen's head was filled with white noise. Todd flashed through her mind, laid out on the restaurant floor.

"I—I don't know."

"I'm going to come with you, okay, Gwen?" Nicola took in a big breath and exhaled, and Gwen reflexively did the same, her chest opening up to a modicum of calm. "Just let me grab my purse. Will you wait for me?"

Gwen nodded as relief flooded her. *This* was why she couldn't and shouldn't push Nicola away, all her confidence in herself slipping out her pores. How was Gwen supposed to handle a crisis? She was useless. She would have gotten Whitney in the car and driven straight into whatever hell awaited them at her grandmother's. She imagined her daughter in tow, opening the front door to the stale silence of a dead house. For all she knew, her mother had been attacked and was bleeding out on the floor. She'd fallen down the steps and cracked open her skull. Against all odds, maybe her mother had been on the roof and fell, her wrecked body awaiting them on the front lawn.

"Ready," Nicola said, returning from her office with her coat slung over her elbow, a purse on her shoulder. In the elevator's mirrored walls, Nicola applied lipstick and Gwen watched the red color smooth across her bottom lip and then the top, parting at the bow to paint the right side and then the left.

Nicola drove at her usual breakneck speed, and as they raced through the streets of Gwen's childhood, her hands were languid on the wheel. "Let me ask you something," Nicola said, and something in the casual tone of her voice put Gwen even higher on alert. "Do you think you'd be happier working somewhere else?"

"*What?*" The question rang in Gwen's head. She didn't understand why Nicola would ask this at such an inappropriate time. Nicola turned and looked at her, and Gwen had to fight not to push her face to look out the windshield. The opposite traffic raced by.

"I just don't think your heart is in it," Nicola said as a pickup truck with a Trump sticker whizzed by, horn blaring.

Gwen didn't know why they were having this conversation now, as they barreled down the suburban streets to whatever awaited her at her mother's. "No. I'm happy at Dacks." She said this even though the night before she'd decided to look for a new job.

"Really?" Nicola asked, and turned the wheel abruptly into Jeri's neighborhood. It was hidden behind a grocery store on a set of streets where all the houses looked the same, and it registered with Gwen briefly how odd it was Nicola seemed so sure of the directions. "Because I wouldn't be able to give you a recommendation. At least not based on your résumé." Her résumé? Did Nicola mean the one she'd doctored? "One call to TeckPocket and it's over, you know?"

"But you're the one—" Gwen started, and Nicola interrupted.

"And who are people going to believe? An out-of-work stay-at-home mom, or a woman who's risen the ranks in her corporation?" Nicola turned onto Jeri's street without turning on her blinker. Gwen remembered her saying that first night in Dayton that she'd gotten Jeri's address from Gwen's résumé, but she'd used her Boulder address, she was sure of it. Sure, Nicola could have found Jeri's address online, but then why lie about it? Gwen realized part of it was that lying came so naturally to Nicola, but also, had she not wanted Gwen to know how much she cared?

Gwen shook her head. All she wanted was to see her mother, to lay her hands on her, because she was convinced now something was horribly wrong. This wasn't a dead cell phone battery, or an extra-long nap on the couch. Something had happened.

Nicola whipped her Prius into Jeri's driveway and turned off the engine. Gwen threw open her door and scaled the porch steps at a clip. She raked through her purse for her keys, grabbing everything but—a pen, her lipstick, a garble of receipts—before seizing the keys, the metal scraping her knuckle.

She unlocked the door and swung it open. An eerie silence permeated the house; dust swirled in the sunlight through the large front window.

"Mom?" she said as she stepped in, raising her sunglasses into her hair and throwing her voice. "Mom? You here?"

A groan sounded from the back hallway and Gwen tore up the four steps of the tri-level, heart pounding, Nicola at her heels.

RULE #4: NEVER LOOK BACK

Chapter Thirty-Five

Gwen tripped up the final step. "Mom!"

She rushed into Jeri's room, confused to find it empty. Then Jeri groaned again, and Gwen followed the noise to the other side of the bed. Her mother lay on the carpet on her back, the oldness of her bare face shocking. Even with her health concerns, Jeri made a point to put her face on every day.

Gwen dropped to her knees and saw a wet stain at her mother's crotch. Jeri tried to roll toward her daughter and promptly flopped back, pain a lightning strike across her face. The smell of shit wafted in the air.

"Oh Jesus," Nicola said, and Gwen turned to see her put two fingers tight under her nose before turning away.

Gwen gave her full attention back to Jeri. "Mom, what hurts?" Jeri groaned. "Call 911!" Gwen yelled to Nicola, who was now in the hallway.

"Chanly," Jeri whispered hoarsely, and Gwen shook her head: *I don't understand.* Jeri moved her hand up with considerable shaky effort and set it on Gwen's wrist, pulling her daughter's hand toward the waistband of her pants. "Change me," she said more clearly this time. It still wasn't evident what had happened to her mom. Had she fallen? Had a heart attack? Jeri's pajamas rested on the unmade bed. Had her mother collapsed this morning and been here all day? Gwen felt a flash of guilt.

"Nicola," she yelled, and Nicola reappeared, grimacing, her phone at her ear, answering the pertinent questions from the emergency call-taker: breathing, conscious. "We need to change her pants," Gwen said as Nicola hung up the phone.

"Ew, no," Nicola said, taking a step back.

"Gwennie," Jeri said, her hands clawing the air.

Gwen couldn't leave her mother in this state. She ran to the small closet and grabbed a fresh pair of sweats and underpants from the shelf and dresser drawer and returned, unsure how to proceed.

"This isn't important," Nicola insisted, but Gwen understood it was, at least to her mom. All she had was her dignity.

"Fine, I'll do it myself," Gwen said, and slid the comforter from the bed. She rolled her mother to the left and tucked the comforter under her to protect the carpet. As she went to roll her mother back, she gasped. There was an open wound on her mother's head, blood matted in her hair and clotted on the carpet.

"Oh, Jesus."

"Cleee," Jeri said, which Gwen took to mean, "clean."

"What the hell happened, Mom?" she asked as she pulled down Jeri's pants, the smell intensifying, and used a corner of the comforter to clean her bottom and thighs. Her mother moaned at the humiliation.

"Nicola," Gwen yelled. "Wet down a towel for me, will you?" Jeri moaned again. "Mom, I need help." She looked around, her eyes landing on the corner of the oak dresser, the sharp edge of the footboard. There on the corner of the nightstand was a smear of blood. Her mother must have hit her head when she fell, Gwen told herself.

Her mother's hand scrabbled through the air and gripped Gwen's weakly. Gwen took a deep breath through her mouth and stroked her mother's thin skin, the veins like tributaries. "It's going to be fine," she whispered to her mother, and meant it. She would will it to be fine.

She and her mother had their differences, sure, but she would never ever wish her harm.

Nicola came in a minute later with two towels—one wet, one dry—wrinkling her nose at Jeri's half-naked form.

Gwen, irritated, concentrated on her mother, reminding herself Nicola didn't have children—she wasn't used to wiping asses, and this woman was a stranger, not the woman who had brought her into the world. Jeri winced as Gwen swiped the cold, wet towel across her skin, cleaning between the folds, and then set down the dry towel where the comforter had been, dabbing at the damp skin.

Gwen could hear sirens in the distance as she clutched the worn, pale-beige underpants she'd grabbed from the dresser. She looped her mom's left foot in a leg hole and then her right. At her ankles, waistband in hand, Gwen shimmied the pants higher and higher, crab walking forward with her mother's body between her legs. The ridiculousness of the scene made Gwen snort laugh and her mother made eye contact, petrified, but then she too seemed to register the absurdity.

"Gurrie," her mom grunted—*Hurry*—which only made Gwen giggle more. Jeri's mouth, despite it all, contorted in a laugh.

Underpants in place, Gwen reached for the sweatpants. She rested the elastic at the ankles and repeated the process, the waistband snapping on her mother's stomach as the front door opened and she heard a noise like a very heavy suitcase rolling in—the gurney.

"Gank ew," her mother whispered, and Gwen squeezed her hand as two EMTs rounded the corner to the bedroom, the gurney left in the hall.

A woman dropped to her knees and secured her hand around Jeri's wrist as she checked the pulse beats against her watch. Gwen moved back to the far wall and watched, her heart hammering. A movement at the door caught her attention.

Nicola clutched the doorframe. Her face was ashen, her blonde hair mussed. Her perfect lipstick was bitten off her bottom lip.

The EMTs loaded Jeri on a board, then onto the gurney, and strapped her in. The female EMT turned to Gwen. "Daughter?" Gwen nodded. "You can ride with us if you'd like."

"I—" She needed to pick up her own daughter; she needed to never leave her mother's side.

"Go," Nicola said, seeming to shake off whatever had paralyzed her earlier. "I'll get Whitney."

"I—"

The male EMT rolled his hand in the air: *let's go.* Gwen grabbed her mother's purse as she tried to sort things quickly in her head, to grasp what she knew as fact. Nicola had been at work all day. There was blood on the nightstand.

She handed the spare key to Nicola. "Will you lock up? You can take Whitney to my house. I'll call the school and authorize you." She paused and locked eyes with Nicola. "And thank you."

Nicola nodded. She, too, looked shell-shocked. "You're welcome," she said, and Gwen followed her mother's prone figure out the front door.

Chapter Thirty-Six

Gwen sat under the fluorescent waiting room lights, one flickering in the corner. She tasted her own foul breath behind her paper mask and checked her watch: she'd been at the hospital three hours already. Jonas had texted when she'd missed their coffee, and she'd responded, asking if he could reschedule for Tuesday morning.

Stuck in the plastic chair outside the ER, mind wandering, Gwen wondered what had really happened to Jeri, replaying the moment over and over when she'd handed her mom's house key to Nicola. She had been in contact with Nicola at least a dozen times since. Nicola sent pics of her and Whitney eating chicken nuggets, the bottles of nail polish Whitney had picked out for a manicure. These photos were proof her child was safe, but pulsing underneath that was worry, a growing thing. They'd had a fight and then her tire was punctured, and the night before, Jeri and Nicola had gotten into it. Could this be a coincidence? Gwen was beginning to wonder if there was such a thing when it came to Nicola.

Finally, twenty minutes later, the doctor appeared. A headache was gaining traction behind Gwen's eye. The doctor was dressed in scrubs and a white coat, a smattering of reassuring gray in his hair. "Jeri Gries?"

Gwen stood quickly, clutching her purse. "I'm her daughter."

He nodded efficiently and started walking. "She's had a pretty bad fall," he said as Gwen followed. "She has a nasty scrape on her head and a concussion. We're going to keep her overnight for observation. And of course this is all complicated by her weight and diabetes."

"Is she awake?"

He nodded again. "She is. We're regulating the pain so she's a little confused, but coherent."

In the room, Jeri's bed was raised at an awkward angle, half sitting up and half lying down. Her head lolled as her eyes connected with Gwen's.

"Gwennie?"

Gwen's own eyes flooded with tears, and she moved quickly to Jeri's side, grasping her hand. "How are you feeling?"

"Like shit," Jeri said.

Gwen pressed a thumb into her mother's palm, swirling it back and forth. "Mom? What happened?"

"I don't really know," her mother admitted. "I'd gotten out of the shower and changed for the day, then boom, I'm on the floor."

"Did something happen?" She leaned forward, holding her mom's hand. "Did someone attack you?"

"Now, Ms. Maner," the doctor said as he picked up the chart at the end of the bed. "Your mom just fell."

"Are you sure, Mom?" Her eyes zinged across her mother's face.

"I—" Her mom's voice caught, spittle drying at the corner of her mouth. She motioned for the water glass, and Gwen positioned the straw at her lips. Jeri grasped Gwen's wrist, her grip surprisingly strong, pulling Gwen so close that their faces were mere inches apart. Her breath smelled like the hospital itself, like death covered by antiseptic. "I don't remember. I was about to make the bed and next thing I knew, I woke up."

Gwen flashed to the plastic rock with the key hidden in the flower bed in front of Jeri's house. She'd pointed it out to Nicola the first night she was in Dayton. "What time was it?"

"Seven. Maybe seven thirty." Nicola came to work around eight.

She lowered her voice. "Mom, is it possible someone attacked you?"

"You're putting ideas in her head," the doctor said, barely looking up from the chart. "A woman gets to this condition"—he pointed toward Jeri like she was an object, part of the bed—"and her balance is off. The diabetes makes her dizzy. It's a classic problem. Besides, the EMT said there was blood on the furniture where she hit her head." He slapped the chart closed and hung it back up, then added his initials to the whiteboard on the wall saying he'd checked on the patient. But had he? He hadn't spoken to Jeri, or asked her any questions about her health. He hadn't even touched her. "The best thing she can do is lose fifty pounds. For starters."

"But she says she can't remember," Gwen pushed back.

"It's consistent with a head injury," the doctor said, smiling tightly. "But if you really think it might have been an attack, Mrs. Gries," he said, finally speaking to Jeri, "we'll need to call the police and start a report. If you're sure." Were people always this condescending to old, overweight women?

Her mother was silent, and Gwen was surprised to look over and see her eyes downcast, focused on her hands, on the wedding ring she still wore along with the tiny diamond. She went to twist the rings and they stayed put, caught in the swollen flesh of her finger. "Are you sure, Mrs. Gries?" the doctor repeated.

Gwen turned back to her mom, marooned in the bed with her face stripped of its defenses. "Not completely," Jeri admitted, and Gwen felt her shoulders slump. It was like watching herself in real time, going from a confident answer to doubting herself.

The doctor left and Gwen smoothed her mother's flat hair across her scalp, then dug in her own purse for a lipstick. She held it up and Jeri smiled as Gwen uncapped the tube and smoothed it across her mother's bottom lip, and then the right and left sides of the top.

Jeri rolled her lips together. "Thank you," she said, her voice clogged with emotion.

Gwen's phone dinged with another text from Nicola, this one a picture of her hand. The tips of her fingers looked like they'd been dipped in a shiny, wet pink, the nail polish almost neon. It looks like I gave Barbie a rectal exam.

Gwen's heart began to hammer as realization took fuller shape: Nicola was alone with her daughter. She couldn't say for sure Nicola was behind Jeri's fall, but Gwen was beginning to recognize the tickle in her gut, the instincts kicking in.

"I need to go," she said. "I've got to get back to Whitney." She knew Nicola hated Jeri and was quite sure she loved Whitney, but whatever was motivating her actions had nothing to do with love or hate. She was not to be trusted with anyone.

"Is she with her?" Jeri asked, and Gwen nodded. There was no need to elaborate. Nicola's name had hung like a poltergeist through most of their interactions and conversations since Gwen had moved home, maneuvering the larger pieces of Gwen's life without her realizing. Her mother squeezed her hand. "Hurry."

Gwen raced through the streets. It was after nine, and the upstairs was dark where Whitney would be sleeping. There was a lamp on in the living room, and Gwen could see the changing blue light from the TV. Nicola was in her house, with her child.

She pulled into her driveway and watched the garage door rise. She drove in, sure to shut it behind her. Nicola was waiting in the kitchen as Gwen walked in. "How is she?" Nicola asked, leaning against the breakfast bar, and Gwen was surprised to see tears in her eyes. Was this genuine concern, or remorse?

"She's stable," she said.

"Did they say what happened?"

Gwen paused. She didn't want to let Nicola know she suspected anything. "The doctor said she fell. Probably dizzy from the diabetes." She set her purse on a stool, exhaustion sinking into her limbs. Gwen didn't want to turn around and look at Nicola. She was afraid there'd be something in Gwen's own eyes, something there that confirmed she no longer trusted her. "How's Whitney?" she asked as she reached into the fridge for a leftover container of linguini. She hadn't eaten since breakfast, since leaving the condo thirteen hours ago.

"Good," Nicola said. "In bed." She held up her hands, the nails and a good amount of skin painted a sordid pink. "Whitney does not have a future in cosmetology."

Gwen twirled a forkful of pasta into a ball and stared at it. She could not look at Nicola. "Listen, I'm beat—" she started, and Nicola interrupted.

"You love her, don't you?" Nicola asked, and Gwen frowned. "Your mom."

Gwen swallowed part of the bite and put a hand in front of her mouth, the rest unchewed. "Of course I do."

Nicola nodded. "I could tell, when we were there. You two started laughing at one point, do you remember that?"

Gwen replayed the terror of the day—finding her mother on the ground, the surprise of the blood, her mother's insistence she be changed and not found that way by paramedics. Gwen had thought it was ridiculous—*who cares at a time like this! They've seen way worse!*—but also felt a grudging respect that Jeri had gone to the trouble to save what she could of her pride. She remembered the waistband snapping into place and her and her mother breaking into giggles. "I do remember," she said. She and her mom had always shared the same grisly sense of humor, but only Gwen had the nervous habit of laughing at terrible moments. When her father had a burn accident years ago, Gwen had been useless. A hand over her mouth to catch the laughter as her mother called 911. The same dumb terror had struck when Todd collapsed, but at least she hadn't laughed uncontrollably.

"My mom and I never would have done that," Nicola said. "About anything. I wouldn't have changed her. I would have left her there to rot." Was this the same woman Gwen had talked to on the phone?

"I'm sure—" Gwen started, but Nicola held up a hand.

"I'm serious. It was nice to see you care for her, but moms are supposed to help us, not the other way around. Mine was nothing but a burden."

"I'm sure she did her best," Gwen said. She knew it was a platitude, but it was late, she was exhausted, and she didn't have the energy for a heart-to-heart with a woman she thought might have attacked her mother. What she wanted was to escort her out of her house, away from her child.

"She didn't," Nicola said, shaking her head. "Not at all. I saw your mom on the floor and I thought, lucky you, but then you helped her." A look of wonder settled in her eyes. Was Nicola that surprised that Gwen loved her mother? If she had done something, did she think she was *helping*?

"Nicola, did you—" Gwen started. Nicola held her gaze, the words waiting to be spoken. *Did you have something to do with this?* But Gwen couldn't do it. She couldn't bring herself to say them. Too much rested on the answer. But she would not leave her daughter alone with Nicola again. The thought that something could have happened to Whitney was like a red film over her eyes.

"Thank you," Gwen finally said. "I appreciate your help tonight."

"You owe me a manicure." Nicola wiggled her fingers and walked out the door.

Chapter Thirty-Seven

Gwen arrived at the coffee shop late Tuesday morning. Her mother was being discharged that afternoon, which meant she could still keep her appointment with Jonas. As she walked inside, she spotted a man in the corner eagerly watching the door. He had a friendly face tinged by sadness, and a forehead covered with floppy brownish-red hair like an Irish setter. Dressed in khaki pants and a fleece vest, he seemed like a guy made to be a dad. He held up a tentative hand to Gwen—*are you who I think you are?*—and she waved back.

She walked over to his table and he pointed to a hot latte and an iced tea, asking if she wanted one. She picked the latte, thanked him, and sat down, apologizing for missing their first meeting, explaining that she'd had to take her mom to the ER.

"Everything okay?"

"I hope so," she said, and they small-talked until Jonas cleared his throat, bringing up the reason they were together. "So you knew Missy in college?"

Gwen confirmed, back during their internship. He asked how she'd ended up returning to Dacks, and Gwen explained about Todd. "That's awful," he said, "but at least you have closure." Gwen flinched. "I'm sorry, I didn't mean to be crass. It's one of the worst things for me about Missy's disappearance." He leaned forward and took a sip of the iced tea. "So you wanted to talk about Nicola?"

Gwen nodded. "Missy's relationship to her, and your own as well."

"In a nutshell," he said, "it wasn't good. It was obvious from the get-go she didn't like me, although I didn't know a lot of that in the beginning. But the first time I met her, I thought the dynamic was weird."

That was what Bethany had said too. "Weird how?"

"Well, we only met once before quarantine, but it was like she was interviewing me to be Missy's boyfriend. We'd been seeing each other a few weeks and Missy said her friend really wanted to meet me, and then it was like Nicola was grilling me. What was my work situation, how much money I made." He looked at the expression on Gwen's face. "Yeah, like I said, it was strange. It reminded me of when I was a lot younger and girls would send their friends over to ask questions. Like we were in high school or even middle school."

"Were they all such personal questions?"

He laughed but without humor. "You have no idea. Did I want more kids? What was my relationship with my ex? What happened to the marriage? Did I cheat?"

"Jeez." If someone had asked her personal questions like that when she'd started dating Todd, well, she probably would have answered them and kept smiling, but now? There was no way.

"Yeah, and I didn't want to make waves because I knew how much Nicola meant to Missy, and I really, really liked Missy, so I tried to laugh off the worst of them. Afterward, I remember talking to Miss about it, saying how odd I thought it was, and she said, that's just how Nicola is. A bit of a bulldog." He took a sip of his iced tea. "I remember her saying, 'She's more like a sister than a friend.'"

"Let me guess," Gwen said. "Missy was an only child."

Jonas nodded. "She said that was one of the things she and Nicola bonded over."

"Actually, Nicola had a sister." She told him about the articles she'd found online, but not that Celeste had also disappeared. She wanted to hear what he had to say first.

His eyebrows shot up, and then he shook his head. "Imagine that: Nicola Kimmel lying. She would always use being an only child as an excuse to Missy. Say it was one of the reasons she misstepped, because she didn't know where the boundaries were. But I think it's pretty obvious asking your friend's new boyfriend if he is a cheat and a deadbeat is overstepping."

"Obviously you didn't trust Nicola."

Jonas answered quickly and definitively. "God no. And I'll be frank, it's the one thing I didn't trust Missy to see clearly. Like I said, a blind spot."

"Trust how?"

"It didn't make sense to me that Missy couldn't see how manipulative she was. The longer we dated, the more she'd tell me what Nicola'd say about me. That I wanted Missy so I could get someone to raise my daughter. That I was a loser who was trying for a sugar mama. I work as a custodian at Glenn State—it's not great money, but it's union and I can take classes for free—so I'm a loser. I admit, I was waylaid out of high school with a drug bust. Spent some time in prison for dealing, but it put me on the straight path. I'm working on a business degree. Eventually Missy started to see that I might be right, and Nicola didn't like that."

"How so?"

"Missy began to distance herself from Nicola when we were in quarantine. During lockdown, someone threw a brick through her window and I would bet money it was Nicola. She came this close"—he held his thumb and forefinger an inch apart—"to hitting my daughter." Gwen thought about Nicola coming after Whitney and felt her eye twitch. "And then when we got back to somewhat normal, Missy kept pulling away from her. More and more time between answering texts. Fewer lunches together at work. Whenever Nicola would ask if we wanted to do something with her and Derek, more and more, Missy would say we were busy."

"How'd that go over?"

"How do you think?" he asked.

"Not well?"

"Exactly. I know that Missy felt like she was going to have to find a new job. She had some feelers out but no real offers yet. That was one of the things"—he cleared his throat—"in the investigation that convinced the police she had skipped town. She was so unhappy at her job." Gwen winced to see his pain so plain on his face; it was what others had been seeing in her own since Todd died. "But it was working with Nicola that was so hard."

Gwen thought again about Todd and how little she'd known about his work and the pressures he had to cover up his failures. But looking back now, she could see the warning signs: the ever-increasing stress, how he ate antacids like candy, how often he'd suggest they eat at home rather than going out.

"I keep wondering if you're going to ask me the million-dollar question."

"Which is what?"

"Do I think Nicola killed her."

He was right. Missy's sudden departure, the brick, the dynamic Bethany described between the two women, the lack of a note in her handwriting. The more Gwen learned, the more she wondered. "And?"

Tears filled his eyes. "I do. I don't know—I don't know where the body is, but I know she killed her. I just can't prove it."

"What do you think happened?"

"Missy had done a great job putting distance between them during quarantine, but Nicola wouldn't stop pushing about the wedding. First, she insisted on throwing an engagement party we didn't want, and then she assumed she was going to be a bridesmaid and was not happy when Missy said it was going to be my daughter. Eventually we decided the only way to keep her from taking over was to have a destination wedding with just family."

Who else did Gwen know who'd had a destination wedding? Something about it rang a distant bell.

"Missy was going to have Nicola over that night," Jonas continued. "To tell her. I asked her if she wanted me to come and be there for the conversation, but she was afraid that might set Nicola off. She was going to tell her about the wedding, and also that she was looking for another job because it was making her sick, being so stressed about running into her at work every day." The similarities to her own situation made Gwen shudder. She, too, had ridden that line between placating Nicola and ending up on the wrong side of her anger.

"But Nicola never showed up?"

"That's what Missy's texts said. She texted me that evening and said she'd canceled on Nicola. She wanted to go to bed early and had some thinking to do. I knew that was off—that talk had been a long time coming and she was ready—but when I texted her back to discuss it, and later to tell her good night, she assured me all was fine. I'm pretty sure now that Nicola sent those texts. The next morning I left I don't know how many voice mails for Missy, and finally I called the police."

"Why didn't they take it seriously?"

"What they saw was a bunch of voice mails demanding she call me back, and a text trail that showed she'd canceled on Nicola and that all was fine there. By the time I talked to the police, they knew about my record and wouldn't let go that I was the number one suspect. Now I wonder if Nicola got to them first and planted some seeds. The detective I was working with basically said, either we close this as a non-case or we come after you. Plus, Nicola had a rock-solid alibi."

Even before Jonas said it, Gwen had an idea who it was.

"Derek," Jonas confirmed. Derek, who had made it clear he was looking out for no one but himself. Why would he have falsified an alibi for her?

"I'm sure that guy had his own crosses to bear being married to Nicola," Jonas said, "but to lie like that? It's unconscionable."

"Why are you so convinced it was a lie?"

"Because he called me the next day to say he'd been home with her. The dude had never called me in his life. The only way he would have gotten my number was through Nicola, and the only way she would have gotten it was from Missy's phone. I am a hundred percent convinced she made him call me and confirm her alibi, and wrote that stupid 'it's all too much' note in Missy's Notes app. This might sound silly, but she'd taken a calligraphy class years ago and loved handwritten notes. There's no way she would have typed something that important." He shook his head. "I'm just glad Nicola hasn't come after us. I think even she can recognize if something were to happen to me, she'd be a suspect."

"You said 'us,'" Gwen said, her stomach dropping.

"Yeah, I mean me and Marlee, my daughter. They didn't spend much time together, but sometimes we'd stop to see Missy at work, and Marlee would run to Nicola's office—Aunt Nicola, she called her—and Nicola would have candy for her and a drawer full of stuff like coloring books, or plastic jumping frogs, or who knows what else." Gwen knew the drawer well; Whitney had run to Nicola's office to see what new items she had in there the few times Gwen had brought her to Dacks.

She thought of Whitney's enthusiasm and how much she loved going to Nicola's house. It was Maxx, of course, but was there more she didn't know about? "Do you think she really would have done something to Marlee?" she asked. "To a *kid*?"

"Yeah, I do. Look what she did to her best friend." He leaned forward. "Why did you really want to see me?" he asked. "Has Nicola done something to you?"

Gwen took a shaky sip of her now-cooling latte. "I think she might have," she started, and told him in more detail what had happened to her mother, as well as her tire.

"You think or you know?" Jonas asked.

Hearing the story out loud in her own voice, Gwen was certain it wasn't coincidence. "I know," she confirmed.

"Then get away from her by any means possible."

Chapter Thirty-Eight

Gwen entered the hospital room and found Jeri sitting on the edge of the bed with her large purse on her thighs, both hands clasped protectively at the top.

"You're late," Jeri said, nodding toward the clock on the wall. It was 2:07. No *thank you*, no *it's good to see you*. She was too tired to tell her about coffee with Jonas, still trying to wiggle something loose in the back of her mind.

"Hi, Mom." Gwen bent down and gave her mom a kiss on the forehead like she did Whitney each night, and the tenderness seemed to take the wind out of Jeri's crabby sails. "How'd you sleep?"

"There was a lot of poking and prodding," her mother said, and then, as if trying to see the good, "but not too bad considering."

"I'm glad." Gwen looked around, unsure what to do next. She hadn't checked someone out of a hospital before. Did they just go? It seemed an awful lot like busting someone out of jail.

She found, though, that she didn't want to ask her mother what to do. What she wanted was to figure it out. Life was full of these small challenges—how to rent a car, hook up the utilities, check someone out of a hospital—and for years she'd slowly been handing the reins of things like this over to Todd. It had seemed sweet, even chivalrous, when he would fill her gas tank or escort her through an airport, but looking back now, it felt like each act had chipped away at her independence.

She was nearly certain this hadn't been Todd's intent, and as with other things, she was learning to take responsibility for her part.

Gwen found the nurse's station and told the woman she needed to check out her mother.

"Ah yes, Jeri. She's a tough old bird," said the nurse warmly. She reached behind the desk and pulled out a thin stack of papers. "Here are her discharge papers and instructions from the doctor." She added another paper to the stack. "You can stop at the pharmacy on the way out for a rolling walker. They rent them next door."

"A walker?"

"She's beyond a cane," the nurse said. "I'm surprised she's gotten along as well as she has."

"What about PT? Can we get her in for that?" Gwen explained to the woman how limited Jeri's mobility had become in the last few years, and that she hadn't managed to address the issue.

"Here," she said, and added another sheet of paper. "These are the instructions to follow if she needs a GP reference or can look out of network. It'll depend on her insurance." And that easily, Gwen knew what to do. How had this task followed her around for so long?

The nurse came out from behind the station and unfolded a wheelchair.

Back in Jeri's room, the nurse helped Jeri lift herself from the bed and sit in the wheelchair, and Gwen was impressed by the muscles that strained within her mom's large body. She recognized how much strength it must take Jeri to haul herself through the world and felt tears prickle her eyes. A tough old bird, indeed.

But still, seeing her mother in the wheelchair, Gwen wondered what she was going to do about childcare. There was the aftercare program at the school, but Whitney had made it clear she didn't want to hang out with those kids a minute longer than she needed to, and she was thankful once again how well Whitney and Jeri had gotten along, despite Whitney's complaints over the weekend.

She left her mother at the front of the hospital with the nurse and went to get the car. Once she was back, the nurse helped Jeri haul herself up, up into the high seat of the Rover. Once settled, Jeri looked around as if realizing something.

"This is where we took your father that time when he had the grilling accident," Jeri said, the SUV now idling. When Gwen was six, her father had been prepping the small Weber grill in the backyard for pork chops, and had accidentally sprayed lighter fluid onto his shirt and lit himself on fire. He'd come into the house and her mother had tried to peel the polyester shirt off, but it had already melted to his skin. Gwen would never forget seeing his mottled chest like a charred marshmallow. She still thought of it at least once a week. She hardly ever ate pork because of it.

On the way to the hospital, Gwen had been in the back seat, petrified, sure her father would die. She'd never seen him cry before. She'd never known he could be injured. When they arrived, her mother shot out of the car and over to the passenger seat where she helped him up. They were halfway to the elevator before she remembered Gwen, who had unconsciously convinced herself if she didn't get out of the car, she would never hear bad news.

"Gwennie?" Jeri said now, and Gwen turned to her blurry mother and realized she was crying. Gwen wiped her wet cheek.

"How did you do it? How did you get over Dad dying?"

"I haven't," Jeri said, and reached over to squeeze her daughter's hand. "It was twelve years ago, and I still wake up thinking he might be there."

"I do that too," Gwen admitted.

"I wake up and think, he's going to be there and you're sleeping down the hall and I'm still in my forties and wear a size ten. But life marches on whether you want it to or not."

"I'm so tired," Gwen said. "And so mad at Todd for dying. And so sad he's gone."

"Of course you are." Jeri curled Gwen's hair behind her ear like she used to when Gwen was a little girl. "But you're tougher than you think, Gwennie. You always have been."

"I was so scared when that happened to Dad," Gwen admitted. "I kept thinking, stay in the car and you'll never hear bad news again."

"Huh," Jeri said.

Gwen turned to her mom. "What?"

"That's not what I remember."

"What do you remember?" Gwen asked.

"That you sat with me that whole night. You had a coloring book with you and you shared it. We spent the night fighting over the yellow and brown crayons to color in those dumb cats from *The Lion King*. I remember being so glad you were there, so glad to have your company. And while I know you didn't want to come back to Dayton and your life isn't what you expected it would be right now, I'm glad you're here. I'm glad I get to see you."

"I'm glad about that too," Gwen said, and she meant it.

At Whitney's elementary school, Gwen followed the white arrows through the driver line, realizing that this was the first time she'd actually picked her daughter up from this school. It was hard to believe something she had done consistently since Whitney started preschool, other than in quarantine, was no longer a part of her day. She remembered how her schedule would center around it; when to start roasting a chicken, or run errands, or even schedule a maintenance call was all determined by that 2:25 p.m. pickup.

And yes, of course, picking her kid up was important, but how had that become her defining task?

Whitney sat on the school steps reading a book, and Gwen tapped the horn to get her attention even though there was a **No Honking** sign posted on the side of the school. She could imagine that her mother, now subdued in the passenger seat, honked that horn each time she'd picked up Whitney, rules be damned.

"I thought about it all night," Jeri said. "I've had dizzy spells and fallen before—"

"You have?" Gwen asked, surprised, and Jeri nodded.

"A few. I broke my wrist about a year ago, and have had a few scrapes." Gwen opened her mouth and Jeri held up a hand to silence her. "We could both do with being a little better about communicating. But I was thinking about it last night in the hospital, and every other time, it was like the world kind of hazed in and out. It went gray then back to normal, and then closed like a pinprick."

"And yesterday?"

"Pain." Jeri circulated her left wrist forward and back. "Yesterday, I felt the blow, I know I did, and the other times, the pain didn't start until I woke up." She looked at Gwen. "You're right," she said. "Someone hit me." Gwen nodded, her worst fear realized. She'd watched Nicola parade back and forth in front of her office door yesterday, but there was no accounting for her time before the office opened.

"What do I do?" she whispered as her daughter finally looked up, saw her car, and plugged her book with a bookmark. Gwen was asking herself more than her mother.

"For now? Keep her away from my grandbaby."

Chapter Thirty-Nine

After dropping Jeri and Whitney at her place—she'd take Jeri home after dinner—Gwen headed for Nicola's condo, knowing she'd be at work for another hour. Derek answered on the third knock, looking much better than the last time she'd seen him. He was showered and out of workout clothes, his eyes bright and clear.

"Nicola's not here," he said by way of greeting. Maxx lunged for the door, but Derek blocked him with his foot.

"Actually, I was wondering if I could talk to you for a sec. Why did you lie the night Missy disappeared and say you were with Nicola?"

He seemed genuinely surprised by her question, a reaction Gwen found satisfying. "How'd you find that out?"

"So it's true."

A grin spread on his face. "I guess I confirmed it, didn't I?" He held the door open and moved aside so Gwen could enter. *What was the harm,* she figured; Nicola was at work.

He offered her a coffee or water, which she turned down as she slid one cheek on a stool behind the breakfast bar, one foot on the floor. She wanted him to know she wasn't planning to stay or making herself comfortable. "So why'd you do it?"

"At the time, I didn't want Nicola poking into my whereabouts any more than she wanted me poking into hers," he said, as if he hadn't compromised an investigation. Men like this never seemed to think too much about the ramifications of their actions. "I was with a woman I had a thing with—someone I'd been seeing for a few weeks. It's over now, in case you're wondering." She hadn't been.

"And where was Nicola?"

"She swears she was here all night." Derek reached under the sink for two enormous containers of protein powder. He set them on the counter, then opened the cupboard and brought down two shake bottles with metal balls inside.

"Did you believe her?"

"By the time she told me the police had questioned her about Missy, she'd already told them she was with me. She implied she did it to protect me, in case they started sniffing around where I was, and she just kept saying it was a big waste of time. That Missy had left to get away from Jonas." He shrugged. "Made sense to me. The guy was a wet rag."

Gwen stared at him. "And you weren't worried about what happened to Missy?"

"I figured if something fishy had happened, the cops would figure it out." He threw the powder and bottles in a reusable grocery bag along with a bag of dog treats on the counter. "But if you're right that Nicola had something to do with Missy's disappearance, then yeah, I'm worried. I'm worried I'm next." Gwen looked around and only then noticed the large black suitcase next to the sofa, a navy duffel on top.

"What really happened that night?"

"I thought Nicola was going to spend the evening with Missy and so I made alternate plans. When I got home around ten, she was already in bed, even though she hardly ever goes to bed that early. I thought it was weird, but frankly, I was relieved I didn't have to talk to her. The next evening, she tells me Missy didn't show up for work, and after that, just never came back."

"And let me guess," Gwen said. "She showed you a text exchange with Missy canceling their plans." Gwen thought how easy it would have been for Nicola to write that exchange after she was there. She imagined her holding the phone up to the dead woman's face to unlock it and shuddered.

"She did," Derek confirmed. "The cops have the transcripts." He pulled a bag of dog food out from under the sink, rolled down the top, and stuck it in the grocery bag. He nodded toward the door. "I hate to be rude," he said, which Gwen knew wasn't true, "but I want to be out of here before she gets home. No use throwing a grenade behind me when I go."

"Okay, thanks," Gwen said, and slid off the barstool. "And good luck, I guess."

"You too." Derek stooped to pick up Maxx so he wouldn't run out when Gwen opened the door, and cuddled him in his arms, kissing the top of his fuzzy head. It was the one thing she liked about Derek: how much he loved the dog.

At the door she paused. "Did you know Nicola had a sister?"
He shook his head. "Nope. Only child."

It took everything Gwen had not to say, *Well, look who's the gullible one now!* but he wasn't worth the energy. "She did. I found out online. She had a sister who just disappeared." She looked pointedly at him. "Like Missy just disappeared? Don't you care about the connection?"

He stabbed his chest with his finger. "Like *I'm* about to disappear." He shook his head. "I'm out of here before she gets home."

He opened the door for her and Gwen walked through, no well wishes necessary. As she turned toward her condo, her stomach dropped. Nicola's Prius was driving down the road. There was no way Gwen could pretend she hadn't walked out of her front door, so she held up a tentative hand as a wave. Nicola pulled into the driveway, shut off the car, and opened the door.

Gwen thought quickly. "I was just checking if you were home," she lied.

Nicola's face was blank behind her mirrored sunglasses. "Why's that? You knew I was at work. Or you would have if you'd come in today."

"I had to pick up my mother from the hospital," Gwen said, wondering even as she did why Nicola assumed she was owed an explanation.

Nicola stood up and slammed the door behind her. "What did you want?" she asked, nodding toward the front door as Gwen crossed her arms against the cold, snow just beginning to fall. The tension was fraught between them, a wire about to snap. "Was Derek able to help you?" Her voice was calm, friendly even, but somehow that made it worse. Did she think something was going on between Gwen and her husband?

"Yes," Gwen said. "Thanks. I just needed some advice." Her mind scrambled and landed on Maxx. "I'm thinking about getting a dog."

Nicola shook her head. "I do not get why people like dogs so much."

"Why'd you get one then?" Gwen asked.

"Because I knew it would make Whitney happy," she said, as if it were the most obvious reason in the world. Gwen had long suspected that was why, and while in the beginning it had felt like an overreach, now it seemed to have malicious undertones. It wasn't Nicola's job to make Whitney happy; it was Gwen's.

"It worked," Gwen said.

Nicola's face stayed flat. "One thing you should know about me by now, Gwen, is that I get the job done."

Despite her fear, Gwen took a step closer to Nicola. "What job? What do you get done?"

"Anything I set my mind to." A car backfired somewhere in the complex, and Gwen's heart stuttered in her chest. She fluttered her hand to her mouth to stop herself from calling out in terror. "You're jumpy," Nicola observed. Her words were even, as if rolled out on an assembly line.

"I'm fine," Gwen said. "Just tired."

"A puppy isn't going to help with that."

Gwen tried to keep her own voice light and steady, hoping Nicola didn't try to check her lie with Derek. "I suppose not. You're right, maybe it's a bad idea."

Nicola's eyebrows shot up. "So you admit it: I still have good ideas. The way you act lately, it's hard to tell." Behind the mirrored sunglasses, it was impossible to read Nicola's expression. It was like looking at a smooth lake as thunderclouds rolled in overhead.

"I need to go," Gwen said, and motioned to her condo.

"Whitney's not home alone, is she?" Nicola asked. She peeled the sunglasses from her face, folded in the temples one by one, and snaked one in the front of her blouse. Her eyes, much to Gwen's surprise, were rimmed with red, the lids thin and tinted blue.

"I'm—" Gwen started, but stopped. She did not need to tell Nicola where Whitney was. For too long, she'd given away information only because people asked for it, but no more. She said goodbye and turned toward the condo, careful to keep her back straight and her head erect.

"Gwen," Nicola said behind her, but Gwen kept walking. "Hey, Gwennie!" It was the nickname her mother used, and out of Nicola's mouth, sounded like a taunt. "Tell your mother I hope she's feeling better."

Chapter Forty

Gwen woke to a scream around four in the morning, and clawed her way out of a deep sleep. By the time she opened her eyes, her system was flooded with adrenaline, heart jackhammering in her chest as she tore out of her bedroom and ran into Whitney's.

Her daughter's eyes were open and empty, her throat already hoarse. Gwen slapped the wall to turn on the light and found Whitney struggling as if against restraints, her sheets wrapped around her arms and one leg. Whitney opened her mouth and screamed again, the primal sound ripping from her throat.

"Whitney!" Gwen yelled, and grabbed her daughter's shoulder, shaking her. Whitney's head bobbed forward and back, and Gwen willed herself to stop shaking. Whitney's eyes fluttered, the whites showing, and then slowly, slowly, began to focus.

"Mom?" she said, her voice pleading, and then, "Mom?" in confusion as she surveyed the room. Gwen held her daughter's shoulders, her hands firm and warm, until Whitney was completely awake, her breath ragged through her mouth.

"I had another one?" Whitney asked, and Gwen nodded. It had been over a week since the last, the longest stretch since Todd's death.

Ten minutes later, they were both under the covers in Gwen's bed, huddled in a tight ball at the headboard. Gwen smoothed a hand down Whitney's hair in a steady rhythm. Her heart was still banging in her chest, and the hairs on the back of her neck had yet to settle. Between Nicola catching her leaving the condo after talking to Derek, and now the night terror, all she wanted was some calm. She thought about just swinging by to get Jeri and leaving town, the price of a hotel room be damned. They could go to the Hocking Hills, or even just Cincinnati. It was Wednesday, and Whitney only had two more days of school before break; Gwen was sure she wouldn't miss much. She could call Bethany and ask to work remotely the rest of the week.

"Maybe we should take a trip," Gwen said. "Get Grandma and start the holidays early."

Whitney turned to her mother, panic clear on her face in the moonlight. "But Mr. TopHat!"

Gwen's hand stopped. Whitney had already cleared a space on her dresser where she'd keep the cage. A Pyrex full of shredded carrots waited in the fridge, a damp paper towel on top to keep them fresh. Last night, Whitney had finished her essay about why she should be chosen to watch Mr. TopHat over break. For the final copy, she'd drawn lines on a piece of printer paper with a ruler to be sure her letters were straight, complete with the dotted line in the middle so she'd know where the tops of the lowercase letters should hit. She then erased the lines, leaving behind the perfect letters and the ghosts of her effort.

Mrs. Toner was to announce the proud caregiver of Mr. TopHat before recess, and Whitney felt confident it would be her.

"Tomorrow," Gwen conceded, but Whitney reminded her that was when she'd be bringing the bird home.

"Right," Gwen said. Mr. TopHat was the one perk at Whitney's school, and Gwen knew how hard she'd worked on that essay. Plus, she didn't want to raise a daughter who ran away and shirked responsibilities. She'd already been a bad enough example of that. "You're right. Once we get Mr. TopHat, we'll leave on a trip."

Whitney was finally soothed to sleep, but Gwen's eyes wouldn't close despite the weight of them. While Whitney's night terrors had grown less frequent, they still put Gwen on edge, and she could tell already it was one of those nights when sleep would elude her. She finally gave up and pulled her hands from her warm child, tiptoeing downstairs to start the coffee.

By habit, she glanced out the window toward Nicola's house, surprised to see the lights on. She wondered if Nicola had questioned Derek about Gwen getting a dog, or if Derek had told Nicola he was leaving. It made her sick to think of telling Nicola something like that, knowing she would hear, "You've lost." Nicola did not like to lose. No one did, but Nicola perhaps pathologically so. Gwen thought of Nicola's passive face behind her mirrored sunglasses the day before, how Gwen had lied about what she was doing there, and then what Derek might say in contrast to her story.

Gwen turned on the coffeepot and went outside to grab the early edition of the *Dayton Daily News* off her now-snowy porch, a welcome-home gift from her mother who still insisted on reading a physical print edition. As soon as it was light out, she'd call and see how her mother was doing, wondering if she should have insisted her mother stay with them at least for a night. She quickly scanned the neighborhood, wondering if she'd see Derek on his early-morning run, if he had chickened out leaving once Nicola came home. Last night, she'd kept an ear cocked toward their house, listening for the telltale signs of his Charger revving to leave the complex, but all she heard was the eerie silence that settles with snow.

She was about to head back inside when movement caught her attention from the left. For a second, she thought it was another woman in the neighborhood—another dumpy mom like herself getting in her steps before the kids ruled her day—and was surprised to see that it was Nicola, dressed in baggy gray sweatpants and an old Def Leppard T-shirt that looked like it belonged to Derek peeking between the open sides of her parka. It was shocking to see Nicola dressed like an average person. No makeup, greasy hair, circles under her eyes. Nicola might not have been a conventional beauty, but she always looked put together, even at her most casual. Now, she looked like she belonged in the aisles of a supermarket, a clutch of coupons in her purse. She looked like the girl from her yearbook.

Gwen felt ashamed, seeing her so diminished; this moment of vulnerability should be private. She wanted to scurry back inside, but it was too late. Nicola was making a beeline right for her, traipsing through the fresh snow in her UGGs. "You okay?" Gwen asked.

Nicola shook her head, her mouth crumpling. "Derek left me." She stepped on the porch, rubbing her hands against her parka for warmth.

"Oh, Nicola," she said. "I'm so sorry." She leaned into sympathy, not wanting Nicola to suspect she'd already known Derek's plan. There were goose bumps on Gwen's arms. She was in just her pajamas in thirty-degree weather.

She thought about her promise not to let Nicola inside, but she had to weigh it against the suspicions she'd raise if she didn't. Nicola wasn't a vampire, she had to remind herself.

She held open the door, and Nicola stepped inside as she wiped a glistening hand under her nose.

Inside, Nicola asked for something to drink, and Gwen poured a cup of coffee from the fresh pot.

"What happened?" Gwen said, doing her best to infuse her voice with sympathy. Her only goal: placate Nicola enough to get her out of the house. She needed time to think. Was Nicola just a friend who oversteps, or was she really a violent threat? Maybe her mom did trip; maybe Missy freaked out and left. Maybe Gwen was scaring herself for nothing, or maybe, just maybe, it was as bad as she thought.

Nicola shook her head: *I don't know.* "When I got home, Derek had packed his bags. He said he wanted to take his Charger coast-to-coast and really take advantage of this gift of time since he was fired." She made air quotes around "gift." "It's not a gift," she added. "Or if it is, I'm paying for it."

"When's he coming back?" Gwen asked evenly, already doubting the story. She knew that Nicola and Derek were beyond reasonable conversation; if they'd talked last night, it had been a fight. Her only advantage was that Nicola wasn't aware Gwen knew this.

"I can't say. He made a point of leaving his cell phone, saying he wanted to unplug. Some real *On the Road* bullshit." Nicola exhaled. "I was up half the night thinking about it. Derek's a dick, and while I'm angry he left and now I'm financing this little midlife crisis, it got me thinking about what really matters."

Gwen felt a sinking feeling. *Don't say me. Don't say me.*

"And that's the people that really support you and lift you up," Nicola continued. "Not the ones that use you for whatever they think they can get from you. Derek's a taker." It was what Derek had said about Nicola, Gwen remembered. "I think I always knew it, even when we were dating. The cheating, the predatory shit at work. I'm not surprised he left, I guess. I hope he stays gone."

"I'm really sorry," Gwen said, an eye on the clock. Whitney's alarm would go off soon for school.

"Like I said, I'm trying to tell myself it's for the best. It's helped me think through some issues I might have." She put a hand to her chest. "I am *not* victim blaming, don't worry, but I've been thinking about other relationships that matter." She looked pointedly at Gwen. "You were right, Gwen. I haven't been fully honest with you about some things."

Gwen felt queasy. Was this about Derek? Missy? She didn't want to have this conversation while her daughter was upstairs within earshot, or when Nicola looked so vulnerable. "Honest about what?" Gwen asked evenly.

Nicola took a deep breath and looked sheepishly at Gwen. "I had a sister."

Gwen blanched but quickly recovered as she turned to grab more creamer from the fridge. Had Derek told her Gwen knew about the sister?

"Why didn't you tell me?" Gwen said, her voice steady, careful to neither confirm nor deny she already knew.

"I loved her so much, but Celeste was starting down the same road as our mom. She had a few guys she was *dating*"—she added air quotes—"and was getting into drugs. She wasn't going to hold out much longer, and then she left me behind and it became easier to pretend she'd never been there. I took my scholarship at Glenn State and left knowing if I didn't, our mom would get her claws into me too." Gwen had the distinct feeling that Nicola was telling the truth, and yet, what was she not saying?

"I loved her so much," Nicola said, shaking her head. "She was the one good thing in my life."

Gwen's heart thudded in her chest. What were the chances two women had disappeared from Nicola's life, and just what had happened with Derek? A thud sounded upstairs and both women looked at the ceiling. It was Whitney jumping from the bed and scurrying to the bathroom to pee. She had to get Nicola out of here.

"Okay, I'll get going," Nicola said, surprising Gwen. "I know it's Mr. TopHat day." Despite everything, Gwen felt a twinge of warmth that Nicola had remembered. "Tell that kiddo good luck." At the door she turned around. "I really just came over to ask if you'd seen the luggage."

"The luggage?"

"What Derek had packed." Gwen remembered the suitcase against the wall, the duffel bag resting on top. Was that really what this visit was about? She nodded. "Okay, good," Nicola said. "If anyone comes sniffing around asking questions, I'm glad I can say you saw it too."

Whitney called down the stairs. "Mom?"

"Sorry," Gwen said to Nicola, and then bit her tongue. She had to stop saying that. She pointed to the ceiling. "I need to get Whitney ready for school."

"Yeah, I need to get back too," Nicola said, and swiped another hand under her nose. "Maxx's probably chewed through his cage by now."

Gwen shut the door behind Nicola, turning the lock as silently as she could. Through the window, she watched Nicola shush through the snow in her UGGs, barely lifting her feet, her back curled against the cold. It wasn't until she turned away to refill her coffee that Gwen remembered: Derek had packed the dog's treats and food.

She was certain now that Nicola had only stopped by so, down the road, Gwen could confirm that Derek had planned to leave. It was just like the text thread between Missy and Nicola the night Missy disappeared, and how Derek had corroborated that Nicola was home. The anonymous website that pointed the finger at Derek and ended with him fired for sexual harassment. How Nicola had walked by her office time after time the day Jeri fell, everyone in the office able to confirm Nicola had been there all day.

There was something else about being at the office. *What was it?* Gwen thought of Nicola dropping her new office key into her palm the first day at work, the click of the door unlocking. What had Nicola said that morning? Something about that memory was working its way to the surface.

Gwen had spun around in her desk chair, elated by her new digs, and then Nicola had told her it had been Missy's office. She'd said Gwen and Missy reminded her of each other, both indecisive idiots in the deodorant aisle, and Gwen had thought about her own wedding. The tiny new potatoes, the salmon. *Tacky,* Nicola had said about Missy's wedding plans. *All those hillbillies on a beach somewhere with their toes in the sand.*

If Nicola had known Missy was planning a destination wedding, that meant she must have seen her the night she died.

Chapter Forty-One

Gwen dropped Whitney at school, her daughter turning at the double doors to give a thumbs-up and mouth, "Mr. TopHat!" All she had to do was hold on through the day, get the bird in the morning, then grab her mom and go. The only thing that made her go to work today was the alarm bells she'd set off in Nicola if she didn't.

At work she busied herself with a pitch deck that she'd be presenting to the board in early 2023 on six ways to earn more revenue. She cleared out her inbox, and emailed Bethany about working remotely the rest of the week. Shortly before noon, Gwen's phone rang, and for a second, she felt a zing of adrenaline, sure it would be Nicola calling to get lunch together. She read the name of Whitney's school on the screen with both relief and a different kind of dread, and swiped to accept the call.

"We have a situation," said Mary, the school admin, and Gwen felt the sick climb her throat. "Everything's fine," she said, and then paused before continuing. "Whitney's had an accident." Gwen leaned over as her stomach cramped. Since Gwen had woken to Whitney's screams, the day had felt too fragile, her skin too thin.

"What happened?"

Mary explained that Whitney had fallen from the monkey bars on the playground, and Gwen struggled to make sense of the words. "A bloody nose, and we think a broken arm. An ambulance has been called and she's on her way to Children's."

"Was anyone else there? Anyone not authorized by the school?"

"Of course not," Mary confirmed. "We have very strict protocols in place."

Gwen scribbled down the address for the hospital with one hand as she grabbed blindly for her coat with the other. "I'm on my way," she said, adrenaline coursing through her as she hung up the phone, her coat on one shoulder, purse on the other. She ran to the elevator, pressing the button with enough force to puncture the wall.

Her blood pounded in her ears; her daughter had fallen. Was this an accident? A coincidence? How many times was she going to ask herself that?

The doors opened and she raced in. Her baby had to be okay. She could not lose her husband and her child in the same year. She could not lose both, period. She tried to reason with herself. A bloody nose and a broken arm weren't fatal, but try telling that to her stuttering heart.

Eighteen minutes later she screeched into the hospital parking garage and barreled to the reception area, the waiting room nearly empty.

"Can I help you?" asked a woman in scrubs.

"Whitney Maner. I'm her mother. She would have arrived from her school in an ambulance."

"Of course." She clicked around her computer and asked for Gwen's ID. It took a moment for Gwen to claw it out of her wallet, her damp hands struggling with the plastic envelope inside. "I can take the whole wallet," the nurse said, and her voice was so understanding, Gwen thought it might break her.

Whitney had lived eight years with barely a scrape, and then her dad died and now there were broken bones.

She turned the wallet to the woman who did a cursory glance—was that it? Had she read Gwen's name that quickly?—and told her which cubicle in the ER.

"ER?" Gwen questioned. Her phone dinged in her purse as the nurse said, "They'll get her transferred to radiology for X-rays soon enough."

Gwen tore through the hallways to the right room, Whitney M written in purple marker on the dry-erase board next to the door.

She took one more deep, settling breath, opened the door, and felt the air choke in her lungs. The room was empty.

Her phone rang and she looked down: Nicola Kimmel.

Chapter Forty-Two

"What did you do?" Gwen screamed into the phone.

She was met with silence and a long pause. "I can explain—" Nicola started.

"Where is she? Where?" A nurse looked over from the main station, a scowl on her face.

"She?" Nicola asked. "What are you talking about?"

"I'm at the hospital. Whitney broke her arm. I'm in her room and—" Gwen burst back into the hallway and saw an orderly rounding the corner, wheeling Whitney her direction in a child-size wheelchair. Gwen's chest collapsed with relief. Whitney's thin legs were visible under her hospital gown, bright pink socks on her feet. Whitney hated pink. Gwen scanned her daughter, trying to take it all in—her arm in a sling, the blood crusted under her nose, the dulled shock in her eyes.

"I have to go," she said, and hung up the phone, dropping to her knees and placing her hands on the armrests of the wheelchair—how awful they made these for children—scared to touch her now breakable child. "Are you okay?" she said. "Baby, are you okay?"

"It hurts," Whitney whimpered, and Gwen swerved a hand over her daughter's head, cupping her chin at the end. She remembered taking Whitney to the pediatrician for vaccines as a baby, how she'd sit on her mother's lap, unaware what was about to happen. There would be a hot, sharp pinch in Whitney's chubby thigh, sometimes more than one, and eventually she became wary, angry at her mother for subjecting her to it.

"Oh, sweetheart," Gwen said. Whitney's eyes were glassy, and Gwen wondered if her daughter was in shock or on pain medication. Could they give her that without Gwen's permission?

The orderly cleared his throat and Gwen stood up, her knees popping. She moved out of the way so he could wheel Whitney into her room and help her gingerly onto the child's bed. Whitney had always been tall, in the upper fifteenth percentile in height, and that, combined with her adultlike skepticism, sometimes tricked Gwen into thinking she was older than she was. It scared Gwen to see her daughter this way, so diminished.

Her phone dinged again and she ignored it, then thought better of it and turned off the sound. She could not deal with Nicola right now. And what had she meant, *I can explain*? Her phone vibrated as she settled at the head of the bed, a protective arm around her daughter as the orderly said the doctor would be by soon with an update.

The air felt awkward and thick as they were left alone in the colorful room, the bright yellow walls reminding Gwen of a false sun.

A woman appeared in the doorway who was vaguely familiar and smiled at Gwen. "Ms. Maner? I'm Ms. Kat. The nurse from the school." She smiled at Whitney. "How you doing, kiddo?"

Whitney looked back at her with widened eyes.

"I think she's in a bit of shock," Gwen said, and moved the bangs from her daughter's damp forehead.

"I'd like to speak with you in the hallway for a minute, Ms. Maner," Kat said, and with that Whitney grabbed on to her mom's arm with her good hand, digging her nails in to the point Gwen winced.

"Stay with me," Whitney said. "Don't leave me."

Gwen gulped to see her tough daughter so needy. "Are you okay?"

"I don't want to be alone." Whitney glanced at Nurse Kat.

"It'll only be a second," Gwen said. "I'll be just outside. You'll be able to see me from the door."

"Actually," Kat said. "It would be great if we could talk privately down the hall. Five minutes, tops."

Gwen glanced from Ms. Kat to her daughter and could read the fear on Whitney's face as clearly as if it had been written with the alphabet. It was the look Whitney got when she'd been caught doing something she shouldn't, and knew if she could keep the adults from sharing information, maybe she wouldn't get in trouble.

"Just down the hall, baby," Gwen repeated. "If you call for me, I'll hear you and come running." Gwen felt an ache anew at being the only parent. Had Todd been here, he could have stayed while she talked to the school nurse.

At the end of the hall, Gwen pricked an ear toward her daughter, confident she could still hear her, and lowered her voice. "Please make it quick." Her nerves were jangled. Something about this seemed too coincidental not to be tied to Nicola.

Nurse Kat bit her lower lip, and mentally Gwen circled her arm like, *Get on with it.* Had one of the kids made fun of her after she fell and she lashed out? Or maybe she'd sworn in pain and they were worried about what the other kids heard? Either way, Gwen just wanted to know.

"Yes?" she asked impatiently, and Kat took in a breath.

"This was more than an accidental fall on the playground." Here it was—Nicola had infiltrated the school, she'd pushed her daughter, but what Kat said next was wholly unrelated. "Whitney kidnapped the class bird."

Gwen blinked twice. It was the last thing she'd been expecting and it seemed to have nothing to do with anything. "What?" Who cared about a fucking bird; her daughter was in the ER.

"Two kids said she snuck him in her backpack and brought him outside." Gwen didn't understand. "She ended up dropping him from the monkey bars and he may not survive."

Gwen shook her head. "She hurt Mr. TopHat? I'm sure that's not right." She knew Whitney loved that stupidly named animal. Next to Maxx, it had been the thing she talked most about, especially in reference to school. No friends, no other kids, not even the teacher. Everything had been about how much she loved the bird. Gwen had signed a waiver recently about the pet, and had to fill out what seemed like a ridiculously long questionnaire about their home and who and what all lived there. They were taking home a bird in a cage, not the king of England, for god's sake.

"She loves that bird," Gwen reiterated, and Nurse Kat gave her a look with so much pity, Gwen wanted to slap her. "Whitney was hoping to get him for holiday vacation." She thought of all the hours Whitney had put into her essay, how much it had all meant to her.

"Yes, and Mrs. Toner picked another child," Kat said.

"Okay . . . ," Gwen said, to show she was following.

"Whitney didn't take it well, to say the least. She threw a tantrum, ripped a poster off the wall, and screamed at Mrs. Toner, who sent her to me. I'm the counselor as well for the third graders. I talked with Whitney and she told me it wasn't fair. That she was the best one to watch Mr. TopHat. Full stop." Gwen shuddered; "full stop" was something Nicola said. "I get it, I do. I know little kids are animal crazed. She calmed down and went back to the classroom, and as is standard procedure, I stopped by about thirty minutes later to make sure she'd reacclimated to the classroom and all seemed fine."

Kat grimaced, and Gwen could tell she didn't want to say what came next. That made two of them. She had the sinking feeling whatever was said was something she wouldn't be able to unhear about her daughter.

"For recess, Whitney put on her backpack, but that's not that odd; the kids often bring out toys or whatnot to have on the playground, but she must have snuck Mr. TopHat in there. Out on the playground, she climbed the monkey bars and that's when one of the other kids saw her take him out of her pack. She threw him in the air. She may have thought she was just releasing him, but she didn't understand his wings were clipped and he couldn't fly. He started to fall and she reached for him, and that's when she fell."

Gwen leaned over, her hands on her knees, the feeling of nausea clawing up her throat. She shook her head and held on to the one good piece of news. "So you don't think she hurt him on purpose?" she whispered.

Kat put a hand on her shoulder, the weight of it warm. "I don't know, Ms. Maner. But either way, this is not a healthy reaction to not getting what you want."

People passed down the hall—a woman in a parka and sweatpants, her hair in a greasy ponytail; a couple in suits and overcoats who looked like they, too, had been called from work. An ER was where no parent wanted to be. She turned her back toward the hallway, away from Whitney's room but still in earshot.

"Where were the teachers during all this?" Gwen asked.

"As soon as they figured out what was going on—two of the kids ran to tell them—they ran over, but Whitney had fallen by then."

Compared to her daughter, the condition of the bird wasn't her main concern, but she had to ask. "How is he?"

"At the vet," Kat said. "Reece took him." Reece was the janitor. "He was breathing when we found him, but may have a broken back."

There was a squeal down the hall, a happy sound. Was it Whitney? Either way, she needed to get back, lay her hands on her daughter. "I have to go," she said. "You've obviously given me a lot to think about. And I'm glad Mr. TopHat is alive." In her bones, she knew Kat was right: even the best-case scenario for interpreting Whitney's actions was not good.

"This isn't about a bird," Ms. Kat clarified. "Two of the things we're teaching kids in school are how to manage their emotions, and how to deal with disappointment. We're trying to figure out why Whitney thought this was the best course of action to handle the situation. The concern isn't Mr. TopHat, Ms. Maner. It's Whitney. These are not the actions of a well-balanced child who knows how to process disappointment."

Ms. Kat cleared her throat. "Ms. Maner, when you enrolled Whitney in the fall, you didn't tell us that her father had died recently."

Gwen turned toward Ms. Kat's empathetic face. "That would have been helpful information. We found out because she disclosed to her teacher a week or so ago. We would have been providing counseling or special services. Why didn't you tell us?"

"I—" she started, but the honest truth was that she had been in denial. She hadn't been able to accept that Todd was gone, and presented with the forms at school, she had skipped the lines for second parent as if that would leave the door open for him to return. She was so embarrassed that she had let her own grief subsume her daughter's needs that her first thought was *run*. She would find a new school district, a blank slate, where they didn't yet know she'd screwed up. She had it in her mind she should get it "right," but what about just doing her best?

And wasn't running to a fresh start exactly what she'd done when she left Colorado? Leaving because she couldn't stand the sympathetic looks of her friends, the shame of not being able to afford the fancy summer camps and premades at Whole Foods? Even so, she was glad she'd ended up back in Dayton, her relationship with her mother now real, if not perfect. With surprise she realized a fresh start was why she'd left Dayton originally. It wasn't only that Todd had wanted to move to Boulder; that had been the end result. She hadn't wanted to face trying to fix what she had—the girlfriends she'd thrown to the side as soon as things became serious with Todd—and instead figured a new start was the answer.

Gwen had been running her whole life.

Kat took a step back and introduced more air between them. "We can talk about this later. I know you want to get back to Whitney." She squeezed Gwen's hand, and in a rush of emotion, Gwen squeezed Kat's back.

"I'm doing the best I can," she said.

"I know that," Kat said, and smiled. "Now get back to your kid."

Gwen said goodbye and tore back down the hall to her daughter, her vision blurred with tears.

She rounded the corner into Whitney's room, and leaning over her daughter was Nicola.

Chapter Forty-Three

Nicola looked over her shoulder at Gwen, wiping the tears from her eyes as she stood up.

"How'd you get in?" Gwen asked, remembering that she had been required to provide ID at the reception area to prove she was Whitney's mother. She looked at her daughter. There was a slight pink to her cheeks, and the whites of her eyes had cleared. Gwen's pulse jumped as she saw her daughter's hand entwined with Nicola's.

Nicola didn't answer the question but addressed Whitney. "Your mom wasn't returning my texts. I was worried about you." This was so typical of Nicola, to find a way to put the blame on Gwen. "But I forgive her," Nicola said. "I know she was worried too."

Gwen felt a fire burst in her gut. Worried *too*? Who was in charge here? It was so clear she didn't need Nicola's forgiveness for this. For any of this. Her priority here was her daughter.

"You need to leave." Gwen's voice was strong and even. Beeps and a steady drone of machines could be heard from the hallway.

"That's a mistake," Nicola said, looking at Gwen. "You're in over your head."

Gwen held eye contact, determined not to look away. "I'm not," she said.

"Mom?" Whitney said.

"You need to leave."

Nicola cocked her head to the side, considering. "Is that really what you think is best?"

Gwen wasn't sure what retaliation might be coming, but she pointed to the door.

"Mom, can't Aunt Nic—"

"It's fine, Whitney," Gwen said. She reached out to put her hand on Whitney's leg and her daughter kicked it away.

"Gwen," Nicola said, her voice reassuring. "I didn't want to have to say this in front of Whitney, but I don't think you're prepared to deal with this kind of pressure. I don't think it's best for your child to send me away. I think you're putting her in danger." Was that a direct threat?

"What danger?" Whitney looked from Nicola to her mom and back. "Auntie Nic?"

"Go," Gwen said, and pointed to the door. She would check Whitney out of the hospital and call a locksmith to change the locks tonight.

"Mom, no," Whitney started, and grabbed on to Nicola's arm.

"Yeah, Mom, no," Nicola echoed, but Gwen could see the steel in her eyes. Nicola leaned over Whitney with an exaggerated scowl on her face. "I'm sure you'll be fine," she said in a way that let Whitney know she thought no such thing, and tears filled Whitney's eyes.

"I want Aunt Nicola to stay." Gwen shook her head and Whitney slammed her head against her pillow. "You're a terrible mom," she said. "I want Dad."

Gwen steeled herself against the words: the one thing she couldn't give her daughter.

"Out," she said to Nicola, surprised this time how forceful and loud her voice sounded as it echoed in the small room.

Nicola kissed Whitney's cheek and whispered something in her ear. Gwen willed herself not to flinch as Nicola pulled her purse onto her shoulder and turned toward the door.

Whitney was screaming now, her own cries ricocheting off the walls like shrapnel. "Let her stay! I want Auntie Nic!" But Gwen held strong. She heard people running in the halls.

Nicola turned at the door and whispered to Gwen so only she could hear over Whitney's cries. "You're making a terrible mistake," she said, and Gwen shook her head.

"It's the best decision I've ever made."

RULE #5: TRUTH, NOT FACTS

Chapter Forty-Four

A locksmith showed up with new locksets for the front and back doors that night, just as Gwen was pulling a frozen cheese pizza from the oven. Whitney and Gwen ate their dinner while the woman worked, Whitney ducking a slice into her mouth with one hand, the other in her new cast. Later, when Gwen walked the locksmith to the door, she handed Gwen the gold keys on a thin ring. "Everything okay here?" she asked.

Gwen remembered the woman from the garage, how she'd told Gwen to make sure she was safe after the tire was sabotaged, and felt a surge as her eyes welled with gratitude. There was a whole network of women out there doing their best to keep each other safe. "I'm good," she said. "Just a precaution."

The woman filled out the receipt, ripped Gwen's white copy from her pad, and handed it to her. "Keep an eye out," she said, and Gwen promised she would. She thought of Nicola leaned over her daughter, the whisper of her lips at Whitney's delicate ear. As much as Gwen had cajoled, pleaded, and demanded, Whitney would not tell her what had been said.

She called the police and left a message for Melinda Willis, the officer she'd dealt with originally, who had notes from their call. In the morning, she would call again and start the process for a restraining order. She'd file the damn paperwork. Hire a lawyer. Raise holy hell. Do whatever she had to do to keep her daughter safe.

She woke early the next morning when it was still dark outside, and left messages at Dacks and the school, saying she and Whitney were staying home. She made the coffee, and the quiet click of her spoon against the side of her cup as she mixed in her creamer echoed through the empty kitchen. It was still before six; the day stretched before her. She knocked on Whitney's door, deciding they'd leave early, get a jump on whatever traffic there might be.

"Whitney?" she said. A drop of unease pooled in her gut as she slowly turned the doorknob, expecting, hoping, to hear her daughter's hair rustling awake. "Honey?"

Gwen peered around the door. The room was empty.

She covered the room in three quick strides and pulled open the closet door to see if by some chance her daughter was hiding. Two Chuck Taylors lay on their sides. Gwen's heart raced as she looked around the room. The bed was rumpled, slept in, and Whitney's latest Percy Jackson sat on the nightstand with a crisp bookmark three-quarters of the way through. Whitney never bent the spines.

Gwen picked up the book and found an envelope underneath. Her breath caught when she saw Whitney's blocky print. *To: Mom. From: Whitney*, with a tiny heart over the *i*. It was the heart that did her in, as recognizable as a fingerprint. She tore open the note.

I'm sorry Mommy! I did not mean to hurt Mr. TopHat I wanted him to live with us so bad. I miss daddy. I will try to be better. Auntie Nic said your very very mad. I will see you when I'm better. Love, your daughter, Whitney Elizabeth Maner.

Tears clouded Gwen's vision: the *z* was backward in *Elizabeth* as it had been since Whitney learned her letters. *Oh, Whitney*, she thought. *You're perfect the way you are.*

There was a cord next to the book and she followed it to the outlet. A phone charger? But Whitney didn't have a phone, or at least Gwen had never given her one. She reread the letter, willing herself to stay calm. Whitney had left because Nicola said Gwen was mad. What other lies had Nicola fed her daughter?

She flew down the stairs, stumbled, and caught herself on the railing. In the kitchen, she dug through the junk drawer, flinging chip clips, pens, birthday candles, and Chapstick to the floor. She grabbed Nicola's spare house key and tore across the three yards to Nicola's house, cast under the first stretch of early daylight.

Gwen's hand stabbed the key at the door—once, twice, three times—before finally connecting with the dead bolt, turning the key so hard she was surprised it didn't snap in her hand. She pushed open the door and screamed "Whitney!" her own voice echoing through the condo.

In Nicola's kitchen, everything looked as it should: the surfaces clean, the cabinets closed, the coffee maker on the counter. Gwen stumbled the stairs two at a time, lungs burning, and scanned the bedrooms and bathrooms. All were empty.

She raced downstairs and opened the garage, surprised to see Nicola's Prius. The stink of garbage climbed in her nose. She opened the large plastic lid on the trash bin in the corner and put a hand above her lip to block the stench. Inside were frozen pizzas and bags of vegetables, three Styrofoam trays of salmon fillets with the cling wrap distended and leaking. They accounted for the smell, but why wasn't this food in the freezer?

The chest freezer sat at the front of the garage, Derek's Vitamix resting on top.

Gwen moved the blender to the floor, her hands shaking as she opened the lid. The suction held a moment before freeing with a pop. Folded inside was Derek, a frozen slick of blood on the side of his face where his right eye had been, a gash in the side of his skull that, even frozen, looked squishy. Gwen's coffee whooshed up her esophagus but she choked it down. He was wearing a short-sleeved T-shirt, and irrational as it was, she thought he must feel cold, the frosty air pluming from the freezer.

Adrenaline flooded her system. An electric panic shot through her: this murderer had her daughter. Her phone dinged and she grabbed it from her back pocket: a text from Nicola.

I'll keep her safe. Don't call the police. You'll regret it if you do.

She dialed Nicola but the call went straight to voice mail. She imagined Nicola driving at her usual breakneck speed, an Amber Alert chiming on her phone and the steering wheel yanked purposefully, decisively, to the right. She couldn't call the police and risk what Nicola might do.

Think, she told herself. Where might Nicola take her?

Back inside, she ripped the house apart. She slammed office drawers, the closets, the hutch in the living room, looking for any kind of clue to show where they might have gone. Upstairs, she tore apart Nicola's bed and through the master bath, flinging open cabinets with Nicola's makeup tucked neatly inside, night cream on the counter. She pulled too hard on a drawer and it clattered to the floor, an eyeliner rolling beneath the sink. Folded at the bottom of the drawer was a deed to a parcel of land in Harris, Ohio. The signature purchasing the land was Nicola's, sold by an Onita Kimmel. The date 2012. She was sure now this was the awful woman she'd met during the internship, as well as the one she'd talked to on the phone a few days ago.

Beneath the deed were a few more folded pages, hospital records for Weldon Kimmel from 1993. Gwen scanned quickly—alcohol levels, broken neck, punctured lung, blood type AB—and the last page, his death certificate. It all seemed to match the obituary she'd read online. Hadn't Nicola said she thought Onita had been the one driving? The paperwork proved nothing, so why was it here? Why was it hidden?

Gwen tried to piece it together—*think, think!* She wasn't sure what it meant, but was sure of this: the answers were on that farm in the past

Nicola thought she'd buried. The one she thought Gwen knew nothing about and would never be able to find.

She took a picture of the paperwork and pulled the deed's address up on her phone; it was just over two and a half hours away. She ran back to her house and grabbed her coat, purse, and car keys. *I'm coming for you, Whitney.*

Chapter Forty-Five

Nicola

Nicola squinted out the windshield, the sun still rising in the east, a pink and gold hue painting the horizon. Her phone rested on her knee. Still no Amber Alert. That was good. Whitney sat beside her with tears streaked down her face, and Nicola wondered if she'd made the wrong decision, but what choice had Gwen given her? Last night, Whitney had texted Nicola from her secret phone and said, Mom changed the locks.

She locked you in, Nicola had texted back. She must be really mad. Of course Nicola knew that Gwen had changed the locks to keep her out, but what kind of a mother did that? Kept her daughter from someone she loved? It was bad parenting; even Nicola could see that.

Whitney had sent back a half screen of crying emojis, and Nicola had texted Whitney that her mother was worse than mad; she was *disappointed.* How had she raised a child so bad? A bird murderer? It hadn't been hard to convince Whitney to outrun that disappointment. Nicola knew that little girls who thought disappointment was bad had never really faced a mother's true wrath.

Early in the morning, with her mother still asleep, Whitney snuck over to Auntie Nic's house. Nicola originally planned to keep Whitney until Gwen woke up and give Gwen the scare of her life, but who was

Gwen to so easily get what she wanted? She'd abandoned Nicola right after Derek had, and Nicola knew the last place Gwen would know to look. She needed Gwen to see her whole life could disappear again, and that there was no Whitney without Nicola. That's how family was.

"Where are we going?" Whitney asked. It was the first time she'd spoken since they'd climbed into the car all those miles ago. Maxx whined on her lap, Whitney's left arm around him and the other in a cast. In the hospital, Nicola had leaned over the little girl and promised, "I will keep you safe."

"You want to see where I grew up?" Nicola asked, and Whitney shook her head. "Yeah, I don't blame you. It's not so great." They were driving the exact roads she'd taken as a child, huddled with her sister in the back seat, as their mom looked for a place to park so that she could play the picture game.

Two nights earlier, after seeing Gwen leaving her condo, Nicola had confronted Derek about why Gwen was there. He told her another lie, and it didn't take long for Nicola to see the packed bags, his Vitamix to the side, the cord wrapped and tucked. She'd gotten it for him for their third anniversary. The industrial grade, no money spared. He'd called her the names she'd called her own mother—psycho, bitch, murderer—and she would have done anything to stop those words from spitting out of his mouth.

Nicola turned off the main highway onto a gravel road and then down the familiar rutted lane, potholed from weather and weeds. She gunned the car and headed straight as an arrow toward her childhood home.

Onita slapped open the screen door, arms crossed and her mouth in a tight, curious line. Her skin was the color of cigarette-stained teeth, and as she raised an arm in greeting, the crepe-like skin of her underarm waggled from her short sleeve. Short sleeves, when it was twenty degrees. Nicola felt a ripple of revulsion snake through her. Jeans hung from her mother's hip bones with thick white stitching on the seams and pockets. Onita bent over and picked up a rock, wiped it on her dirty jeans, and set it in her mouth. The rough pebble rolled cheek to cheek at the direction of her tongue and Nicola could nearly taste the gritty dirt.

Nicola stopped the muscle car and they both climbed out, Whitney blocking Maxx from jumping down with her hip as he whined in the passenger seat.

"Who's this?" Onita asked as she scratched at a red spot on her arm. The scab caught on her fingernail, and a bead of blood oozed. "Why'd you bring her to this shithole?"

Whitney looked at Nicola with large eyes. "Auntie Nic? Where are we?" All that remained on the land was the crumbling farmhouse and once-red barn, the cracked and weeded concrete of the hog pen further upended by years of weather and neglect. Everything in the landscape was gradients of gray and brown, fields stretching beyond.

Onita raised her eyebrows. "Auntie Nic, is it?" She bent at her knees to look Whitney in the eye, her scraggly box-dyed blonde hair falling in her face. "That makes me your grandma."

Whitney scrunched her nose. "This is your *mom*?"

Onita stood up as if slapped and Nicola wanted to laugh, but Onita's face hardened as she turned to Nicola. "I'm guessing you're not here to bake Christmas cookies," she said.

Why *was* she here? Nicola wondered, and only then did she know, deep in her lizard brain. *Because this is where it started.* She had come to free herself from Onita, once and for all, one way or another.

"I want you gone," she said to her mother.

Onita laughed, the rock on her tongue. "I'm not going anywhere. I've got my insurance policy, remember?"

Eight months ago, Nicola had been home to bury Missy a few yards away from her sister. That wedding. That stupid destination wedding. Nicola had gone to Missy's apartment to say she was fine with not being a bridesmaid—give it to his dumb kid, who cared?—but then to not even be *invited*? The first strike had been an accident as they both reached for Missy's phone, an elbow to Missy's windpipe. The second was to stop Missy from lunging for it a second time. After that? Nicola found her hands around Missy's neck, struck by the intimacy, the pressure. Why didn't friends touch more? When she and her sister used to sleep in the same bed as kids, they'd often wake entwined with an arm around the other, a leg flung here or there. Nicola had squeezed until she saw sparks behind her eyelids.

An engine gunned from the road. Nicola turned to see a white SUV career from the rutted road and onto the private lane, Gwen at the wheel. Nicola was shocked to see her there, but also impressed. *This* was why she'd put her chips on Gwen. She'd seen such potential.

"Who's that?" Onita asked. Nicola ignored her, but Onita put two and two together. "Ah," she said. "Someone's here for the kid." She looked at Nicola, a rotten grin splitting her face. "She's in pretty high demand."

In a surprising surge of both speed and strength, Onita grabbed Whitney, pulling her against her bony body in the same fluid movement with which she pulled a knife from her front pocket. Nicola flashed back to her mother and sister in the hayloft, the knife clattering to the ground. She should have known her mother would have a weapon.

"Who is she?" Onita demanded, one crooked tooth escaping between her lips as she held the knife against the tender pink skin of Whitney's neck. "What'll you give me to get her back?"

Chapter Forty-Six

GWEN

As Gwen's car bounced across the uneven ruts on the driveway, Whitney seemed to recede farther in the distance, held captive by a thin woman who was pulling her toward the old red barn. A glint of sunlight caught under Whitney's chin and Gwen saw the knife. She gunned the gas and shot the Rover forward. Gwen could imagine the foulness of the woman's breath, someone who looked like she was rotting from the inside out.

The woman slid inside the wooden door with Whitney against her as Gwen tried to calm her raging mind. What horrors could be inside the barn? She slammed on the brakes and threw the car into park.

Gwen's hand shook as she opened the door and slapped it shut, the metal sound reverberating in her ears. Nicola stood frozen, terror splashed across her face. Her cheekbones, usually so intimidating, looked gaunt, her face collapsing much like the older woman's. How had Gwen not realized how empty, how broken Nicola was?

"What's she doing?" Gwen demanded, and Nicola shook her head, mute. Gwen grabbed Nicola's shoulders. "Nicola! What is she doing with Whitney?"

The wind caught her words, flicking them toward the harvested cornstalks. "The hayloft," Nicola said, and pointed a slim finger toward the barn.

Gwen pushed her aside and ran. She felt the pull of her own body, propelled forward, as she tried to get to Whitney. Inside the barn, she paused as her eyes adjusted to the darkness. Small shafts and bullets of light broke through the wood planks. The smell of dust thickened the air along with something heavier and alive: the shit of decades-gone animals, mold up the walls.

"Whitney!" Gwen yelled, her word echoing off the concrete floor. She looked up and saw a dry catch of straw fall like the twirling, winged seeds of the maple she'd admired when she was a girl.

She flew to the wooden ladder and climbed.

There was a *thunk*, followed by whining, and then a muffled "*Mommy!*"

Gwen's heart slammed in her chest as she grabbed the last rung, a splinter sinking into her palm, thin as an eyelash but sharp and painful.

There was a large hay door swung open to the north, the sun rising to the right on the blue-white horizon. Gwen scanned the space, littered here and there with old bales and a ratty afghan, but no Whitney. She ran across the wood floorboards to the open door, gasping at the quick, unrepentant drop. She had expected a ledge, something, but there was nothing. The rough concrete ground loomed below her, and she could see Nicola pointing frantically up to the sky.

Gwen rotated her head and saw the dirty bottom tips of two smooth flip-flops peek over the roof. Whitney screamed. The flip-flops shuffled back. Gwen held her breath as her daughter's body dangled over the edge, still in the grip of the old woman. Whitney's thin body bobbed, every limb erect with fear. She wore loose jeans, a tiny white sliver of skin visible at the ankles.

"No!" Nicola screamed, and then her own name, like a loud, feral howl. "Niiikkkkki!"

Whitney remained, suspended, two craggy hands under her armpits. "What's she worth?" the old woman yelled back.

A quick scan of the barn's exterior showed Gwen no foothold, no latches or gaps by which to hurl herself up the side. Adrenaline coursed hot in her veins. Whitney still in her periphery, she glanced back inside and saw another ladder, this one leading to the roof.

The hardest thing she'd ever do was take her eyes off her daughter, but she had to. Gwen snuck across the loft and climbed quickly, quietly, up the second ladder. At the top, she burst through the hole in the roof, and the woman turned her head to see her. Up close she could see the woman's eyes, wide and unsettled, the whites the color of cat pee on an old sheet.

Gwen stepped onto the rickety roof, surprised by the slip of the shingles, worn as smooth as metal. Whitney remained still. Her hands clenched in fists at the cuffs of her winter coat as she dangled over the edge.

"I'm here," Gwen said, her voice low and even, purring. She took in the woman and her wild eyes. "I'm here for my daughter." She heard the *thud thud thrum* of blood through her body.

"Daughters aren't anything but trouble," the woman croaked, her voice jagged in the cold. Her lips curled inward, pouched and wet. She held Whitney against her now, the knife warbling under her chin.

Gwen locked eyes with her daughter and was in motion before she realized it, all the moving parts simultaneously obeying an order she didn't know she'd given.

As she lunged, the old woman turned. The blade glinted. Gwen saw every thick white stitch on the woman's jeans, her curled toes grasping her grimy flip-flops, the toenail paint chipped and the color of old blood.

Onita's skinny arms shot forward and Whitney blurred.

Gwen grabbed for the woman and yanked her back. She was lighter than expected and Gwen stumbled. Her mouth opened in a jumbled, frantic scream.

Whitney was airborne, over the edge, skinny limbs and the white slip of her ankle, a ponytail against the backdrop of the pink-and-red sky.

Chapter Forty-Seven

NICOLA

Nicola stood near the edge of the barn. She had been standing there for fourteen years, since her name had been Celeste. Nikki, Nicola . . . hurled through the air. She screamed her sister's name.

The sun blazed behind her, but the cold of winter still seeped through the thin flannel of her shirt. In the distance, Christmas lights danced.

She held out her arms and ran forward as the body floated down, like cotton, like a dream. How many nights had she fallen asleep to this moment only to shudder awake, screaming, as the body landed on the ground?

But now—

She felt the full force of her sister's weight land against her as their bodies slammed down. Air left her lungs. A crater of wrecked concrete dug into her spine; another, her hip bone. The body collapsed against hers, and her own hand tangled in her sister's hair as her arms encircled her bones. Fact was, when her sister had died that day, so had she. But now, she caught her.

Not Nikki. But Nikki.

She could still see her sister, hurled over the edge, her ruined body impaled by the rebar.

She squeezed her eyes, her face and skin tight from the cold.

A thud rang out.

She turned to see Onita lying next to her, her eyes wide and yellow. Air leaked from her mother in a long, slow wheeze, but she didn't blink. Somewhere in the world, Gwen screamed, a retching sound, and Nicola looked up to see her head over the side of the barn, hair obscuring her face in the wind.

She disappeared inside and a moment later flew from the front door, collapsing next to Nicola, ripping that weight from her chest.

Not Nikki. But Nikki.

Gwen held her daughter against her so fiercely, Nicola worried she would hurt her, but Whitney clung back, scrabbling up her mother's body, desperate to get closer. She flung one arm around her mother's neck, the broken one pressed between them. Gwen stood and Whitney wrapped one leg and then the other around her hips. Nicola's arms were empty. She looked over at her mother and felt nothing but a shadowed grief.

Gwen's mouth moved, but Nicola couldn't hear anything. She watched her friend run her nose against the smooth shine of her daughter's hair and breathe deeply. Nicola's own lungs felt empty, deflated. She tried to remember how her sister had smelled. Like dry straw, like powdered milk, a body too long without a shower. God, how she loved her.

There was a noise at a frequency Nicola could barely hear, like words said underwater. She looked at her mother: dead. Gwen said her name, but not her name. "Nicola. Nicola."

Gwen turned to her, and whatever she saw on Nicola's face softened hers. She held out a hand. "Here," she said. "Let me help you up."

Chapter Forty-Eight

GWEN

May 2023

Gwen sat in a pair of jeans and a T-shirt, her ankles one behind the other, six bags of Wint-O-Green Life Savers purchased at the vending machines on the table in front of her. The first time she'd come to Marysville, she'd brought snacks from home along with celebrity gossip magazines and a paperback novel. All of it was confiscated before Nicola even skulked through the concrete doorway in her orange outfit, a stretched white T-shirt peeking out from the V-neck. Now Gwen knew to leave everything in the car but her key, jacket, ID, and her money card for the prison. She'd buy the snacks there.

Nicola had pleaded guilty to Derek's murder. She and Gwen told the same story to the police about what happened at the farm, mere days before Christmas. How Onita had thrown Whitney over the edge, and how her flip-flopped foot had lost all traction, the momentum of it hurtling her own ninety-pound body over as well.

The cops had their questions—why was her body so far right of where Whitney landed in Nicola's arms?—but they were satisfied by easy answers: Onita must have slipped in her trajectory and rotated somehow. Did they see the bottom of those smooth, worn flip-flops? These cops, they knew Onita well. She'd grown up with some of them and had dated them in high school. Others knew her from her steady stream of arrests. Either way, it was one less meth-head to worry about.

Nicola came into the waiting area, her white smile flashing, and Gwen held up one of the bags of Life Savers. Nicola unwrapped three in quick succession, throwing them in her mouth one by one. She bit down with her molars, the candy upright. "Did you see a spark?"

Gwen shook her head. "God," Nicola said between crunches. "I never ate sugar like I do now, but they took away all of my vices." Even so, her teeth were still a perfect white.

Every month or so when Gwen drove up to the Ohio Reformatory for Women, her mother would ask her, "Why do you visit her? What can you possibly get out of that?"

"I don't know, Mom," she'd say. "Maybe because it's a nice thing to do. She's not a monster, she's a person." But Gwen knew it was more complicated than that.

Jeri was living in a senior facility now. Independent living, but with other phases to come. Gwen had taken over power of attorney, and each week she spent at least two hours on hold organizing her mother's PT or insurance claims or prescriptions. She'd moved into her mother's old house, the four walls of her childhood. She'd torn down the heavy dust-mite-covered curtains that had blocked most of the natural light in the home. She'd rolled paint on the walls, cutting in the edges with a brush, and let Whitney pick her own bedroom color: Flyaway Blue. Sometimes, after her daughter was in bed, Gwen would drink out of the amber-gold juice glasses she'd known her whole life. They were the same ones Jeri had had for thirty years, and Gwen had to work not to hurl them against the wall, her life having come full circle when she'd expected an arrow pointing up.

But her daughter was there. Their health was good. Her mother was safe. She had wanted a perfect life but ended up with this one.

"How's the job?" Nicola asked, and before Gwen could answer, added, "I still can't believe you let a good thing go."

In the new year, after the dust had settled, Gwen had made an appointment with Bethany and told her about the fraudulent résumé Nicola had submitted, and admitted that she had been complicit in giving it to the board. A part of her knew she could have gotten away with it—it was amazing, Nicola had once said, what people could get away with—but that wasn't what she wanted. She wanted to own up to her mistakes, learn from them, and move on. She was of course asked to resign, but they wanted to hush up that they hadn't done their due diligence and sever any apparent ties to Nicola's bad behavior. Bethany was good enough to give her a reference, and she'd secured a support position at a private equity investment firm downtown that was more in keeping with her experience and abilities, but her time at Dacks had taught her to push for more, to expect more of herself. Already she was gunning for a promotion, her eye on office manager.

During Gwen's visits, Nicola told her all about the women on her floor and said the prison shows on TV were full of lies. "Where do those women get access to skin care?" she said, pointing at her own face, which Gwen could tell had aged in the past five months without daily access to collagen and fine oils. It made Nicola's white teeth stand out even more, and Gwen marveled that she hadn't noticed they were fake long before.

At some point in the visit, she would ask Nicola one of the questions she always asked her: "How could you push my mom? What *did* you do to Missy? What if you hadn't caught my daughter?" Today it was "Do you regret anything you did?"

Nicola rolled her eyes. "Where would that get me? Jesus, Gwen, have I taught you nothing? Never look back, remember?"

And the thing was, Gwen did remember. As much as she didn't want to admit it, the rules Nicola lived by held some wisdom. *Never*

Look Back. Don't Let Anyone Make You Feel Small. Gwen wanted to live by these, or at least try.

She and Bethany stayed friends and had a standing lunch date every other Wednesday, when they'd almost always go to Uno for a salad or Fly Pie for a slice. Bethany was a talker, an extrovert. Everyone thought all extroverts were socially savvy, but Gwen thought Bethany was boring. She told Gwen about the bird feeder her husband had gotten her for her birthday. It had a camera that connected to both their iPhones and took pictures of the birds, identifying over six thousand species. Every lunch she shared a new picture. Gwen knew Bethany was the type of woman who would never say anything that surprised her. And she supposed there'd been a time when she'd been fine with that, but Nicola had spoiled her. She'd been routinely surprised by what Nicola had to say, and by how loudly she'd proclaim it to the world. Don't like the job you're applying for? Cheat on your résumé. You want a dog? Buy a dog. Husband's an asshole? Well, she'd certainly solved that problem.

After the incident at the farm, Gwen and Whitney had celebrated Christmas. In the week before the holiday, Gwen had found herself obsessing on Amazon, finger on the "Buy Now" button, wishing she could hit it harder. She ordered a birdcage for Whitney and imagined how her daughter's face would light up when she told her she could pick out her own Mr. TopHat as soon as the pet store opened. She wrapped the cage, along with bird toys and birdseed, in the bright Christmas paper she also added to the order, stacking the gifts one on top of the other like Legos.

Gwen had begun to understand on some level why Todd had kept their debt a secret, and why she had let him. He'd wanted to be his best version of himself as a husband and provider, even if that version was a lie. Now she wanted the same, but the day before Christmas, she unwrapped the gifts to return them later that week. She couldn't afford them, and while she was still working to accept that, they were only things. Instead she bought those dreaded gifts that bordered on practical: a sweater, new shoes, a book, and a toy.

One of her greatest regrets, one of the things she mourned most about Todd, was that they hadn't known their real, messy selves. What would he have made of a true, vulnerable Gwen? Of a woman with opinions and strength who also brought a cardigan wherever she went. She wondered sometimes if it was possible to love someone you didn't fully know, and other times she wondered if it was the only way.

Gwen glanced at the large white clock screwed to the wall; she had to leave soon to pick Whitney up from school. "I need to get going," she said. She would not say Whitney's name to Nicola.

Nicola reached out to hold Gwen's hand, and Gwen had to fight not to pull it back. She didn't want to touch this woman. Nicola had saved Whitney's life, and for that Gwen would always be grateful, but she would never ever let Nicola near her family again. But there were other reasons to visit her, secrets Nicola now held about her.

"I'm proud of you," Nicola said. "You did what you had to do." She said it every time, and whether she really was or she just wanted to remind Gwen of what she knew, Gwen couldn't say for sure. "You know, we're not that different when it comes to protecting the ones we love."

"Um, we're a little different," Gwen said, and motioned around to the prison.

She left a few minutes later, breathing deeply the outside air on the way to her car.

When Nicola was arrested, Gwen had stopped by the HOA office to say she was breaking the lease, and while she was there, she told the woman she hoped this wouldn't discourage them from renting to others since she'd been the first. "Where'd you hear that?" the woman had said. "Most of the condos here are available to rent." Another lie from Nicola that she'd swallowed whole.

Gwen climbed into her car to drive the hour-plus back to Dayton from the prison, through cornfields similar to the ones she'd raced past in December, desperate to save her daughter. Some nights, Gwen could still feel Onita's bony back against her palms, the ribs curved and sharp under the skin. She'd weighed barely anything at all. It had been like shoving a ghost, rage and adrenaline coursing through Gwen's body like a possession. Some nights, Gwen would wipe her hands against the hips of her sleep shorts over and over again, trying to get rid of the sensation. Other times, she'd get out of bed and run her hands under scalding water until they turned pink, but the itch of that feeling never fully went away.

That day at the farm, before they'd called the police, the two women agreed: Onita had fallen on her own. She didn't visit Nicola out of a sense of obligation, although that's what she told Jeri. She did it because Nicola knew her secret, and with that secret came a sense of kinship. Gwen finally understood how you could love someone so much you'd do anything you could to keep them.

But in return, she had a copy of Weldon Kimmel's hospital paper-work, his blood type AB. It wasn't impossible he could have a daughter who was a universal donor, but rare enough she could convince some people to do some digging. It had been one of the boring tidbits about herself Nicola had let slip. And what they'd find was that Celeste had been the one to commit identity theft the last fourteen years, no matter who shoved the real Nikki over the hayloft's edge.

Gwen unrolled the window and hung her hand out, toggling it up and down in the wind current, the warm air blowing up her cuffed sleeve. Her own life, while free, was not the one she'd imagined, but she felt alive, scrappy, thankful. She'd been happier before, but not content. Gwen checked her watch. She'd make it just in time for Whitney's pickup.

At the school, she turned on her blinker and swung the Rover around back, quickly tapping the horn. Her daughter looked up, sun-shine spreading across her face.

Whitney turned to Shasta and hugged her goodbye. Shasta and her family had moved to Dayton at the start of the calendar year, so she hadn't been at the school for Mr. TopHat's calamity. It was a fresh start for Whitney to make a friend.

"How was school?" Gwen asked as her daughter clambered into the back seat, lunch box and backpack in tow.

"Good. I told Shasta all about Maxx," Whitney said. When Nicola went to prison, someone had to take the dog. Whitney slept with him every night, her night terrors receding further into the distance, although sometimes Gwen woke to the dog's whining.

Whitney asked her mom to flip the radio from NPR to a pop station and Gwen obliged. "She's excited to meet him." The girls had their first sleepover scheduled for this Saturday, and Gwen and Whitney had already planned the menu: a Domino's pizza for dinner, extra cheese, and an egg-and-sausage casserole for breakfast. When Shasta's mom had first texted about the sleepover, she'd offered to host, but Gwen wasn't ready to have Whitney out of her sight and offered to have the girls stay at her house.

Whitney smiled at her mother, slipping on a pair of plastic sunglasses with daisies at the corners. "She doesn't have any pets at home, but she really wants a kitten, two of them. A white one and a black one so she can name them Salt and Pepper." It was the happiest Gwen could remember her daughter being since the accident, although *accident* wasn't quite the word for it. She was so excited about her new friend.

"Those are cute names," she said, encouraging the prattle.

"I don't know," Whitney said. "I think they're kind of stupid, but whatever, they're not my cats." She grinned at her mom. "Her parents told her no-go on the kittens, and I told her, if you want those cats, there's always a way. Just because they said no, doesn't make it a fact."

Gwen gripped the steering wheel tighter. It was reminiscent of one of Nicola's rules: *Truth, Not Facts.* She racked her brain but couldn't remember a time when Nikki had said this to Whitney. Just how much time had Nikki spent with Whitney that Gwen hadn't accounted for?

Gwen fought to keep her voice light, her hands at ten and two. Sometimes when she woke to Maxx's whining in the night, she'd bolt up in bed from a dead sleep, a scream caught in her throat. "What do you mean, it's not a fact?"

"Truth is," Whitney said, "if Shasta wants two kittens, she can make it happen. There's always a way."

"But how?" Gwen asked, her palms slick on the steering wheel. How much had Whitney been shaped by Nicola? Gwen knew she owed Nicola for surviving Todd's death and her own grief, gaining the confidence to start a career, becoming a better role model for Whitney. It was a snake eating its own tail: if Gwen had never met Nicola, she never would have been strong enough to survive her.

Whitney laughed. "I don't know. I'm just saying, I wanted a dog, and you said no, and now I have a dog." Her voice softened and she smiled at her mother in the rearview mirror, the plastic sunglasses guarding her eyes. "And I love him so, so much."

ACKNOWLEDGMENTS

Thanks to Wright State University for continued support and to my wonderful, weird, creative students. What a joy it is to talk fiction with you!

Big heartfelt thanks to my agent, Jill Marr, who is an inspiration, a cheerleader, and a partner. I cannot thank Jessica Tribble Wells enough for believing in this book and for her smart edits, as well as Celia Johnson for helping me shape this into the thing it is today. Ploy Siripant, this is the cover of my dreams. Thanks to Grace Doyle, Tamara Arellano, Tara Whitaker, Heather Rodino, Iris Winslow, Sarah Vostok, and Sarah Shaw at Amazon Publishing, as well as everyone else I've encountered at Thomas & Mercer. I've long said I don't want to be the smartest person working on one of my books, but it's humbling and inspiring how far down the list I fall.

I'd like to thank all my girlfriends—past and present, good and bad—for their friendship. In particular (and in the categories of good and present) Christina Consolino, Meredith Doench, Katrina Kittle, and Jess Montgomery for helping me think up this story and for trusting me to execute it. And to Charlotte Hogg for being the best friend I could imagine, and for in no way inspiring this book.

And of course thanks to my extended family, starting with Gene Milligan and all the Milligans in perpetuity. To my folks, Judy and Ken, for always believing in me despite evidence that might not be the best idea. And to Kelly Hansen, my sister and my favorite matchie. Big thanks, too, to her and her husband, Doug Hansen, who are the benefactors of the Hansen House Writing Retreat, a celebration of creativity and Cheez-Its and laughter and hard work. Without their generosity, this book wouldn't exist. For real.

To my kids and their partners—Ellen Milligan, Nat Henry, Neil Milligan, Katie Smith, and Cora Dunekacke—who always make me laugh and always make me proud. And finally, my husband, Barry Milligan, for Wednesday nights and all the nights. But especially the Wednesdays.

And to the readers who pick up this book or any book—thank you.

ABOUT THE AUTHOR

Photo © 2022 Art Smaven

Erin Flanagan is the Edgar Award–winning author of *Blackout, Deer Season*, and two short story collections, *The Usual Mistakes* and *It's Not Going to Kill You, and Other Stories*. She's held fellowships to Yaddo, MacDowell, the Sewanee Writers' Conference, the Bread Loaf Writers' Conference, Ucross, and the Vermont Studio Center. An English professor at Wright State University, Erin lives in Dayton, Ohio, with her husband, daughter, two cats, two dogs, and her friendly, caustic thoughts. For more information, visit www.erinflanagan.net.